T0083608

'If poetry was the supreme literary form of the First World War then, as if in riposte, in the Second World War, the English novel came of age. This wonderful series is an exemplary reminder of that fact. Great novels were written about the Second World War and we should not forget them.'

WILLIAM BOYD

'It's wonderful to see these four books given a new lease of life because all of them are classic novels from the Second World War written by those who were there, experienced the fear, anguish, pain and excitement first-hand and whose writings really do shine an incredibly vivid light onto what it was like to live and fight through that terrible conflict.'

JAMES HOLLAND, Historian, author and TV presenter

'The Imperial War Museum has performed a valuable public service by reissuing these four absolutely superb novels covering four very different aspects of the Second World War. I defy you to choose which is best: I keep changing my mind!'

ANDREW ROBERTS, author of *Churchill: Walking with Destiny*

MR BUNTING AT WAR

Robert Greenwood

IMPERIAL WAR MUSEUMS

First published in Great Britain in 1941

First published in this format in 2022 by
IWM, Lambeth Road, London SE1 6HZ
iwm.org.uk

© The Estate of Robert Greenwood, 2022

About the Author and Introduction
© The Trustees of the Imperial War Museum, 2022

ISBN 978-1-912423-50-7

A catalogue record for this book is available from
the British Library.

Printed and bound by CPI Group (UK) Ltd, Croydon CR0 4YY

Every effort has been made to contact all copyright holders.
The publishers will be glad to make good in future editions
any error or omissions brought to their attention.

Cover illustration by Bill Bragg
Design by Clare Skeats
Series Editor Madeleine James

FSC
www.fsc.org
MIX
Paper from
responsible sources
FSC® C171272

About the Author

Robert Greenwood (1897–1981)

ROBERT GREENWOOD (1897 –1981) was a novelist and writer. His first novel depicted the family and working life of the eponymous *Mr Bunting* (1940). His next novel, *Mr Bunting at War* (1941), continued this story in the first two years of the Second World War. *Mr Bunting at War* was subsequently made into a film the following year entitled *Salute John Citizen* (1942), which proved tremendously popular at the box office. Greenwood's other novel about the war was *The Squad Goes Out* (1943), which depicted the work of a voluntary ambulance squad during the London Blitz. Greenwood wrote eleven novels in total as well as a number of short stories, including *Mr Bunting in the Promised Land* (1949) which tells the story of the Bunting family in the immediate aftermath of the Second World War. He died in 1981.

Introduction

One of the literary legacies of the First World War was the proliferation of war novels, with an explosion of the genre in the late 1920s and 1930s. Erich Maria Remarque's *All Quiet on the Western Front* was a bestseller and was made into a Hollywood film in 1930. In the same year, Siegfried Sassoon's *Memoirs of an Infantry Officer* sold 24,000 copies. Generations of school children have grown up on a diet of Wilfred Owen's poetry and the novels of Sassoon. Yet the novels of the Second World War are often forgotten, particularly those based on the home front.

Robert Greenwood's *Mr Bunting* was published in 1940 but was really a depiction of the Bunting family's life in the 1930s. Much in a similar vein to R C Sheriff's *The Fortnight in September* (1931), it tells the story of the 'average' suburban family. *Mr Bunting at War* continues the story of this family during the first two years of the Second World War. Specifically, it is the tale of George and Mary Bunting and their three children: Ernest, Chris and Julie. They live at Laburnam Villa on the outskirts of London in the fictional location of Kilworth in Essex. Due to wartime staff shortages Mr Bunting has returned to his former work as manager of the ironmongery section of Brockleys in London, while Mary looks after the family home. Initially their sons Ernest and Chris run a laundrette and garage respectively, whilst daughter Julie is looking for employment, having previously been employed at a solicitor's. Throughout the course of the novel the reader sees how the war impacts the whole family and ultimately endows Mr Bunting with some quiet dignity. In the final pages we are left with admiration for his stoicism in the face of the impact of the conflict.

The novel begins during the first few months of the 'Bore War', a period of relative inactivity (except at sea), which was subsequently dubbed the 'Phoney War'. In these first few chapters of the novel, the war itself seems very far away and life more or less continues as normal for the Bunting family. Indeed, at the end of Chapter

Three we are told, 'the boredom of the war once more descended on Laburnum Villa'. However, on 9 April 1940, Hitler's armed forces invaded and quickly overwhelmed Denmark, which surrendered within the day. At the same time, neutral Norway was attacked, and despite an Anglo-French attempt to land troops on the mainland, it was largely lost by May. As a result, Prime Minister Neville Chamberlain came under sustained criticism.

Yet worse was to come. On 10 May, Germany launched its westward invasions of the Netherlands, Belgium and France. On the same day, Chamberlain, unable to retain the support of the House of Commons, resigned. Winston Churchill assumed the prime ministership. Within days, it became clear that the fighting on the Continent would be no repetition of the stagnating Western Front of the First World War. By 20 May 1940, German troops had reached the Channel coast, dividing the Allied forces in two. Plans were hastily made to withdraw the British Expeditionary Force. This culminated in the 'miracle of Dunkirk' in which from 27 May to 4 June, a brilliantly improvised naval operation extracted more than 338,000 men, and brought them safely back to Britain. Some 850 vessels, including steamers and fishing boats, took part in Operation 'Dynamo'. Both sides interpreted Dunkirk as a victory, Churchill, however, pointed out that 'wars are not won by evacuations'. It is against this backdrop that Greenwood's novel is set. As the months of 1940 progress and the British situation becomes worse, we see increased mention of war news in the text (such as Mr Bunting reads in his beloved newspaper the *Siren,* and the family listen to on the wireless together).

On 22 June 1940 the French signed the armistice at Compiegne in the same railway carriage that the Germans had signed the armistice in 1918. This surrender is shown to severely affect Mr Bunting, as the war suddenly takes on a new reality:

The French surrender came to him with a shock beyond anything in his whole life's experience. He heard of it with a sickness of the heart which, he felt, would lay its mark on him for all his days.

As the news bulletin ended he switched off the wireless and, with a stunned mind, stood at his French window looking down the garden. It was a still June evening, his roses shone in their beauty and beyond the bright red roofs, and over the wooded hills the sun was sinking slowly as though reluctant to leave a land so lovely. But Mr Bunting's thoughts were not stirred, his mind was frozen. Nothing moved within him except his heart, which seemed to expand and contract, as though it were an independent living thing lodged in his breast. He looked at his wife and daughter, methodically laying supper. Didn't they understand? Was he the only one with thoughts and feelings? He sat down with them, but could not eat, though he drank copiously and immediately felt sick. For a moment or two he wondered whether he were ill. But he knew he was not ill.

By the summer of 1940 the situation for Britain was grave, and the novel depicts this worsening state of affairs as slowly the Bunting children become more involved in the war effort, having previously declared, 'it's men of father's age who are responsible for the war – not us'. In particular Chris, who has always had an interest in aviation, makes the momentous decision to volunteer as a sergeant pilot in the Royal Air Force: 'He had piles of flying journals, *The Aeroplane*, *Flight* and *Aeronautics*, in his bedroom, not one of which would he surrender to the nation for salvage. His sole interest was flying.' Although in the earlier stage of the novel Mr Bunting has been depicted in a slightly pompous manner, both his and Mrs Bunting's reactions to Chris's news are particularly poignant:

With an air of not being noticed Mr Bunting went through into the kitchen. His wife was standing by the sink; their glances met and he put his arm around her shoulder. Swallowing something in his throat, he whispered: 'We mustn't try to stop him if he thinks it's his duty.'

'No!' softly, with a hint of tears, but much to his relief. There seemed little else to say.

'Don't let him see we're upset.'
'No. If other parents can, we can, George.'

This passage epitomises the resilience of Mr and Mrs Bunting throughout the war. Mr Bunting is initially regarded as a 'fusspot' by his family over his insistence on air raid precautions, gas masks and the blackout, all of which contribute to his somewhat comical character construct. However there is an underlying emotional depth too, aptly illustrated in later passages of the book. It is changes occasioned by the war – such as Chris joining up and Ernest's marriage – which lend Mr Bunting more dignity than the reader might first expect:

Mr Bunting sat by the fire, close to its dying embers. It was late, but he had no desire for sleep. He had a lot to think about, but he thought about it aimlessly. Emotion more than thoughts possessed him. He sat with his feet inside the fender, the faint glow of the fire lighting his full, gingerish cheeks, his cold pipe held in his thick fingers. The home was breaking up. After these many years he had reached the moment that had been inevitable from the start. His sons were going out into the world, his daughter in her turn would follow, and he and Mary would be left alone, old people at the fireside. It was the end of a stage in life's journey.

Yet he seemed to have got so little out of all these years. His memories of family life were contracted to a few vivid scenes and a host of things he had forgotten.

Your best hopes were like a tree you planted. You watered it and pruned it, and staked it against the storm. You waited eagerly for the first blossoms, and how their loveliness gladdened you, like the first almond blossoms of the spring! But the next time you passed the petals were already strewn upon the grass.

Mr Bunting rose and put out the light; the last ember in the grate winked and went out.

* * *

German plans for the seaborne invasion of Britain – codenamed Operation 'Sealion' – included attaining control of the British skies and the destruction of the RAF. Throughout the summer of 1940, the Luftwaffe attacked shipping in the English Channel and mounted an all-out assault on the RAF's fighter bases, in the great and sustained aerial conflict known as the Battle of Britain. Almost every day between July and September 1940 fleets of Luftwaffe bombers departed from airstrips in Occupied Europe heading in search of targets. In response, the RAF's thinly stretched squadrons of Fighter Command did everything they could to stop the bombers getting through. Having volunteered for the RAF, the Buntings' son Chris is therefore at the forefront of his parents' minds during this period – they are ultimately devastated when their worst fears are realised and they receive a telegram with the news, 'Regret to inform you that Sergeant-Pilot C R Bunting...'

One of the successes of the novel might be said to be the way it intersperses comedy (such as friend Bert Rollo's hopeless attempts to court Julie) with the pathos of Mr Bunting's role as a father who feels he has been misunderstood and left behind, and who ultimately loses a son to the conflict.

Frequently during these early days he [Mr Bunting] *found himself standing trancelike, some train of business thought having merged into a speculation as to how Mary got through the days alone. It was hard for her, ever in the same place, with all Chris's things about her. Recalling himself with a start, he would look over the partition at the clock, and finding it had not moved, compare it with his watch, not able to understand that these trances were but momentary. Then he would focus his attention doggedly upon his letters, reading them slowly and carefully till everything grew clear to him.*

Almost the first person at the firm to speak to him directly was Mr Bickerton. He called at the cubby-hole before going to his office upstairs, and Mr Bunting received him with a conscious stiffening of moral fibre. Standing, he listened to

*his chief's words; they were sincere and kindly, they were
everything that words could be, and what could anyone
bring him now but unavailing words? Mr Bunting listened,
enduring them patiently, his glance steadily adhering to his
blotter till the chief ceased speaking. Then he looked up and
said:*

    *'Thank you, sir. 'Preciate it. Course, nobody knows what
it means to lose a son till they lose one of their own. I don't
expect them to, really. It's something his mother and me have
to face, not losing heart, if you understand what I mean, sir.'
Had he known it, he was touched during these few minutes
with true and natural dignity, as a man may wear laurels on
one occasion in his lifetime.*

In the first paragraph of the novel the reader is told he is 'not a
dignified person' but, in fact, perhaps he is.

After Chris's death, Mr Bunting joins the Civil Defence, an
organisation responsible for air raid precautions that would prove
essential during the Blitz. The Blitz represented Germany's sustained
commitment to decimating London and other British towns and
cities, commencing on 7 September 1940 with the bombing of
the East End and parts of the city. Indeed 'Black Saturday' was
succeeded by 71 consecutive nights of bombing (with the exception
of two due to bad weather) and London received 354 aerial attacks
between September 1940 and May 1941. By the end of September,
three weeks into the Blitz, 5,730 had been killed and over 9,000
wounded. Even a full year after the declaration of war, the conflict
had produced a higher death toll among British civilians than among
British soldiers. Written in 1941, the novel itself is very much of its
time and thus extremely patriotic in its depiction of the reaction to
the Blitz, as well as showing Mr Bunting's own fears:

*There had been hundreds killed in Stepney; bodies flung on to
the roofs of churches. He had heard the most terrible things.
Heard, too, the most amazing stories of the inhabitants'
behaviour. Stepney was by no means cowed this morning; it*

was defiant, angry, even cheerful, anything but cowed. Such people must be vastly different from himself, he thought: it amazed him how anyone could stick it.

Yet perhaps it is Mr Bunting himself who epitomises this resilience during the war, summing it up as 'how needlessly lives were wasted in the war and on what slender threads they hung'. The novel can be viewed as a tribute to the Mr Buntings of the world, and some of the final lines evoke a moving patriotism:

Bunting! He believed they called this stuff bunting; common, tawdry, ordinary stuff. Yet out of it were made the banners of victory.

The film of the book, *Salute John Citizen*, heavily featured the Blitz in London and added some additional plot points such as a wedding in a bombed-out church, in a particularly poignant scene. It featured Edward Rigby and Mabel Constanduros (as Mr and Mrs Bunting), Jimmy Hanley (as Ernest), and the likes of Dinah Sheridan, Stanley Holloway and George Robey. Both the film and the book were propagandist, depicting an ordinary family living on the outskirts of London and 'sticking it out' during the Blitz. However they also importantly demonstrate the significance of the home front in the wider narrative of the Second World War: a microcosm of suffering and sacrifice, and an illustration of the resilience it takes to make it through.

Alan Jeffreys
2022

ONE

IN HIS blacked-out kitchen, under the shaded light, Mr Bunting was on his knees before the boot cupboard. He was middle-aged and shortish, with a gingerish tinge in his full cheeks, and a grey eye, whose stare was sometimes disconcerting. He was not a dignified person; his round head, his stockiness, and his whole mien denoted practicality and a certain pertinacious quality; but he never remembered his personal dignity until, as now, he had lost it in pursuit of some more immediate aim. At the moment, crouching before the boot cupboard and peering alertly into its interior, he was conducting an investigation into questions of expense.

Though these investigations of Mr Bunting's had always been a feature of life at Laburnum Villa, he now considered them as part of his war effort. Usually, they coincided with his recurrent attacks of dyspepsia. Driven by this gastric demon, he became restless and began to prowl, and not often did he prowl very long or very far before his natural instinct for the detection of extravagance led him to the most recent, and what he invariably described as the most outrageous, example of this family failing. He had, by one of those mischances which so often wrecked domestic peace, discovered a pair of Julie's shoes worn till they were past repair through sheer laziness and neglect to take them to the cobbler. They were fit for nothing but salvage. The country was at war, and Mr Bunting believed in salvage as a national necessity, but he objected to the salvage of any article that had the slightest vestige of use left in it for himself. From Julie's shoes he had passed on to an inspection of Ernest's and Chris's shoes, and then proceeded systematically and persistently – for persistence was one of Mr Bunting's characteristics – to an examination of every pair of shoes in the house. Finally he reached the boot cupboard.

Kneeling on the tiles, with a face that grew redder from exertion and emotion, he emptied the cupboard of every pair of ancient and forgotten boots and shoes, finding only one pair honourably patched and stitched – his own. He was particularly incensed to observe that he alone recognised the merits of Baxter's rubber soles.

Mr Bunting knew he was unceasingly criticised merely for insisting on reasonable economy. That he was thus being criticised at this very moment he was perfectly aware. Julie, who had lately taken to eating nothing but fruit and nuts, had come into the kitchen for the apple which she was required by some esoteric rule of diet to consume between seven and eight pm. She had seen him on the floor surrounded by a tattered company of misshapen footgear. Immediately she began to hum in a light-hearted absent way, irritating as the buzzing of a bluebottle to an occupied mind. And brightly and innocently she greeted him, ''Lo, daddy darling. Looking for something?' Then, stepping over the vulgar objects on the floor, she had gone out with her apple on a plate. The fact that she needed a plate and a knife to eat an apple was itself an indication of a finicking habit of mind out of keeping with these sterner times.

As the front room door closed behind her Mr Bunting raised his head, straining to hear what was being said beyond it, but relying chiefly on his imagination. And his imagination immediately supplied the hum of facetious comment which followed a report of anything father happened to be 'up to'. His lips pursed and his moustache took on the peculiar bristling appearance of his warmer moments. Then he flung the shoes back in disorder and rose, rubbing his knees. A tenderness had developed there, a stiffness; one should always use a kneeling mat, he remembered. There was, he believed, a complaint called housemaid's knee, brought on by neglect of this very precaution.

Thoughtfully he mixed a draught of carbonate of soda and water in a teacup. His children, he reflected, didn't realise there was a war on. They never did realise anything unpleasant. Any fortunate event, as when he received a legacy under Aunt Annie's will, caused an instant reaction; the house was filled with a continuous buzz of hopeful speculation, everybody eager to adjust life to more opulent standards. But when the clarion call came... Even to describe anything as a clarion call was to invite his family to ignore it.

It was Mr Bunting who carefully perused the official booklets on air raid precautions, and made notes in them. It was Mr Bunting who, night after night, examined the effectiveness of the blackout and who, before retiring, collected all the gas masks and hung them on the hall stand ready for instant assumption. It was true that, up to now, no bombs had been dropped in Kilworth, and very few in England. No gas bombs had been dropped anywhere in Europe. They were, as Ernest pointed out, forbidden by the Hague Convention. This reasoning did not lull Mr Bunting's suspicions of the enemy. When the Government gave you a gas mask the proper thing was to hang it at all times where you could instantly snatch it up if need arose, and, if need did not arise, to examine it at intervals and polish the eyepieces. All of which Mr Bunting did for the entire family. And his reward? The disrespectful epithet 'Fusspot' had floated round the edge of the front room door to his reddening ears as he fixed a shade on the upstairs landing light. He had been hurt and startled. Too hurt even to remonstrate with Julie, whose vulgarity had shocked him. But he complained to his wife.

'Somebody's got to see to these things,' he said, reasonably.

'I know, dear. But they get tired of always hearing about the war.'

It was this kind of remark that made Mr Bunting sigh so heavily that his chest visibly rose and fell on a wave of suppressed emotion.

It never occurred to anyone, he supposed, that he got tired of doing the scores of extra jobs the war imposed upon a householder; filling in identity and ration cards, registering for fuel, sticking anti-splinter on the windows. They got tired simply hearing about it.

It was sometimes suggested, and particularly by Ernest, that Mr Bunting's abundant interest in the war, and the rejuvenating effect it had wrought upon him, were the result of his unexpected promotion at Brockleys. The war had crippled Ernest's business at the laundry, and almost extinguished the garage Chris shared with Bert Rollo, but had unfairly rewarded Mr Bunting with promotion and financial benefit. That was why, according to Ernest, father so completely realised there was a war on.

When war broke out Mr Bunting had been employed in the warehouse at Brockleys in the city. It was believed by his children that he wore a long white overall like a grocer's and, what their imaginations could but faintly picture, trundled a small truck like a porter's trolley about the basement. He also, and much more credibly, exercised sole dominion over a youth named Charlie, into whom he sought to instil ambition. Mr Bunting had, however, not always been a mere storekeeper. He had worked forty years for Brockleys, and for twenty-five of them had held the solid position of manager of the ironmongery department. Mr Bunting's knowledge of ironmongery was, in fact, encyclopaedic, and he had been highly esteemed by old John Brockley, the founder of the firm. But when old John died Mr Bunting's world collapsed about him.

Up till then Brockleys had been proud of being an old-fashioned firm. It never advertised, its windows never startled passers-by with shrieks of tremendous bargains, it never condescended to 'move with the times'. A sign over the entrance said simply and inclusively: 'Brockleys for all household goods – Wholesale and Retail,' and when you bought household goods at Brockleys you paid top price and you got the best. They lasted all your lifetime, and were honourably mentioned in your will, for to wear out a Brockley article was too much for one generation. Rooted in this principle of quality, Brockleys endured through good times and bad as an evergreen endures when blighting winds bring down showier trees that flourish only in the sunshine. Year after year discerning buyers made a track to its doors. But only after some other discerning buyer had supplied them with the address.

After old John's death a human whirlwind descended on Brockleys – Mr Ventnor, apostle of the smart and new. To Ventnor business was as much a science as modern warfare, which he seemed to think it resembled. Advertising was his propaganda; sales he spoke of as 'campaigns'; high-pressure salesmen drove home his attack. His objective was to reach 'saturation point' in any line of commodities, and he often talked about 'sales resistance' and 'sales prospects'. Mr Bunting prided himself on his vocabulary, and often added to it out of the *bijou* dictionary, but these neologisms stunned him. His friend, Joe Corder of the rug department, whose words were inextricably mingled with those of Shakespeare, was difficult enough to follow; but Ventnor was incomprehensible. Often Mr Bunting left the manager's office convinced only of one thing: that Ventnor was barmy, an impression which his general air of protest did nothing to conceal. Nor could he rid himself of his hatred of the shoddy, nor of his attachment to the slow and exact methods of a lifetime. There was no place for him in this speeded-up and bustling world. Brockleys had never sacked an employee because he'd reached a certain age till Ventnor sacked Mr Bunting.

But he went back. His reinstatement, even as a storekeeper, seemed in some way to justify a moral principle. When Ventnor vanished, and the directors set about recovering their lost reputation, they found a post for Mr Bunting. Not, alas, his old position of authority – that had been filled by a Lancastrian named Holroyd – but in the stores, where he earned enough to help his boys set up in business, and where he was much happier than he had been in his fallacious retirement. For Mr Bunting had odd, out-dated principles of loyalty. He belonged to Brockleys; he was as proud of his association with a house of quality as ever Tybalt was of being a Capulet.

The first hint of promotion came whilst he was in the warehouse imaginatively disposing the heavier stock where it would afford most protection from the blast of enemy bombs. Ever since war broke out Mr Bunting had given much thought to methods of outwitting Hitler. Hearing what sounded like a few bars of grand opera, he turned and saw Corder standing at the foot of the basement stairs with a more than usually theatrical air.

Lively and loquacious was Joe Corder; the poets echoed in his mind continually, and through him, though a little jangled, in Mr Bunting's.

'I bring thee glad tidings,' announced Corder. 'Thou wilt soon cease to be a troglodyte.'

Mr Bunting turned interrogatively, wanting a clue to this remarkable word.

'The usurper Holroyd appears to have been an officer in the territorials. He's joined his regiment.'

'Been called up?'

'As I said. George, your old job's vacant.'

Mr Bunting's heart leapt like a girl's. 'Is it 'ficial?'

'Yes, and I thought I'd pop up to the old man and remind him that here, dwelling in a den and cave of the earth, there still exists George Bunting, an example of unregarded age in corners thrown.'

'He knows I'm here, don't he? He knows I used to be in the iremungery,' said Mr Bunting, reflecting, however, that storekeepers were as grasshoppers in the sight of the chief, passing out of mind much more quickly than departmental managers.

'I'm going up to remind him,' said Corder, vanishing. 'Leave all to me.'

Balanced on the edge of hope and fear, Mr Bunting gazed doubtfully after him. Corder was a good chap, none better, but he never could deliver a plain unvarnished tale; he was far too literary. It was likely that if he talked about disregarded troglodytes Mr Bickerton would have little more idea of what he meant than Mr Bunting had.

Enduring all the sensations of a prisoner who knows the jury have just been locked in, Mr Bunting sat on a crate to await the issue. Thought was impossible now, he was all emotion. Resolutely he strove to blot from his mental retina the alluring picture that hope painted there; the old familiar cubby-hole, the long salesroom, himself installed securely in the seat of authority. A dryness of the throat affected him, a strong desire for forbidden tobacco. He got off the crate, lit the gas ring, and filled the kettle at the sink.

Whilst it boiled he examined himself in the tiny mirror. He straightened his tie, brushed his coat lapels, and looked himself in the eyes. There were things one naturally couldn't say to other people, but privately Mr Bunting classed himself as a good type of fellow. Not showy, nor brilliant (he prided himself on knowing his limitations), but a good average Englishman – sane, practical, and steady, and not this morning very well shaved.

Hearing footsteps on the stairs he turned off the gas and, with a swiftness that betokened long practice, silently slid the kettle out of sight behind an empty box conveniently placed for that express purpose.

'Mr Bickerton wants you,' piped the office boy, coming no further down the stairs than was absolutely necessary. Mr Bunting nodded gravely at him over the edge of a stock book.

After an interval calculated to give an impression that he had been actively busy below, he presented himself in the manager's office. Old John Brockley's photograph still hung above the fireplace; something like a look of recognition passed between it and Mr Bunting. Except for Corder and himself hardly any one now at Brockleys remembered its founder as he was pictured there. Irascible, kindly, strict, and humorous, Mr Bunting had never known a man who could get through so much work without ever appearing in a hurry. There were none like him nowadays.

Mr Bickerton was writing swiftly, his pink, bald head shining under the green-shaded light. He glanced up sideways, picked up a jotting, looked at Mr Bunting as though he were another jotting in human shape, and made the necessary mental connection.

'I want you to take charge of Mr Holroyd's department whilst he's away,' he said briskly.

'Certainly, sir. Only too pleased.'

'Carry on as far as you can in the way Mr Holroyd has been doing,' pursued Mr Bickerton, letting his clear, large eyes rest on Mr Bunting thoughtfully. 'It's purely a temporary arrangement. You'll receive the appropriate salary.'

'Thank you, sir,' said Mr Bunting. In his overflowing gratitude it hardly seemed enough; one ought to add some expression of – well, some expression. Unable to conjure an appropriate one he stood there faintly beaming and most honestly and unaffectedly filled with a determination to prove worthy.

It was clear, however, that on the manager's side the interview was at an end. No time these days for the smallest seasoning of ceremony. He might never have known that for twenty-five years Mr Bunting had controlled what was now called Mr Holroyd's department, that Mr Bunting indeed had served Brockleys since he was a boy. He might have been a stranger, any hireling who could be attached to Brockleys by bonds of so much work for so much pay.

Still, he could show he was a person of intelligence, above the mental level of the stores.

'I've been wondering, sir, if you'd ever thought of making an air raid shelter in the basement.'

'An air raid shelter!' repeated Mr Bickerton, surprised. 'Whatever for?'

'Well – air raids, sir.'

'Surely you're not nervous, Mr Bunting?' There was a faint irony in his tone.

Mr Bunting disdained nervousness. 'I thought you might want to consider it, sir.'

'I'm not having any one here getting hot under the collar about air raids,' pronounced Mr Bickerton with the blue glitter that occasionally lit his eye. To thaw the frost of this rebuke, he smiled for a split second, then waved Mr Bunting away with his pen.

Delightful as it was to emerge from the gloomy darkness of the cellar and walk again the quarter-deck of his own department, Mr Bunting assumed that, to others of the staff, it would be merely another wartime readjustment. He was prepared to be quite matter-of-fact. But immediately he entered the familiar salesroom he had a sense of the spotlight being upon him. Corder had been there with a palm-scattering of news, preparing for his arrival. As Mr Bunting passed between the rows of counters he got a welcoming word and handshake at every one. He proceeded down the long room in such a confluence of smiles and good wishes, all so transparently sincere, that his easily moved heart was warmed to its core. He would never have believed his old assistants would have been so glad to see him. Ah! If only Chris and Ernest could witness scenes like this and learn that, whatever they pretended to think of him at home, in the outside world of maturer judgment, their father was a highly respected figure.

But (as he reflected) their only conclusion would almost certainly be that Holroyd must have been a bit of a blighter to work for.

Having made a brief exploratory tour of the department, Mr Bunting retired to the cubby-hole to straighten it up and make it really his own. He was just unpinning from the partition a picture post card of the park gates at Rochdale (one of Holroyd's treasures) when old Turner came to say his private and particular word. Old Turner – he had been so designated for many years though actually he was younger than Mr Bunting – was one of the lurking figures in the shadowy background of the department devoted to stoves and iron piping. He had grey, watery eyes and a fluting voice, supposedly developed by long service as a church tenor. He was a man of rigid principles, to which he made more constant reference than his colleagues thought entirely necessary. He came, he explained, to set Mr Bunting's mind at ease in this matter of the managership.

'You needn't think there's any jealousy on my part, Mr Bunting. None whatever. You've been put in charge, and you can rely on me to back you up. Anything you want doing – don't hesitate to tell me.'

Having reinforced his message by an earnest, if watery look, and a firm, if chilly handshake, Turner departed, leaving Mr Bunting staring amazedly at his retreating back.

'Jealousy! Don't hesitate!' For a moment his powers of comprehension failed him. Then, like a slow dawn, the incredible, the diverting truth, filtered through. Almost automatically he slid off his stool to pass this huge joke on to Corder. Turner, the old tortoise, to think he might be put in charge and George Bunting left forgotten in the cellar. It showed how men whom you have all your life regarded as intelligent often secretly harbour the most asinine notions.

Meanwhile, for the duration at any rate, he was installed. He sat very firmly on the cubby-hole stool determined to continue in the methods of Holroyd, if Mr Bickerton so desired it, but to make improvements by the way.

That evening, before sitting down to tea, Mr Bunting announced his promotion from the centre of the hearthrug, which was his domestic rostrum, and waited for the acclamations. None came. The Bunting children were a little staggered, as they often were by the way events conspired to bring father out on top. Chris's garage business was fading out, and Ernest found the laundry making very heavy weather, but Mr Bunting was to ride above the storm, his star in the ascendant.

A silence fell upon the tea table, an unnatural pause, that gave Mr Bunting a sensation of having thrown a stone into a pond and seen it vanish without sound or splash.

Chris was the first to recover. 'Fine! Congratulations, dad,' and Ernest murmured self-consciously over his teacup that he was delighted to hear it.

'Yes, back in the old place,' went on Mr Bunting briskly. 'And not before time, considering the way things are going with you two boys. How's business been today, Chris?'

'Hardly taken a pound. Can't get petrol.'

'Other garages get plenty. Can't think what you're doing, Chris,' observed Mr Bunting, and passed through into the kitchen, which he preferred to the bathroom for his personal ablutions. Back to the tea table, where certain implications of this change were being gloomily realised, came the sound of splashing at the sink, mingled with intermittent bursts of song.

'That's what the war does, Chris,' remarked Ernest. 'Chaps like you and me get our careers messed up, and chaps like father get whacking good berths out of it. Yet, it's men of father's age who are responsible for the war – not us.' He cut a slice of cake as though he knew in advance it would contain too many caraway seeds.

To Ernest, the war was something that had first and foremost complicated the affairs of the Eagle Laundry Company. They had been complicated enough before. To an outsider it would have seemed incredible that a concern so small should have room in its affairs for such extraordinary complications. With Mr Eagle, aged and cautious, obstructing all improvements, the morose engineer eternally demanding repairs, the migration of laundresses, and the complaints of customers, Ernest's post as manager was no sinecure. There were, he believed, men earning thousands a year who never faced a fraction of the problems he daily coped with at the laundry. His chief sustaining thought was that very few fellows of his age could do it. Ernest had always known he was extraordinary.

But the complications of peacetime had been nothing to the ones that had arisen since the war. The whole of Ernest's waking thoughts were now given to the laundry, and he often delivered a problem over to his subconscious mind before he went to sleep. Quite frequently he was so deep in business thoughts that Chris was moved to inquire whether he was brooding over the loss of some girl's cami-knickers.

'It seems to me,' went on Ernest, glancing at the kitchen door, 'that we're going to hear a lot from father about keeping the home fires burning. You know what that leads to.'

'Reasonable 'conomy,' said Julie, who had a gift for mimicry, not always kept in check.

'But if the laundry does badly it'll hit father, won't it?' asked Chris. 'After all, he mortgaged the house to put money in it when you went there.'

'I know that,' said Ernest, who was sensitive on this point.

'So it's a good thing he's got his old job back, isn't it?'

'I know that too,' said Ernest. 'Only it seems to me so – so unfair. You work and plan to do something useful and along comes a war that nobody wants and takes it out of the younger generation.'

'That's just what I told Mavis,' said Julie, who admired Ernest's capacity for developing well-rounded sentences.

Mrs Bunting came in with sausage rolls hot from the oven. Mr Bunting, ruddy from his vigorous rough towelling, followed her, his nose and eyes appreciating the principal dish.

'Now, that's what I like,' he remarked, sitting down. 'Nothing like a hot sausage roll. Wonder you don't make them oftener, Mary.'

'Because they're bad for your digestion, George.'

'Not they,' said Mr Bunting, spearing two of the larger ones. 'In any case – special occasion.'

He launched into an amplified version of his discussion with Mr Bickerton. He was supremely happy and confident and just a shade inclined to draw the inevitable moral. In times of stress send for the old and trusted.

''Course I've got more responsibility,' he proceeded, lest he should give an impression of having been called to a post of ease. 'We've got a lot of stuff in for air raid precautions.'

'Do you really think there'll be air raids, daddy?'

'I don't know, but we've got the stuff. Scoops for incendiary bombs, stirrup pumps, salving hooks, portable sirens – all manner of stuff.'

'It doesn't seem right to me,' interposed Ernest, 'that private firms should be allowed to make money out of things like that, even if they're necessary. You can't open a paper nowadays without seeing advertisements for war stuff. It's getting to be a proper racket.'

'Not at all,' replied Mr Bunting, ''gitimate business.'

'Course it's 'gitimate,' agreed Julie. 'It's about the 'gitimatest thing anybody could think of.'

Mr Bunting gave her a sharp sidelong glance, and bestowed a longer one on the carefully composed faces of his sons.

'I can never understand,' he remarked, 'why, as soon as anybody begins a sensible discussion in this house, you all start grinning like a lot of asses. If you're refusing war work at the laundry, Ernest, no wonder you've had to cut your own salary.'

Having thus pointedly put an end to the discussion, Mr Bunting rose from the table, undid the top button of his trousers, and, relieved to that extent, settled into his fireside chair.

He sat there finishing the *Siren*, and keeping his pipe alight with spills. Chris and Ernest, he supposed, had gone out or were in the front room with Julie; at any rate none of them were present to disturb him; quietness filled the living room. In this delicious quietness Mrs Bunting was laying out the mended washing on the table. It always pleased him to watch her at work. She knew every vest, sock, and handkerchief; she apportioned each to its owner's pile as though she were playing patience with the household linen. The concentration she brought to the simplest domestic task always faintly amused Mr Bunting, and filled him with a sort of pride and tenderness. At such moments his emotions would suddenly come to the boil and he would give her a playful unexpected smack.

Watching her, as he was doing now, was like looking in on one of her private moments, when they were apart. He might have been miles away at Brockleys, and she here quite alone. Thus happily occupied she lived and worked in her own domestic world where violence and terror had never entered, where the doings of the world outside were no more than rumour.

There must have been rooms like this, he thought, women like Mary, in those towns and villages of Poland where, without warning, bombs had come crashing through the roofs. Mr Bunting had very little idea of bursting bombs, but there was present to his imagination just then an idea of noise and flash, smoke and dust swirling back from some sickening spectacle, as it might be here in the living room of Laburnum Villa. Such things happened, were happening even now, as the *Siren* faithfully reported and frequently illustrated with photographs. Mr Bunting had grown accustomed to seeing photographs of bombed houses, houses ripped open and indecently exposed, many of them respectable, decent ones like his own.

With an effort he banished these unwanted thoughts and fancies. Where they came from he did not know. They arose in the mind without cause, and filled you with a vague dread that some deep-rooted racial instinct was at work, that they were premonitions of disaster and warnings and things a sane man knew they could not be. One had to shake them off. It was more likely, as faint familiar symptoms warned him, they were mental accompaniments of undigested sausage roll.

'I'll have a soda mint,' he said, reaching this specific off the mantelshelf. The *Home Doctor*, which had no more interested reader than Mr Bunting, was silent about soda mints, but definite in its warnings about too much carbonate of soda.

'Will you get your old salary, George?'

'Yes,' he told her, and became judicial. 'Don't know whether it will start from today or tomorrow. I'll see what Corder thinks.'

'I'm glad you're out of that unhealthy old cellar anyway. Why, you look brighter already.'

'I feel brighter,' he declared. But his sunnier mood had deeper roots than his physical liberation from the cellar; his mind and spirit had been emancipated.

'For all that,' he said sincerely, 'I want to see the Germans beaten and Holroyd back. I'll be as glad to go back into the cellar as I was to come out of it. If need be, that is. But we've got to lick these Germans.'

He stood firmly and squarely on his hearth, puffing his pipe and thinking about Hitler, and how little Hitler understood the spirit he was up against.

TWO

THE FROSTY PAUSE that succeeded Mr Bunting's announcement of his promotion expressed his children's instant realisation of the complications that would ensue. Regarded as a fact in isolation, his promotion was a stroke of family fortune, and the difficulties of Chris and Ernest's businesses made it timely. But it could not be regarded in isolation because of the peculiar defects of Mr Bunting's character. As far back as they could remember he had carried the family's financial burden on the understanding that he was, in consequence, entitled to dictatorial powers.

The days were not far distant when father earned all the money and asked all the questions about where it went to; when he used to follow his children about the house switching off lights and pointing out what the current cost per unit; when he would take Ernest's new trilby off the hat-stand and criticise it in the full daylight of the living room as being of superior quality to his own. Lately there had been less of these indignities, but they were by no means forgotten, and in a world turned topsy-turvy it seemed possible they might return. Their warning shadows even now fell chilly on them. It was one of the minor consequences of the war which they had overlooked.

It was true, and most generously admitted, that Mr Bunting had helped his sons towards independence by investing in the laundry, and by converting his cottages at Linport into a garage for Chris. Their guileless young hearts had accepted his assistance as a sign that a new era was about to dawn. But its dawn had cast a false, illusory glow. More and more frequently was it pointed out when they were in committee (for one should think realistically and without sentiment) that Mr Bunting would not have sponsored these enterprises had he not been certain that financial advantage would accrue. His interest in them did, in fact, wax and wane according to the rate of the financial benefits. And the total effect of his sleeping partnership was sensibly to extend his dominion over what should have been their free young lives.

Mr Bunting was now able to criticise the decoration of Ernest's office as extravagant and to take up with Chris the folly of wasting money on advertisements. Nor did either of their businesses ever receive a setback that could not have been avoided had Mr Bunting been asked for his advice in time.

Sometimes the Bunting children, smarting in their thraldom, wondered whether beneath father's simplicity there lay concealed a streak of shrewdness superior even to their own. Or (a revised opinion) whether by the vagaries of chance events worked out to give his decisions an effect of far-sightedness he could not possibly possess. This fortuitous promotion at Brockleys was a case in point; it arose out of the war, their own business difficulties arose out of the war, neither had anything to do with possessing guts and determination or any of Mr Bunting's favourite Victorian virtues. The facts were plain and simple; but not so Mr Bunting's interpretation thereof.

Already he was beginning to stand on the hearthrug jingling his change, particularly at moments when Ernest was trying to think, beaming and satisfied as a man who has got safe ashore, and cannot understand why anyone should still be struggling in the water. He continually urged his sons not to let their difficulties overwhelm them – they should show more initiative, take arms against their seething troubles, and grapple with hooks of steel, as the poet said. If the laundry and the garage were not paying there was one unfailing remedy, the recipe of the older generation: to put their backs into it.

When Mr Bunting delivered himself of a pronouncement of this kind he invariably assumed that, if the difficulties in question were not swept away, it was because of failure to act on his advice. They had evidently not put their backs into it, or not sufficiently, or not in the way Mr Bunting would have done; had, in fact, often done when he was a younger man. None of his *obiter dicta* failed for want of repetition.

He was, indeed, once more, as Mrs Bunting had touchingly assured them, his old familiar self. As Chris remarked pensively, if business didn't improve he would soon be unable to go out unless father bought him another pair of braces. For Mr Bunting's interest in small economies had been revived, and dedicated to the service of the empire. No one could make the fire up without being reminded that coal trucks were needed for the transport of munitions, and every particle of uneaten food became a text for a lecture upon the vital need for shipping space. Now was the time for self-denial and for effort! As to business difficulties, Brockleys had business difficulties and were making efforts to surmount them – most active efforts, on a vastly larger scale than they could have the least idea of.

Between whiles he went up and down the stairs humming like a bee, wondering a little at his freedom from dyspepsia. His nerves probably. Psychological. He took down the *Home Doctor* and turned the pages, softly whistling.

Ernest heard him as he sat one evening at the front room table working out, in his neat figuring, the comparative cost of blacking out the laundry with different widths of material. Though the necessity for this unproductive expenditure irritated Ernest, it was the kind of task he liked, and he calculated accurately and to the finest detail. Behind these calculations odds and ends of thought wandered through his mind as they did when he was playing the piano. The laundry skylights, newly put in to effect a permanent saving of electric light, would now cost several pounds to black out. Mr Eagle, who had been opposed to the skylights, had drawn attention to this fact today, rather unfairly, Ernest thought. Mr Eagle had, in fact, been a trifle sarcastic, as though amused to see one of Ernest's fine ideas recoil so disconcertingly upon him. It was now proved that the laundry, which had never had skylights, would have been better without them.

This, and endless other difficulties, arose out of the war. Had they arisen out of some national effort to do those simple things that were needed to make life better, no one would have sacrificed for them more willingly than Ernest. But they were all waste; all the feverish activity visible around him was worse than waste, it was positively destructive. A bomb cost hundreds of pounds, he supposed, and the damage it did amounted to thousands. All over Europe, where the need was for better hospitals and better houses, for more laboratories for research, men were making bombs. When they got them they used them to destroy the hospitals and the laboratories. If that was what patriotism demanded, Ernest had no use for it.

Thoughts like these never troubled Chris, who was entirely single-minded. At the moment he was studying the new tail plane of the Blenheim bomber in a recent copy of *Flight*. Having superficially absorbed the technical explanation he turned to an illustration of the cockpit of a Hurricane fighter, experiencing the immediate thrill of 'that's where you sit'. To examine the dashboard of a super-car was a sensation that faded into nothing. Chris had, in fact, ceased to read motoring journals, he now brought home nothing but flying journals. He had piles of flying journals, *The Aeroplane*, *Flight*, and *Aeronautics*, in his bedroom, not one of which would he surrender to the nation for salvage. His sole interest was flying. His mother had long feared that he and young Rollo (known to be a little mad) would construct a homemade plane and embark on suicidal adventures. But his father's criticism was more cogent. When Chris was in Barclays Bank he studied nothing but motorcars, now he was in the motorcar business he studied nothing but aeroplanes. The only way to stop him studying aeroplanes was, obviously, to get him a job in a factory where they made them.

Spasmodically cutting across Chris's concentration on the Hurricane was preoccupation with his pipe. It was his first, a bulldog, short and blunt and admirably suited to a man of fifty. He tried it first at one corner of his mouth, then at the other, then in the centre. He had never imagined that the art of pipe-smoking presented so many points of practical difficulty, the paramount one being that of keeping the pipe alight. Frequently he had to abandon *Flight* altogether and puff determinedly for a good half-minute, after which he felt an excoriating sensation in his throat and a faint dizziness. He was inclined to think he had got the wrong tobacco.

'Better let me dump these matches before father comes in,' said Julie, examining the ash tray.

'They're not his matches.'

'But don't you realise there's a war – '

At this mimicry of Mr Bunting Ernest rattled his papers as a reminder that brain-work was in progress.

'Where did you get the pipe?' she whispered. 'Did Marvellous Monica buy it for you?'

'Yes,' said Chris composedly.

'Did Marvellous want her Christopher to look a proper he-man?'

'Yes. Shut up!'

'Oh, damn!' exploded Ernest.

Julie raised her brows at him. 'Now what on earth's the matter?' she inquired.

'How do you think anyone can concentrate when you're gassing and talking?' he demanded, and began to collect his papers and slip them into a business-like manilla folder. He was surprised that his voice should have such a blurting tone when his thoughts had been so very lofty. But he had been struck once more by a thought that always came to him with a touch of irony. All his energies, all his time and talent, were now devoted to a laundry. The laundry was all right, and he liked to make a success of it, but it was no great concern; it looked much smaller and less important than it used to do as he walked towards it every morning, and it made no demand on his special abilities. All that mattered of life had to be built out of what was left of time and energy when he had finished with the laundry; which these days, he thought bitterly as he scanned his papers, was precious little.

His life seemed utterly futile sometimes. The war was turning the whole of life to drudgery. One thought and worked and planned not to build something better, but as the servant of a vast conspiracy of vandals bent on wrecking the best things we had.

Straying down these avenues of speculation Ernest would pull himself together, and, remembering his psychology books, wonder whether his mind had been simply wandering or whether he had been surrendering himself to the voice of the unconscious. Merely to dream was to fail in thought control, which Ernest assiduously practised, and was rather good at really; at least, he could do all the exercises. For a time this question of what his mind had been up to banished the earlier ones, which came back to him presently unanswered and unanswerable, as though life held problems not to be solved by mere mental efficiency. He heard the kitchen door close and Mr Bunting's footsteps as he walked round the house examining the blackout and, no doubt, critically scanning the entire avenue.

Nothing in life seemed real these days; the streets were dark and empty except for an occasional warden cycling past with his steel helmet and gas mask like a tangible ghost. The searchlights' beams went creeping eerily about the sky, and indoors the radio's voice went suavely on reporting on a world of evil phantasy. Men and women were reduced to the helplessness of automatons moved by lunatic masters.

He crossed to the piano and sat down to play.

If, in every country, there were men who devised bombs and mines, there were also men who made music. Ernest's saddened heart often turned to that for comfort.

'That's a nice piece,' said Mr Bunting, coming in. 'I heard it outside. New, isn't it?'

'Yes, it's by Otto Reinberger – a German. I suppose you'd call him a Hun.'

'I would,' said Julie. 'I'd like to spit in his eye.'

'That's enough, Julie,' said Mr Bunting, who nevertheless thought Ernest's remark unnecessary, to say the least.

'No reason why Hitler should rule us because Otto can write a bit of decent music, is it?' asked Chris. 'You're always so keen on these foreign Johnnies. Why shouldn't a chap with a name like Parkinson turn out as good stuff as your old Beethoven?'

'I don't know. They never seem to. Parkinson's sonatas. Good Lord!'

There developed an argument about Parkinson's sonatas which grew more heated and wandering and incomprehensible to Mr Bunting. He turned his head this way and that following the speakers, but without learning who Parkinson was, or even whether he was a reality or a myth. He agreed with Chris that Ernest would be unlikely to buy, play, or even listen to sonatas by a chap called Parkinson; but, apart from this, he regarded the whole discussion as silly and unpractical.

'Say what you like,' declared Ernest, 'the Germans are a great people and supreme in music.'

'I don't see that they are,' put in Mr Bunting. 'Some of their music's rotten. Bach, for instance – all them fugues. And those silly twiddling 'tudes – '

'Chopin. He was a Pole, of course.'

Mr Bunting spared Chopin further comment, but pertinaciously returned to Bach. 'Can't understand why you play 'em, Ernest. Ain't we got British music?'

'Art,' quoted Ernest, 'knows no frontiers,' which Julie, with an effect of egging everybody on, echoed with 'as the poet said'.

'I can never understand your attitude towards Germany, said Mr Bunting. 'Anyone would think you weren't patriotic.'

'I don't think I am, really.'

Mr Bunting was deeply shocked; he crimsoned slightly. 'I never thought I'd live to hear a son of mine say a thing like that. You can't mean it.'

'I think for myself,' said Ernest.

'Not under Hitler you wouldn't.'

'Under Hitler, or anybody. Not that I want to see his methods over here. I believe in democracy.'

'Ah!' said Mr Bunting, perceiving with relief that Ernest's remark had some obscure meaning perceptible only to highbrows. Speaking for himself as a practical man, it was a straight issue, the empire against the Huns. He remembered the last war, lots of things that had lain buried in Mr Bunting's memory had received a resurrection: the *Lusitania*, Belgian atrocities, the whining after the war for money, and the swindle in which it vanished. There were lots of things Ernest didn't know; he wasn't old enough.

Ernest interrupted him at this stage. As it happened, he knew a great deal about the last war and what followed it. He knew much more than his father; was prepared to argue him to a standstill.

'If we'd given them a square deal – '

Mr Bunting grew heated. He had been heated before, but with an effect of restraint, now he grew heated with an effect of unleashing righteous indignation.

'A square deal! What sort of a square deal would they have given us? What we ought to have done was to sit on their heads.'

'Hear! hear!' exclaimed Chris, giving his father unexpected support, which would have been more welcome had he not immediately followed it with: 'I'm looking forward to when I can join up.'

'Very well,' said Ernest. 'But you'll see when all the slaughter and destruction is over we'll have to sit round a table with the Germans and start the world running again. And if there's more injustice there'll be another war, and another; and so it'll go on.'

'We haven't got them beaten yet,' put in Chris with some practicality. 'Wait till the Luftwaffe gets busy.'

'We'll beat them right enough,' said Mr Bunting, scenting defeatism. He felt annoyed with both his sons and rather more with Chris for always bringing in the Luftwaffe. It had taken him some time to discover that this peculiar word only meant the German Air Force. Then why not call it the German Air Force, or better still the Hun Air Force, using 'lee mott just.'

He felt that, as far as Laburnum Villa was concerned, he was the only person really keen on beating the Germans, the only one who stood four-square and defiant in the true spirit of John Bull. A war was like all other things, he told them; to win you'd got to put your back into it.

THREE

AS MR BUNTING walked up Cumberland Avenue the following Saturday afternoon a faint tinkle of glass was audible in his leatherette case. This tinkle, musical in itself, and particularly so to Mr Bunting's ears, was caused by the knocking together of two bottles of 'Bonnie Prince Charlie'. Two bottles! For a long time he had not had even one, but today he had drawn his first salary as manager of the ironmongery department.

Mr Bunting took whisky for purely medicinal reasons connected with the lining of his stomach. It was a demulcent or a carminative – to speak the truth he forgot what it was, but he knew the *Home Doctor* regarded it with reasonable favour subject to certain warnings against excess, which, of course, did not apply to himself. What exercised his mind was the second bottle, which, he feared, would carry with it a suggestion of extravagance. It had been purchased because of his suspicions of the forthcoming war budget. More than once had the Chancellor of the Exchequer forestalled him in this matter of whisky, taxing where further taxation had seemed inconceivable. Mr Bunting's motive had been economy. To explain this to his family would, he feared, not only be to invite scepticism, but also to present his children with a reason for buying all kinds of articles which the Chancellor would certainly ignore. The wisest thing would be to secrete the second bottle in the cupboard of the spare bedroom.

He climbed the hill more steadily than usual; the tinkle was just loud enough to caution him against haste. Besides, there was plenty to see in the familiar road now changing day by day. There were sandbags round the callbox, sandbags round the warden's post, sandbags barricading windows. A white strip edged the kerb and encircled the base of every tree. The effect was rather pretty – struck him vaguely as continental. Here and there he saw a garden dugout or an empty house with battened windows. All these changes had the effect of novelty, for throughout the week he walked home in the primeval blackness of the evening, flashing his torch on the pavement.

As he passed the pillar box he gave it a suspicious look, fixing its position exactly in his memory, for there had been collisions.

It was mildly cheering to see even these modest signs of the war being taken seriously. Ever since he opened the morning's *Siren* a fog of doubt had settled in all the chambers of his mind; his thoughts had been dismal. Mr Bunting's faith in the *Siren* was naive and complete, but he could never understand why it painted a rosy picture of the path to victory one morning and a gloomy one the next. Today, the special correspondent had given a disheartening conspectus of the European diplomatic scene. His change of tone was most upsetting. Mr Bunting always looked forward to the diplomatic correspondent's Saturday article; it was cheerful and sprinkled with heartening suggestions that what looked like British blundering was really diplomatic finesse cleverly disguised, and the Government's apparent inactivity was but a mask concealing astute moves behind the scenes. To read these articles was to be convinced every weekend that Hitler was being led up the garden. The damaging revelations of this morning were tantamount to an admission that a trap had been sprung, and Lord Halifax, not Hitler, was inside it. This far-seeing commentator, whose writings suggested a perpetual hovering about European chancelleries, seemed ruefully to confess he had not seen far enough nor calculated rightly.

Mr Bunting perceived that even the diplomatic correspondent was a man like unto himself and capable of error.

'Bound to have set-backs,' he thought, stoutly striding along. A set-back never did the British any harm. Mr Bunting privately believed they thrived on them. He sighed, nevertheless.

Carefully he changed the attaché case from one hand to the other. He had borrowed a strap from old Turner to safeguard its precious contents. Turner was a teetotaller; his watery eyes had widened disapprovingly at the bottles of 'Bonnie Prince Charlie' on the cubby-hole desk. He seemed to conclude that Mr Bunting was travelling to perdition at an increasing pace, and that he was culpably aiding and abetting in a rake's career. Mr Bunting had, in fact, feared for a moment that Turner would countermand his offer of the strap; he was the sort of man who would have called the snapping open of the attaché case an act of God.

A measure of acerbity had crept into his relations with old Turner. Turner put things in the wrong boxes, dispatched orders to wrong addresses, and he was generally jumpy and forgetful. Moreover, Mr Bunting had seen him slip out several times lately to buy the four o'clock *Standard* in the street, and return with it imperfectly concealed beneath his coat. Such actions were bad for discipline, and Mr Bunting had lately grown very strong on discipline. Occasionally he wondered whether the welcome he received on his return to the department had not been a shade too warm and friendly, suggesting that here was someone lax and easy. Holroyd had been by no means easy, but a martinet, his surly silences broken only by a voice of nutmeg-grater quality. Therefore, at intervals during the day, Mr Bunting pulled out the bottom drawer of the desk, levered himself cautiously upon it, and surveyed the salesroom, searching it from end to end. This phenomenon, known in the past as the 'turnip sprouting,' had developed a stealthiness like the action of a rising periscope. Sometimes he would enter the cubby-hole and immediately appear bolt upright above the partition, discovering several delinquencies by this new tactic.

'Thank God for weekends!' he thought, as he passed through the green and white gates of Laburnum Villa. This moment of arrival home was the high spot of Mr Bunting's week, his mood was that of a liner captain docking after a long voyage. Chris and Ernest drifted in with no more spirit of festival on Saturdays than they did on Mondays; but Mr Bunting bustled in humming and greeting everybody loudly and cheerfully, not at all like a man who had parted from his family as recently as breakfast time.

'Here we are!' he exclaimed, bouncing into the kitchen to greet his wife. 'Everybody home? Good! I'll just take my collar off,' which he proceeded to do, unmindful of Julie's lips compressed in protest. Julie often wondered how, if ever she became engaged, she would break in her fiancé to her father's lack of refinement.

'Rabbit pie!' he exclaimed, dexterously piercing as fine a piece of pastry as even Mrs Bunting had ever produced. As recognisable portions of the carcass were uncovered Julie shuddered.

'Ugh! Dead rabbit! Disgusting!'

Thunderstruck, Mr Bunting turned on her. 'What's the matter with rabbit pie?'

'She's gone vegetarian,' explained Chris. 'Picked it up from her boss at the office.'

'It's hateful killing things,' said Julie. 'What right have we to kill innocent little rabbits just to eat them?'

Mr Bunting paused in his serving to stare at his daughter. Here was something new. She had made her protest, and sat haloed with moral courage, her young face reddening. Apparently she was developing on the same lines as her brothers. Instead of becoming more sensible as they grew older, their ideas got sillier and sillier, till they passed the confines of common sense and reason.

'Serve the pie, George,' said Mrs Bunting.

'Should jolly well think so.'

He objected most strongly to the suggestion that he was not humane because he ate rabbit pie. He was exceedingly humane. Many a morning he wasted several minutes rescuing a spider from the empty bath, and depositing it carefully on the windowsill outside. But a rabbit playing on Kilworth Common and a rabbit in a pie had, as far as he could see, only a sentimental connection. A pie, to Mr Bunting was a pie, a most enjoyable thing.

'I wouldn't take too much pastry, George. It doesn't agree with you.'

'I know,' he retorted with some crispness. It annoyed him to be warned against dishes he particularly liked, yet it was all Mrs Bunting did warn him of. When they had a chicken nobody suggested that his indigestion entitled him to a liberal portion of the breast.

'How's business, Chris? Got any petrol?' he inquired presently.

'No, but I've filled a form in.'

'Filled a form in. That's some good, isn't it?'

'It's what you have to do anyway.'

'All the Government thinks about,' remarked Ernest, 'is filling in forms. Just a lot of red tape. And when you've filled your forms in they go and lose 'em.'

'I expect it's worse in Germany,' said Mr Bunting, striking the patriotic note. 'What's that Julie's eating?'

'Nuts.'

'And very appropriate,' remarked Chris.

Mr Bunting regarded Julie's plate. They were nuts, certainly – fried nuts, a sort of rissole. Although the whole thing was a silly fad, they looked by no means unattractive. He had never considered the possibility of cooking nuts.

'Be better with a bit o' batter,' he observed thoughtfully.

Julie suddenly choked with laughter. 'Oh, daddy! You say the funniest things.'

Mr Bunting stared at her, stared at all of them. What funny things? He wondered. He deliberately said funny things quite often without any effect whatever. But when he made a perfectly straightforward remark... As one who ignores folly, he inquired: 'What's for pudding, ma?'

'Rice. Julie made it.'

'Oh, lor!' exclaimed Chris, sitting back; and Ernest observed: 'Now we're all going to have indigestion.'

'That's quite enough,' said Mr Bunting decisively. ''Mazes me you children can never agree. Your sister's got to learn to cook some time. You should have seen the stuff we had to eat in the last war.'

'The war to end war!' put in Ernest, with sarcasm.

'Look here, Ernest – '

'Please! No war talk,' interposed Mrs Bunting, to his great relief, for though he had been going to remonstrate with Ernest he had no clear idea how his remonstrance should develop. He stirred the pudding gently and helped himself out of the very centre.

'Pity we can't have more peace and quiet in this house, especially in wartime. None of us know what might happen before it's finished.'

'You're right, George,' said Mrs Bunting, with a sincerity of agreement which he found altogether pleasant. It would have a better effect, he thought, if she displayed such prompt support a little oftener.

It occurred to him, as he finished his after-dinner cup of tea, that it was time Laburnum Villa began to dig for victory. Now was the season, according to the gardening articles, to prepare the soil and make it friable, a word Mr Bunting had at first taken for a misprint, but later discovered in the *bijou* dictionary. His old boots in the cupboard, mentally assigned for salvage, would do excellently for gardening. This was in itself a cheering thought, and he assumed them in the spirit of a soldier girding on his weapons to have a crack at Hitler. But he did not immediately proceed to operations on the soil. The first essential was planning; when he considered the actual digging his thoughts turned to Chris and Ernest. Planning, however, was something he could do himself.

Mr Bunting's garden had passed through many stages, but had never been completely subdued. Gardening, to his thinking, was a hobby, and a man should indulge his hobby or leave it alone according to his mood. Admirable as this principle is when the hobby is stamp collecting or astronomy, it is difficult to apply successfully to gardening. Nature, unlike Mr Bunting, would not leave the garden alone. Weeds sprang up and flourished, their seeds were blown into Oskey's garden next door, and arguments ensued.

Oskey was at this moment parading his garden, hoe in hand, like a sentry with fixed bayonet. Let the tiniest unauthorised green shoot betray its presence and Oskey's hoe dexterously uprooted it. He had a swift, spearing action, as though attacking disappearing targets. He kept his eyes open for various kinds of insect pests with which Mr Bunting was frequently and condignly visited. These insects, none of which could hide its identity from Oskey, were alleged to come through Mr Bunting's fence and attach themselves to Oskey's vegetables. He dispatched them as dexterously as he did the weeds, but with more venom, knowing their origin. Oskey's garden was, in fact, the most highly cultivated piece of ground for miles around, and he was proud of it. Weedless and thriving, it shone as bounteous proof that everything promised on the seed packets was possible to skill and industry.

'Going to make a dugout?' he inquired, after a spell of watching Mr Bunting pacing up and down measuring out distances.

'Going in for more vegetables. 'Tensive cultivation. Help the country.'

'If I were you I'd make a dugout,' said Oskey, as though directing

Mr Bunting to something within his competence.

'Why? You don't think they'll come to Kilworth, do you?'

'Can't trust Germans. You want to go down six feet, roof over, and cover with eighteen inches of earth. You can grow marrows on the top.'

'I'm not very keen on a dugout,' said Mr Bunting, whose private thought was that it would spoil the garden. As this was hardly the sort of reason he could give to Oskey he sought for another.

'I saw a case in the papers of a council increasing the rates on people who had built dugouts. That's the sort of thing a council like ours would do. Any excuse is good enough for pushing up the rates in Kilworth.'

'All the same, you ought to have a dugout,' persisted Oskey, whose method of argument was to return continually to his original assertion. 'It's not just bombs, Bunting, it's splinters off the ack-ack. What goes up has got to come down.' He mentioned this with the air of opening up a more original line of thought. 'Do you know the velocity of a piece of shrapnel falling four miles?'

'No. What is it? And what's this ack-ack business?'

'You see! You don't know nothing about it, and yet you argue. Build a dugout, like I said, and see it's properly covered over.'

Mr Bunting watched him clump away to duty at the wardens' post. Poor old Oskey, he thought, a man whose mind was eternally occupied with technical details. His entire leisure was devoted to gardening, and he followed it, not light-heartedly, but with unswerving adherence to strictest rule, like a man doing penance. Oskey had a way of looking over his fence as a Nazi might look across his frontiers, offended by the free and easy life of the adjoining territory. He would interrupt Mr Bunting in the performance of certain processes to tell him that science and the season required the performance of quite different processes – and usually ones Mr Bunting had no mind for at the moment. He would carefully prune Laburnum Villa's two apple-trees according to the best utilitarian principles, not knowing that Mr Bunting prized them chiefly for their blossom. All that gave Mr Bunting's garden its enchantment, as when he planted a thing like an onion and was rewarded with a daffodil, was lost on Oskey, who attributed everything to phosphates in the soil. A man without poetry, who called a columbine an *aquilegia*.

Still, Oskey's garden looked strange without his lean, perpetually occupied figure. For the first time since the war, it occurred to Mr Bunting how much Warden Oskey must miss his weekends in the garden. "Course, everybody 's got to make sacrifices,' he thought. He disliked feeling under any kind of obligation to Oskey. He had never regarded him as being particularly patriotic. Probably Oskey had joined the wardens out of an intense personal dislike he had conceived for Hitler, mainly, one gathered, on the grounds of his facial appearance. No doubt he welcomed an opportunity of acquiring technical knowledge and passing it on weightily in his official capacity, as in this matter of the dugout. It was not long since Oskey, speaking as an ex-soldier, had declared that the safest place in an air raid was the first bomb crater. They could never drop 'em in the same place twice because, as he said (anxious to be fully grasped), an aeroplane is a moving object.

Mr Bunting's thoughts returned to the question of the dugout as he sat by the fire later in the evening. A dugout would cost not less than twenty pounds. It was only necessary to mention this fact to set everybody in the house clamouring for one to be provided. Ernest could be relied on to enlarge on the value of its psychological effect. There were many arguments which could be put forward in favour of a dugout (and that was why he did not raise the question), but the principal argument against one was that it might never be used. There might never be any bombs dropped on Kilworth or, if there were, not on the Cumberland Estate. Even assuming bombs were dropped actually in Cumberland Avenue, wasn't it reasonable to assume they might miss the house and hit the dugout? The whole question was exceedingly complex and uncertain in every aspect except one, that twenty pounds was twenty pounds, and, Kilworth builders being what they were, might easily become twenty-five.

So Mr Bunting meditated and waited for the wireless news. There was none in the *Standard*, except what he had read already in the morning's *Siren*. There was no reference anywhere to the disclosures of the diplomatic correspondent which had disturbed him so deeply that he had at once looked for sensational developments in the evening headlines. Reassured that national collapse was, at any rate, not imminent, he gave himself up to smoking. In this he was conducting an experiment. For years he had smoked nothing but Paradise Mixture. He had started when it was eightpence an ounce, stuck to it through successive tax increases till it got above a shilling, and even after that. But he was not prepared to pay one and tenpence. Not for all the Chancellors of the Exchequer who ever lived would George Bunting pay one and tenpence for tobacco. He had, in consequence, begun a systematic testing of the cheaper brands, filling Laburnum Villa with a variety of pungent odours which, it was complained, got into the curtains and made the place smell like a taproom. Some of them were, indeed, not pleasant, and he had recently given much tobacco away as unsmokable – but only to men in the forces.

'Better go back to your old sort, George,' said his wife. 'That stuff's terrible.'

'Not at one and tenpence. Anyway, it's better than dock leaves, what the Germans have to smoke.'

'I thought it *was* dock leaves,' said Ernest, over the edge of his book. He spoke in a detached way, his intelligent eyes in his pale, restrained features riveted on his book. Mr Bunting assumed this was a joke. Ernest never smiled when he made jokes; his smile at all times was quick and momentary. Chris sat with his feet on the couch, snuggled almost out of sight behind the *Aeroplane*, his brows furrowing more and more as some technical article took him increasingly beyond his depth. Julie sat upon the stool distributing her attention between a khaki sock and the instructions how to knit it, breaking off now and then to straighten out and murmur at the wool she had inexpertly tangled. All were silent, occupied, self-absorbed. Saturday evening in wartime! In the past Mr Bunting had often wished to have his family round him instead of seeing them run off to silly films. When the blackout came he imagined they might have some old-fashioned sit-round-the-fire evenings, happy and jolly. But instead they got this gloomy isolation and boredom. It seemed he could sit there a week and nobody speak to him.

'Ah, well!' he sighed, and with a sort of inspiration got up to black out the bedrooms and do a little prowling after gas masks.

He found Chris's gas mask under the kitchen table with his boots, one lying on its side; his raincoat hung lopsidedly on its peg, his hat on the handle of his father's umbrella. Even there it had a slightly dashing tilt, as though proclaiming its ownership. With an indrawing of his breath Mr Bunting corrected these errors. It passed the time.

The BBC time signal greeted him as he returned to the living room. He stood still, waiting with the recurrent slight apprehensiveness for the announcer's voice.

'*There is nothing to report on the western front –* '

'Oh, damn!' he thought. 'They'll never finish the war this way. Why don't they get at the blighters?'

'Switch off, dad. There's nothing fresh.'

Mr Bunting sat down again. He liked to hear the wireless news. It was never accurately reported to him; Mrs Bunting's inaccuracy was quite astounding. But he switched off. The boredom of the war once more descended on Laburnum Villa.

FOUR

SUNDAY DAWNED BRIGHT for Chris, who was going to see Bert Rollo, home on his first leave. He ran the Conway out before breakfast, and attacked that meal with so much haste that it was accompanied throughout by a parental monologue on the results of imperfect mastication. If Mr Bunting had never understood the origin of his own indigestion he had a clear idea why indigestion attacked other people. Chris heard him with a cheerful heedlessness, and before the rest of the family had reached the stage of toast and marmalade was chugging down to Linport, the site of the Snappy Service Garage.

This undertaking needed to be viewed with the eye of faith that sees the acorn in the oak. It had potentialities. As the Linport Estate grew, so would the business, drawing its sap from ever-enriching soil. At present it consisted of a reconstruction of three old cottages acquired by Mr Bunting under his sister's will, and its architecture was preponderantly domestic. But it was camouflaged by a plentiful display of peppy slogans in the American style. Bert, who admired everything American, added to them from time to time and strove to introduce pep into the business generally.

No motorist pulled up at the garage without being impressed by its efficiency. One of its chief objects was so to impress him. With his petrol he received a leaflet explaining what Snappy Service 'stood for'. He got his tyre pressure tested, his oil checked, the correctness of his route confirmed, and his attention drawn to any sound of wear in the engine. He couldn't fail to realise as at last he drove away that he had been in touch with first-class people.

Right up to the outbreak of the war Chris would sooner have spent an evening at the garage with Bert Rollo than anywhere on earth, unless it were with Bert's sister Monica, to whom he was, in a manner of speaking, engaged. Even this latter pleasure he would forgo rather than disappoint a customer over a repair. At the garage there was plenty to do, plenty to talk about, plenty to plan for. It was their own enterprise and adventure, and the centre of their lives.

But the war had changed all that; knocked the sense out of every workaday endeavour.

There were times these days when Chris had nothing to do, when he sat about, or read, or spent hours in aimless thought. There was a loneliness about the garage since Bert enlisted. It stood at the cross-roads, a mile out of Linport, well placed to catch traffic when there was traffic to catch; but now, since private motorists had almost vanished, a lonely, isolated spot. There would be hours without a caller or any sound except the rattle of lorries driving past, or the drone of an aeroplane in its own loneliness overhead. At this sound Chris would stare up from the road, blinking sunwards in an effort at identification and, with a stirring of the heart, watch till the plane became a black speck dissolving into the horizon's blue.

It was Rollo who had decided, with some sentiment, that their reunion should take place at the Snappy. Chris never analysed his feelings, but he knew he was driving down to Linport in a happier mood than he had made the journey lately. His spirits rose with every mile, and as the variegated signboards came into view he thrust the accelerator hard down and gave a blast on the horn like the oncoming of John Peel. He pulled up with a spectacular skid and screech, his bulldog pipe impressively smoking.

And there was Bert, in khaki. He looked taller and ruddier, and even more confident than ever. He had a military poise.

'Oh, boy!' Bert exclaimed, taking Chris in (pipe and all) with a sort of brotherly affection. There followed a slight, awkward pause, arising out of a fear that either of them might betray emotion. A handshake would have bridged this pause between adults, but Bert and Chris had not got beyond the stage of exchanging playful whacks on various parts of each other's anatomies. So there was this breath-space of embarrassment, and Chris took advantage of it to relight the bulldog. Then he unlocked the garage for Bert to enter and inhale its well-remembered smells.

'Ah!' exclaimed Bert, walking round the repair shop, going in and out of the storeroom, staring from floor to ceiling, and at the benches, visibly stirred by recollections. Amidst the questions and answers of this home-coming he stopped suddenly, and pointed to the stripe on his arm.

'See that, comrade? Lance-Corporal Rollo. Since yesterday. Only two more and I'm a sergeant. Drive my own tank.'

Chris betrayed surprise, envy even. His tone was puzzled. 'But I thought you were working in the repair shop?'

'Not this baby. I told the army guys when they enrolled me – "I don't want to march, and I don't want to ride a horse," I said. "Gimme a tank."'

A faint stirring of jealousy moved Chris, an emotion so foreign to his nature that he hardly felt its flames before they were extinguished. Nevertheless, the picture of Bert swaying and swerving across country in a tank whilst he decarbonised bakers' vans was altogether too painful. A little more of the departing lustre vanished from the garage then.

'Gosh!' said Bert, 'I'd like to take you for a run in "Daffodil". Driving cars is kid's play after tanks. You don't stop for nothing. I've drove through walls – through 'em, mind – through hedges, over ditches, through a blazing cottage. Coo! The stuff I've knocked sideways since I joined the tanks. You gotta be tough. I guess you'd certainly get one big thrill, comrade. 'Course, I couldn't take you. You're a civilian.'

Chris reddened slightly.

'When you know the fuss the police make about a scratch on a lamp post in civil life,' mused Bert. 'Makes you think, brother.'

They wandered towards his working bench, at which he gazed as though it were his desk in the old school, an illusion robbed of complete verisimilitude by the gallery of photographs affixed to the whitewashed wall. These were of Rollo's lady friends, and the extent and variety of the collection were evidence, not only of his susceptibility, but also of his catholic taste. Often, when working in this corner, he would be struck for the first time by something in the face of one or other of these charmers, some plain indication of the sulkiness or cockiness from which he had lately suffered, and which had precipitated the final disruptive evening. Then he would detach the photograph and scan it closely, wondering a little at his previous blindness before he dropped it in the stove. But from his wistful scrutiny it seemed that, if there were some he but faintly recollected, there were also one or two who had left wounds upon his heart. His chief regret just now was that none of them could see him in his beret with his stripe up.

'Still getting on all right with our kid?' he asked.

'Yes.'

'Swell!' said Bert, though not with complete sincerity. Throughout their conversation he had been listening with half an ear for the sound of Monica's arrival in the family car. She did far too much of this muscling in on him and Chris already. In some mysterious manner Chris could always distinguish the sound of Monica's car from all others, and would quietly put down his spanner and go out to meet her. Then Bert had the mortification of waiting, with his half of the job suspended, and of watching his sister descend from the car and look this way and that (to show off her profile) and smile in an actressy way till he veritably blushed for her. It amazed him that Chris, an intelligent chap and the best at crown-wheel work for miles around, hadn't the sense to recognise all this posturing as affectation, not even when his attention was drawn to it in a friendly way. Other fellows had developed a similar blindness towards his sister in the past, but none had gone so far as Chris, who had actually bought her a ring – an amethyst ring which she wore publicly because it was her birthstone, but which he knew darn well was an engagement ring and had set Chris back twelve and sixpence. Never would Bert Rollo have locked up capital like that. As he remarked at the time, there were eleven other months in the year, and swell dames with birthdays in every one of 'em.

'If it hadn't been for her keeping you out of the Terriers,' he remarked, more regretfully than by way of criticism, 'we might have been together in the Tank Corps.'

'How did I know there was going to be a war? Why doesn't your father put old Rutherford down here to run the garage? I'm nearly due to be called up. I don't want to be pushed into anything.'

'You can't get any sense out of the governor these days,' declared Bert. 'He lets the business run itself and all he thinks about is civil defence. There's a proper school of 'em – all his pals from the bowling club – and everybody knows that all they do is play darts at the police station. He says he's enrolled old Rutherford as a stretcher bearer. He's got everybody enrolled for something, even mother. I'm darned glad I got out of it into the army.'

Chris knitted his brows over this obstacle. He admired Mr Rollo, and the Snappy Service Garage was as much indebted to him for its start as it was to Mr Bunting. Even now it was run as a subsidiary of the huge Rollo garage in Kilworth. Time after time, speaking calmly and between the puffs of his black cheroot, Mr Rollo had informed Chris that the garage must be kept going by one partner if the other joined the Forces. Later he would make proper arrangements. When approached about these proper arrangements his mind came back from a spell of imaginary and highly successful dart-throwing at various objects in the office, and he gazed at Chris absently, though with patience. For Mr Rollo was a sportsman, and often went through sporting motions with his walking-stick or his ruler or whatever happened to be handy, striking imaginary balls with amazing precision down imaginary fairways, being often so absorbed that you have to repeat what you said to recall him to the actual. But he never lost his temper.

Chris, who had hitherto admired Mr Rollo's imperturbability, was now discovering it made him more difficult to deal with even than his father. Still, Montague Rollo didn't possess all the strength of mind there was in Kilworth. By no means.

Chris's manner took on a resemblance to Mr Bunting's in his most stubborn moments. 'You can tell him that if he doesn't make some arrangements soon about the garage, I'm going to shut it up and clear out. We can start again after the war. But I expect things'll be a bit different then.'

'They certainly will,' agreed Bert cheerfully. 'Say, what about me coming round to your place? They've never seen me in my uniform. I could come up for tea.' He made this as a fair offer, not to be passed by.

Duly he appeared, very spick and span, gliding along Cumberland Avenue in Mr Rollo's monster car, and arriving just as Julie was returning home from her Sunday afternoon walk with Mavis. Seeing this magnificent vehicle halt at the green and white gates, and having glimpsed a uniformed figure at the wheel, her pulse quickened; her steps also, for there are few of man's creations more socially impressive than a Corton-David 24, especially to the owner of a flivver. Julie approached it with a proper sense of awe.

Before the Buntings bought a Conway any make of car seemed almost as good as any other; the essential thing was to own a car of some description. At the time the Conway had been a marvellous acquisition; glamour surrounded its ownership. Since then, however, they had learnt to make comparisons, and the Conway had grown antiquated. You could tell by the bonnet it was seven years old at least, and it was dented in the wings by reason of Mr Bunting's frequent miscalculations whilst reversing. Julie, in particular, was rather ashamed of being seen in it near her own home. But a car like Mr Rollo's! She paused to covet and admire.

'Oh, I say!' she exclaimed, approaching to inspect its interior luxury. She hovered a little, diffusing a certain fragrance and charm. 'What can she do, Bert?'

Bert was moved to admit that, if coaxed, she could burn the road one small trifle.

Her voice flattered him; it sank to the intimate: 'I say, can you teach me to drive some time?'

'How can I, kiddo? You can't get a licence till you're seventeen.'

There was a sudden stiffening, an almost electric tension. It occurred to Bert that he must have said the wrong thing. Two pink spots appeared on Julie's cheeks, her glance ran over him witheringly. She contrived to give this glance a crushing effect of looking down disdainfully from superior heights.

'What are you talking about, not seventeen? I'm eighteen – will be in January. And don't you forget it, *Herbert*!'

For all his experience of women Bert was momentarily nonplussed; he even blushed slightly. He had never witnessed quite such a lightning change from blandishment to the inimical. Neither had he been called 'Herbert' since he left the grammar school.

'Okay! okay!' he said peaceably, and observed her in greater detail. Silk stockings, high-heeled shoes, an insouciant hat with a sprightly feather. This was Julie Bunting. He got her into focus, as it were, at a second attempt. The last time he remembered noticing her she had been wearing the blazer and straw hat of Miss Morgan-Dell's Academy, a mere leggy schoolgirl in black stockings. Feminine transformations were apt to be startling.

'Certainly I'll teach you to drive,' he said, as they walked up the path, his boots ringing enormously on the concrete. 'But how can I? I've only got two days' special leave.'

No answer from Julie. They reached the front door and she stood there, neither knocking nor opening it, but aloofly waiting and tapping her small foot.

'Do you mind?' she asked archly, indicating that a door, even of her own home, should be opened for a lady. With a countenance now unmistakably red, Bert performed this office, wondering where she could have picked up such high-flown ideas of etiquette. 'Reads novels, I expect,' he reflected.

It gave him some relief to walk in behind her, and a moment in which to remember that, after all, he was a soldier, and by tradition a man of nerve.

Once inside the house he recovered his self-confidence, which at all times was considerable. He remembered the uniform and the stripe. Mr Bunting came forward to shake hands, a signal honour, and seemed inclined to treat him almost as an equal.

'I hear you've been going in for a bit of promotion,' he said, for he approved of young men making headway. 'Rising on steppingstones, as the poet said.'

'I'm sure Bert would like his tea,' said Mrs Bunting, who never saw a boy in khaki without wanting to mother him. She had fed many soldiers in the last war, and always conceived it to be a woman's duty to push all the food possible into them whilst they were on leave. She had the meal already laid and brewed the tea the instant she heard his voice. Bert might have been coming to her from a beleaguered fortress.

'I'm sure they can't feed you properly in the army,' she said, as she bade him draw up to the table.

'Nothing like hard living, for all that,' declared Mr Bunting, adding: 'if you've got a young stomach.'

Looking at Bert across the table took his mind back through the years. He had been living at Camden Town in the last war, and round this very table which, when its leaves were extended, had almost filled the living room, he remembered the faces of other men in khaki. Faces with the newly acquired ruddiness of camp life, faces that went with odd provincial accents and interesting private histories. He had brought soldiers and sailors home from chance encounters in the street, and from station waiting rooms, men far from friends and home. There had been hot suppers and talk and singing and wonderful evenings of good fellowship. There were faces he recalled without names, and names without faces. The boys of the last war! Dead, some of them, for more than twenty years. One came across their photographs in old books and forgotten corners, saw a once familiar face smiling from a post card, tried to remember who it was and what had happened to him. To some you gave a smile and a glance as though saying: 'You are not forgotten.'

Looking at Bert he had a strange feeling that one of them had come back, youthful and smiling as of old.

'I'm glad to see you, Bert; I am, prop'ly. Help yourself to anything. Pass Bert the scones, Julie. No margarine in them, my boy.'

'These tanks now,' he recommenced. 'Got some improvements, I expect.'

'I'll say we have,' said Bert, and began to explain what tanks could do, and in particular what 'Daffodil' could do, with capable handling. There were points about tanks that were military secrets, and which couldn't be divulged even at Laburnum Villa; but after he had explained what they could do it seemed likely that anything left over as a secret must border on the miraculous.

'Did you come on leave in it?' asked Julie softly.

'Now, Julie,' warned Mrs Bunting, and Chris advised his friend not to take any notice. Mr Bunting, aware of a slight tension, and the mumbling about which he frequently complained, glanced interrogatively at his wife, but received no enlightenment.

'Why "Daffodil"? That's what puzzles me,' inquired Ernest, who disapproved of Bert's bloodthirstiness.

'It should be "Vindicative" or "Repulsive,"' said Julie. 'Or the "Scorpion". Something that *means* something.'"

'"Repulsive" would be exactly right for a tank,' said Ernest.

'Couldn't call it the "Scorpion,"' objected Mr Bunting. 'Name of a blow-lamp. But "Daffodil"'s too poetic.'

There ensued an informal competition in the invention of suitable names for tanks. None of the results were striking, but there was tacit agreement that they were all more appropriate than 'Daffodil'.

Bert grew rueful. 'I couldn't think of anything, I guess. So I called it after one of the governor's old motorbuses.'

'What does it matter what it's called so long as Bert came safely back in it?' said Mrs Bunting. 'That's the principal thing.'

'Hear! hear!' said Mr Bunting. 'And now that he's home on leave we ought to have a jolly evening in the front room. Ernest can play the piano and we'll all have a sing-song. What d'you say, Ernest? Not snarters and 'tudes. Something with a jerk in it.'

He rose and led the way, anxious for everyone to be merry and bright instead of sitting about arguing about trivialities. It was a funny thing, he thought, that no matter what subject was started at Laburnum Villa it always led to argument.

'Now,' he said, opening the piano, 'what about a song, Julie? You can give us that one you learnt at school. The delicate lass with the hair – you know. Got them nice runs in it.'

'We haven't got the music for that one, daddy.'

'Oh!' he said, disappointed. 'What we need here is a few good old-fashioned songs. One of those albums. You ought to get one some time, Ernest.'

'I'll play anything you like,' offered Ernest, determinedly non-committal to this effort to revive the drawing room brand of joviality which Mr Bunting remembered from his youth. Ernest didn't think much of it, but he would go as far as the rest of them. A pity his father didn't sense the feeling of the company, which was becoming unmistakably uneasy.

'That's a fair offer,' said Mr Bunting, who was in the mood for song and tried a few rumbling notes in the lower compass. No one ever sang *The Village Blacksmith* nowadays. You never heard it even

40

on the wireless, and these young people would think it out of date. But it was a good song, and he had rendered it with considerable effect at smoking concerts in his bachelor days.

'What's that?' he said, inclining an ear towards Chris. 'Got an appointment? Bert shouldn't have appointments for Sunday evening. Ought to be free to enjoy himself.'

'No, dad; it isn't that sort of appointment. It's a girlfriend.'

'I see!' exclaimed Mr Bunting, staring. But Chris was perfectly composed, so was Bert; it was only Mr Bunting who felt embarrassed. Worse than that, he felt rather silly for overlooking the possibility of his jolly evening not being wanted.

'He could have brought his young lady up here. Be pleased to see her.'

'It's not his young lady exactly. We sort of planned to go out together. You don't mind, dad, do you?'

''Course not. I was trying to – sort of – ' He broke off. He felt rather hurt.

'It's jolly decent of you; but, you see, we'd fixed up.'

'That's all right, Chris. I don't mind. Go off and enjoy yourselves.'

'Goodbye, Bert,' called Julie. 'All the best, if I don't see you.'

She came to the door and waved him down the path as he left with Chris. Haughty as she pretended to be, it was evident she was not immune from the effect of uniform. She was only a kid, of course, but he gave her a military salute, just as he might have given her a bag of sweets had she been a trifle younger, for she was by no means unpleasing to the eye.

'Keep it under your hat, comrade,' he told Chris, as they drove off in the monster limousine. 'My crowd's going to Norway. Some of our chaps are there already. Going to tan the hide off the Bosche.'

'Norway!' exclaimed Chris. A pang shot through him. He glanced sideways at Bert, booked for the great adventure, and his heart was heavy with the heaviness of youth in chains.

FIVE

ERNEST SAT IN the twilight of the front room playing the piano. He had come home tired and depressed by things great and small: by the moroseness of the morose engineer, the decline in business, the rise in the cost of soap, the war, and the dreariness of life in general. He came to the piano as to an altar of comfort. His fingers wandered over the keys and his thoughts amongst his problems.

There was in Ernest's sensitive soul a steely streak which he thought of as strength of will and which his father called simple obstinacy. The voice of the press, the pronouncements of the Government, of his family and friends, the whole articulate world might declare in favour of certain opinions, but, if Ernest thought differently, he stuck to his own, and not silently, either. In season and out of season he spoke with the voice of conscience and, he claimed, with that of reason also. Hence his loneliness in a wartime world where he was out of key. Ernest was against the war, was against all war, he regarded war as something insane that should have vanished from the earth a thousand years ago.

Too free utterance of his views in the office had led to a passage of arms with Mr Eagle this very afternoon. Mr Eagle had lived through many wars; he had fought in the Boer War and remembered it vividly. He could remember even earlier campaigns against Zulus and dervishes, and other odd people who had opposed the British. War was nothing new to Mr Eagle, neither was it anything to make too much fuss about, being inevitable and likely to diversify man's story until the dawn of the millennium. What was new to him was a point of view like Ernest's, a weakling willingness to reason with the king's enemies instead of giving 'em the bayonet. Pacifists he regarded as creatures lacking in manly courage, to be visited with condign contempt.

'You needn't worry, my boy. You won't have to go,' he said, not without sting. 'You're in a reserved occupation.'

Recalling this innuendo, Ernest flushed. He was exempt from military service, not because of his opinions, but because Mr Eagle had represented him as a key-man at the laundry. But was there ever a minority that was not attacked unfairly? What Eagle really feared was that the indiscreet propagation of Ernest's views might lead to loss of business. Any loss of business caused by the war he was prepared to endure like a stoic. It was 'for his country'.

No remark could have more quickly set Ernest's mental teeth on edge. In a world of diminishing spaces one had to look beyond the narrow boundaries of one's country to the Federation of the Nations.

Ernest knew what he was talking about. He had attended lectures and had a library of political booklets. He had even bought *Mein Kampf* and read as far into it as most people, which was not quite to the middle. He meant to finish it some time. Give him liberty to explain and he would reduce the world to logic.

Ernest knew about the injustices of Versailles and why Germany so understandably went Nazi. He knew Britain's share of responsibility for the failure of the League. If he sometimes argued the German case, it was with no sense of disloyalty to England. Such an accusation stamped you in Ernest's mind as a fossilised reactionary; what you had to get at was the truth. The old national loyalties were the roots of war, just as family loyalties were the springs of vendetta. Man needed a larger loyalty, bounded by no frontiers, extending its embrace to the brotherhood of all mankind.

This ideal of a world without frontiers, governed by one human family, Ernest held with a tenacity that nothing could shake, but he knew it could never be attained by force of arms. Only by keeping inviolate one's faith in it, and awakening a like faith in others, could any new world order be brought to birth, after long years perhaps, and many generations, in the slow way of human progress. But he never doubted it would arrive, and how blest would be the generation that lived to see it!

These ideals were a candle flame in a tempest now.

The trouble with most people, Ernest considered, was that they didn't think. They accepted a war as though it were a natural catastrophe, like an earthquake, not the result of human blundering, like a railway accident. They devoted themselves to national service in wartime with a courage and devotion one rarely saw displayed in time of peace. They made sacrifices which, rightly directed, would have ushered in a golden age. And they became utterly gullible, the prey of rumour.

One had only to read the leaders in such papers as the *Siren* to estimate the depth of public credulity. According to the *Siren* all Germans were bloodthirsty barbarians except when it suited to describe them as nose-led sheep. Hitler was as crafty as a horse dealer, a man without honour, who lied and swindled deliberately and as a matter of policy. This sort of statement made Ernest stare as though he lost hope in human intelligence. It was true these statements were supported by news items in the paper, but Ernest was not inclined to believe everything he saw in print. Hitler was the leader of one of the world's greatest nations, their chosen and approved representative; the lives and happiness of millions of his countrymen were his responsibility. To Ernest, it was fantastic to imagine that any man holding such a position could be a liar and a swindler.

Sitting at the piano in the darkening front room, playing but scarcely knowing what chords he touched, Ernest contemplated the tangled world. It was a world gone astray and old in misery, cut across and fought over by narrow-minded, uncompromising men. They sat round tables in portentous conference, their weightiest argument being always the bombers waiting to take off. Such were the leaders of twentieth-century Europe, and a thousand years hence their actions and their standards would seem incomprehensible. It was true enough the world needed mending; how to mend it was, indeed, one of Ernest's intellectual hobbies; but he knew, at least, that the task required everything man had of disinterested humanity and honesty of soul. At worst, its problems could be left to the slow instincts of the race to work out without obstruction. But today paid propagandists blared their skilful lies from continent to continent so that the echoes of them never slept.

Against this seething background Ernest saw his own life, a mere speck on the canvas. And yet – a life! Surely one could not respect the rights of others who thought meanly of his own. But he was just a speck, no more than a midge in the sun, except in the recesses of his mind and heart where there should be something to sustain him, and where he found nothing.

For a moment or two he sat silent, these confused unhappy thoughts dying as he ran his fingers up and down the keys, like rippling them through water. He had considerable musical skill and possessed a good ear. The old family piano wasn't up to much, though; when he and Evie married they would have a Missen. It was included in the budget of the ideal home in Ernest's pocketbook, along with the brick fireplace, the Medici prints, the add-on bookshelves, and a great many other items of obvious good taste. Ideas for the ideal home floated to Ernest from time to time, and he captured and set them down in the pocketbook, a whole domestic inventory of a superior kind. Formerly he could be seen in his spare moments examining the pocketbook, and adding a note here and there with his fine-pointed pencil. But he rarely looked at it now. Like most other things it had lost interest and immediacy since the war.

Nevertheless, the ideal home existed so completely in Ernest's imagination that he often came home to it in fancy, went from room to room, and had tea with Evie at the gate-leg table by candlelight, thus enjoying a brief, imaginative respite from the shortcomings of Laburnum Villa. Up to a few months ago he had been so obsessed with its details that he could have compiled a handbook on house planning and furnishing, and on the business side of marriage. Now it was Evie herself he thought of more and more, Evie his heart clung to, Evie dark and gentle, to whom his secret mind and heart lay completely open.

For there might be no after the war for him, no marriage, no home, nor any future. The young men of his generation stood nearer the edge of the grave even than the aged. Beyond it waited oblivion, into whose black jaws the last war's millions had vanished. There were thousands like himself whom the war would blot out as though they had never been born, with all their dreams, desires, and hopes so like his own.

With a great sigh Ernest banished these thoughts. He felt the aloof anger of those intelligent, if self-centred, people who regard themselves as spectators rather than participants in a mad world.

One sank to the depths during these meditations and then rebounded. Some law of compensation, he supposed, a kind of emotional purging. Blake mentioned it in his *Psychological Studies*. Whatever it was, he felt brighter, with a new mental appetite. Now he would have some music! He switched on the light negligently, having complete confidence in someone else's blackout arrangements.

He re-seated himself at the piano, and in this familiar attitude became, rather more than he knew, an ordinary young man. Sailing expertly into Bach's 'Forty-eight' he soared with equal ease above the worrying minutiae of his business life and the world's distress. Nor could he help thinking, as he attacked the severer passages with spirit, that he played rather well. He enjoyed the isolation of the front room, but he would have liked an audience too. There were times when he imagined an audience, felt the listening stillness behind him, succeeded by a spellbound pause, then a storm of clapping. It was rather vain to pretend such things, he thought sometimes; on the other hand it bucked up your playing tremendously.

He did not reflect that he had an audience in the living room, in the fireside chair, an audience of one person only, the man who had paid for the piano and occasionally regretted it, not having the cultivated taste with which Ernest endowed his imaginary audiences.

Mr Bunting had, in fact, been listening to Ernest for the last half-hour, not willingly but with the enforced attention one gives to sounds that distract the eardrum. Defeated in his attempt to read, he occupied his thoughts in wondering what kind of classical music Ernest was playing, just as Oskey sought to identify a garden pest, so that he might lavish his dislike more solidly upon it. It was not solemn enough for a 'snarter,' nor twiddly enough for a ''tude.' By the way Ernest's hands followed one another up and down the keyboard, in a kind of musical paperchase, he was inclined to think it was a fugue. If there was one variety of high-brow composition Mr Bunting detested above all others, it was fugues, and he applied this term of loathing indiscriminately amongst the classics, but with particular emphasis to the ones he thought most rotten.

He put down his paper, glared at the partition wall through which the noise proceeded, and made a grimace. Why, he wondered, couldn't Ernest sometimes play one of the pieces he got when he was pianist for the Harmony Five? It was only jazz, he knew, and not to be compared with the good old-fashioned stuff, but it was better than fugues.

'Fugues!' he remarked, bitterly. 'Haven't we enough to put up with in wartime without fugues?'

Neither wife nor daughter answered him. In the screened pool of light above the table Julie was writing a letter. Her lips were compressed, her head tilted, you could see her forming her large, round capitals with effort, not like a girl who has had the advantage of an expensive education.

Mrs Bunting was doing something, he knew not what, with bits of coloured wool out of her work-basket. She examined each knot with her slow housewifely scrutiny, no more aware of him than Julie was.

As for Chris, he was not yet home, but from the attention he had given his hair, teeth, boots, and tie before he went out, it could safely be predicted he was meeting Monica Rollo. The development of this affair was known to Mr Bunting only by a sort of instinct; the same instinct told him he was supposed to know nothing about it, and to imagine that Monica came to Laburnum Villa merely as Bert Rollo's sister and a family friend. Well and good! Their smiles at his blindness (which he did not miss either) were nothing to the deep interior smiles that flickered across his face only in his private moments.

The fugue ended during these meditations, and there was a brief respite of silence during which Mr Bunting returned to his paper. But not for long. With a series of chords, so dismal they would have frozen every smile in a Cochran beauty chorus, Ernest began on Beethoven. For Beethoven – a name Mr Bunting pronounced as spelt, preferring British ways to foreign ones – he had a particular detestation. He considered him the gloomiest man who ever sat on a piano stool. In Beethoven, Ernest tore the heart out of the piano. He went stumbling and crashing on, as though searching amongst all the chords that still slept in blessed silence, for something more harrowing than all that had proceeded, sinking now and then into

47

a grumbling *adagio*, during which the exhausted Beethoven got his second wind, before setting off on another clanging bout amongst the discords.

'Lovely, ain't it?' said Mr Bunting, stung at last into speech. But no one heard him.

Throughout a trying day he looked forward to these few hours by his own fireside, and then he spent them in a sort of isolation. Nobody spoke to him; he might be no more than a salary-earning automaton that came home only for refuelling. Driven from his paper and rebuffed in his conversational advances, Mr Bunting produced the distended pocketbook in which he made managerial jottings, and which was his last resort in boredom. As always, when he opened it, several slips of paper fluttered to the floor. These he read with close attention and put one by one on to the fire. There were notes in the pocketbook of Holroyd's price-marking system, the principle of which he had so far failed to grasp. The ironmongery trade not being sufficiently complicated already, Holroyd had complicated it still further by marking everything with cabalistic signs, a kind of arithmetical shorthand. Once again Mr Bunting examined these signs, not so much in the spirit of an earnest student, but of a critic who demands first of all to know what no one can tell him: what is the sense of the whole business.

Taking swift advantage of one of Ernest's pauses, Mr Bunting switched on the wireless. It was a strategic move, a pouncing upon and seizing of the silence as of briefly unoccupied territory. There floated to him the voices of three young women singing in what he believed was picturesquely called, probably so that it could be palmed off on the BBC, 'close harmony'. They had shrill young voices; voices too shrill and girlish, he thought, to sing the sort of words they did sing, leering love songs, not half so good as *Honeysuckle*. But he kept them on as a protective barrage against the fugues and to assert his right to amuse himself in his own house.

Throughout Ernest's performance Julie had been absorbed in letter writing, and deaf to all extraneous noise. Now she turned with a protesting look.

'Oh, daddy, turn it off. I'm writing!'

'Well, go on writing.'

She put down her pen, shook back her hair, sighed, dipped, and returned to her paper with every symptom of the impeded literary mind.

'Mother, make him turn it off.'

Thus appealed to, Mrs Bunting gave a critical five seconds to the Swinging Sisters, and 'couldn't think why they put such people on the wireless'.

'Wait till the news comes on, George,' she suggested.

With some asperity of movement Mr Bunting switched off. He knew if he tried further he would be accused of messing with the wireless.

How wearily flat and stale was this unprofitable world, as the poet said. Bored in the house, bored if you went out, bored by the monotony of the papers. To look out of doors gave you the creeps: not a spark of light anywhere; the town was entirely blotted out, the landscape dark and desolate as a moor. You had a peculiar sense of thousands of brightly lighted interiors hiding and waiting in that primeval blackness, a whole world gone to ground. You came indoors to a stuffy, closed-in room, where the papers and the wireless bored you with endless reiteration of the name of Hitler. You sat there disregarded, but not in peace. The peace was shattered by fugues and sonatas.

And they said the war would last three years!

'I suppose we can stick it,' he ruminated. 'Got to, I expeck. Stick it longer than they can, anyway.' He wondered why the Germans didn't rise against Hitler and stop the war. He understood they had been on the point of rising for years now. Hadn't got the guts, probably.

There was the sound of Chris whistling up the path, and in he came, pink and cheerful, a figure eternally welcome to his father. His very hair was cheerful, it sprang up when he took his hat off, thick and fair, exhibiting all the resilience of Chris's spirits. There was none of that highbrow stuff about Chris, no fads nor fancies. Care lay on him lightly as a shadow.

'Hear any Germans about, Chris?'

'Germans? Good Lord, no, mother!'

Whatever his thoughts had been since he parted from his Monica, they had not been of German bombers. He came in with his clean scrubbed look and his misleading smile of innocence. As he passed the table he said unexpectedly, and in a tone of declamation: 'My darling Bill!'

'You pig!' exclaimed Julie, covering her letter with the blotter.

'Who's darling Bill? Do we know him?'

Julie stared, pink-cheeked, round-eyed, acutely aware of the forward-leaning attitude of her father.

'He's a lonely soldier, if you want to know!'

'How can he be lonely in the army? There's about a million other fellows in it beside him. Do you send him cigarettes?'

'I might.'

'Why, you silly young ass, that's what these lonely soldiers write to you for. It's a racket. You should see the fags Bert gets.'

'Bert Rollo's nothing to go by.'

'Bert's okay.'

'Not so much of the okay and racket business, Chris,' protested Mr Bunting mildly. ''Tain't English.'

'Course 'tain't,' said Julie, with an air of hearty agreement. With considerable presence of mind Mrs Bunting realised the clock was due to strike and switched on the wireless. Mr Bunting turned towards the receiver for the news. Not that he expected any.

'Ask Ernest if he wants to hear,' he directed in an undertone.

At the first words his face grew blank. He looked silently at his wife, at Chris, even at Julie. They stood round the set, tense and rigid. In a growing apprehension, which the announcer's impersonal tones did nothing to diminish, they heard the story in stoic silence to the end. Then Mr Bunting switched off firmly.

'So our chaps are being turfed out of Norway. Something's gone wrong prop'ly. Why, they've hardly got there!' He looked extremely serious.

'Isn't that where Bert 's gone?' Julie asked Chris.

'Yes. How did you know?'

'Oh! I knew.'

'I don't like it,' said Mr Bunting, now on his feet on the rug, brushing aside any personal viewpoint. 'I don't like it at all. Been some blundering.' Not since the war began had they seen him look so grave.

'I'll make supper,' said Mrs Bunting practically.

Even this did not move him to his usual inquiry whether there was anything special. Instead he presently followed her into the kitchen and hung about in one of his awkward attempts to help in assembling a meal. Nothing could have more clearly indicated his distress of mind.

Into this newly diffused atmosphere of calamity, and startlingly breaking up its silence, came a knocking at the door. Not the ordinary knock of moderation, but a resounding thud, as of some official summons. Every head turned towards the door, all movement, and even breathing, suspended till Chris exclaimed: 'Crikey! What's happened?' as the knocking was more urgently repeated. There seemed some sinister connection between this summons and the Norwegian disaster.

Oskey stood there, the moonlight shining on his steel helmet.

'Showing a light!' he announced succinctly.

This was too much for Mr Bunting. Thrusting Mrs Bunting aside, he took possession of his doorstep; stood there as though prepared to defend it against all comers.

'Kitchen light's showing,' said Oskey, with official impassivity.

Without a word, and in his slippers, Mr Bunting preceded him to the back of the house. He was certain there could be no light; very positive indeed. But, standing where Oskey directed him to stand, he saw one – a faint yellow line down one side of the window. Usually the curtain was kept in position at this point by the soapflake tin. It was easy to see what had happened, someone had moved the tin and here was Oskey. Nevertheless, Mr Bunting stared at the window and demanded: 'What light?'

'There! *There*, right in front of you. Giving the position of your house away.'

The light was the merest gleam, but Mr Bunting recognised the reasonableness of Oskey's complaint. Nobody more particular about showing lights than he. Still, he felt inclined to argue. He had experienced a jolt, and to be rattled made him obstinate. Besides, one of his objections to the warden system was that it gave the wrong people authority to intrude into your affairs, and to address you in this official voice of Oskey's. A stranger would instantly have met compliance, but Oskey was the man next door.

'What do they want to know the position of my house for, anyway?'

'Navigation,' said Oskey, adding as explanation: 'That's how they navigate.'

'I see! They look over the side of their aeroplanes, and they say: "That must be Laburn – "'

'I'm not going to argue. Just a plain question. Are you going to put it out?'

Out went the light. Some pacific listening presence, probably Mrs Bunting, had turned the switch.

'Good night!' said Oskey, in the hostile silence. His heavy feet, as though encased in gardening boots, clumped off into the darkness.

What Mr Bunting wanted to know was, who had moved the soapflake tin? But he didn't ask. He came indoors perturbed in spirit. He fancied, moreover, that he had inadvertently moved the tin himself during his preoccupied activities in the kitchen.

'Who does he think he is?' he grumbled. 'With his old tin hat. I'll bet he sleeps in that tin hat. Wonder he don't find fault with the glow-worms.'

Mr Bunting's best flashes of wit always came, alas, too late, but he occupied himself for some minutes forming a really piercing comment with glow-worms as a verbal arrowhead.

'Where's Ernest?' he snapped, as he sat down for supper. 'Why's he always got to be fetched?'

Ernest was sitting in the darkness of the front room. He had put out the light when Mr Bunting opened the front door, and during the argument he had felt the draught swirling about his legs, a breath from the cruder outer world. For the last half-hour Ernest had completely forgotten the war. Now, in the extinguishing of light and the silencing of music, it had come back to him.

SIX

AS HE CLIMBED on to the cubby-hole stool next morning Mr Bunting felt a painful twinge strike down his spine into his legs, and knew it as an aftermath of his labours on the dugout. Following the prevailing fashion, Laburnum Villa now had a dugout, and most of his weekends had been devoted to its construction. After discharging an individual who had described himself, with some exaggeration, as a working man, Mr Bunting decided to tackle the job himself. He actually began himself, though only in a pottering manner, until Chris and Ernest came out to assist, impelled by the moral pressure of his solitary exertions.

The successful completion of the dugout was due chiefly to Chris's practicality and staying power with the spade. He had shown much more intelligence as a dugout constructor than Ernest had. In spite of the undeniable fact that he was the one with brains, Ernest had been unable to grasp the simplest practical operation, or even to keep his sleeves rolled up. His final role had been hander-up of tools and timber.

When all was finished, and Chris and Mr Bunting were reclining on their chairs exhausted, Ernest went into the front room to start work on some laundry accounts. He had said no word about laundry accounts, had chosen to hang ineffectively about the dugout perpetually rolling up his sleeves. 'Just like Ernest,' thought Mr Bunting with irritation. He could have been excused from doing anything about the dugout. But Ernest, having satisfied his conscience, worked on at the front room table till the last account was done, and came into supper so white and strained that Mr Bunting looked at him with anxiety.

It could be safely assumed, however, that Ernest had awakened this morning with no twinges in his back and legs, such as his father had.

Having painfully assumed the stool, Mr Bunting's first action was to pin his new war map on the cubby-hole partition. In the woodwork, almost lost beneath the varnish, there were some old pin holes, which he looked at closely and with interest; pin holes probably of his maps of the last war. The names on the new one were quite familiar – Arras, Cambrai, Ypres – names that carried an association of mud and blood and sodden human misery, such as he had believed would never be laid on any future generation. But here, once more, was the old familiar country and the same invaders. Place names long dead to memory sprang to life as he examined it, names even of obscure hamlets – Loos, Poziéres, Bullecourt – to read them was to recall the ghosts of a forgotten army.

A queer lot the Germans, he thought. Must be a queer lot. Couldn't stay in their own country. They figured in the European story as endless hosts of jackbooted columns streaming down the straight continental roads, spreading like a green-grey blight over peaceful lands, their only appropriate setting the charred and shattered buildings seen in the sickening, matter-of-fact official photos of German 'victories'. In this generation and the last, even before that. And for what reason? What was the sense of it? 'Beats me,' Mr Bunting sighed.

Down the centre of the map ran the Maginot Line, about which he knew a great deal from photographs and articles. The Germans weren't up against ancient forts and hastily dug trenches now. There was something to stop them this time. There was, of course, the Siegfried Line – it ran a little nearer his right thumb – a hastily constructed imitation of the Maginot. Hitler designed it himself, and it was full of water, the German garrison wading in puddles to their knees. The thought of them resigned Mr Bunting to every pouring day.

But this morning he was depressed in spirit. His aching limbs had kept him wakeful, and his brain had been busy with questions of strategy. Mr Bunting gave a lot of thought to strategy; he had bought the war map for the purpose of studying the strategy of this Norwegian affair. He often thought of ways in which the Allies could get at the Germans which the general staff seemed never to think of. Some of these ideas of his seemed so obvious and so sensible that he searched the *Siren* for a hint that action was being taken on the lines of his own thinking. Finding no such hint, he would declare in mystified tones: 'Can't imagine what our people are thinking about,' and murmured against the methods of the old school tie. And there were other times when he lay awake, his imagination full of stratagems which the U-boats might employ against the Navy; cunning, low stratagems that the bluff, honest sailors at the Admiralty would never anticipate. The silence and loneliness of night gave such forebodings an ominous credibility. Tossing and turning in his bed, it seemed most urgent that he should write to the Government at once pointing out these hidden dangers.

The thing uppermost in his mind this morning was the reverse in Norway. It had penetrated Mr Bunting with disquiet and gloom. Official news was brief and guarded, but Chris said young Rollo had never even landed in Norway, but had returned to Scotland, presumably with his tank. This bit of private knowledge was a damning commentary on the whole affair.

Nevertheless, in spite of the alarming headlines, it was easily seen that Joe Corder was undisturbed, even happy. His eye was as lively as ever, his glance keen, as he came across the salesroom floor, a man full of gestures. He pulled up in the cubby-hole door, smiled, grimaced, and inquired what was the matter with his melancholy friend.

'Art thou pale for weariness, or is it indigestion?'

'I'm fed up!' replied Mr Bunting, making rare confession. 'What sort of a weekend have you had?'

Corder had experienced a very disappointing weekend, but it was not clear from his narrative where his disappointment lay. On Saturday he had bought a book by a man called Herrick, an ancient, dog-eared book, which he had lost on the way home. This battered volume had held such extraordinary interest for Corder, manifestly outweighing his interest in national disasters, that he had spent the rest of the weekend calling at lost property offices in search of it. He admitted, however, that the thing had cost him only ninepence.

Mr Bunting listened to this trivial story with impatience, the point of it entirely escaping him.

''Course, if you hadn't read it – '

'Not read it? Not read Herrick? O God! O Montreal! I've had the complete half-guinea edition for years. That's not the same thing.'

''Speck not,' said Mr Bunting, who had wanted Corder's opinion about Norway, not about Herrick. He had never even heard of Herrick. All that was clear to him was that Corder had lost the ten-bob book but got his prices mixed, which was bad in a businessman, and a habit that would lead to trouble if extended to the carpet department.

'The thing is, George, you're not a bibliophile.'

'I've been everything else you can think of, Joe,' sighed Mr Bunting, 'so you might call me that as well.'

Corder was another person who didn't realise there was a war on. All he thought of was reading books, none of them on practical subjects. Too complacent. The whole country was too complacent, the Government and the newspapers were the same. This rot about England always starting badly, as though they were proud of it. A good start was as necessary in a war as it was in the Derby.

'Work's got to be done anyway,' he murmured, with thankfulness. There was endless satisfaction in work. Kept you from worrying about things you couldn't mend. After all, what could a man of his age do to help his country? Nothing but keep business moving as briskly as possible by attending to the ironmongery department, and that meant serving customers himself, nailing up crates, packing, and doing a lot of things a manager didn't ordinarily do, even down to dusting boxes, because young men were at the war.

Cheered by these reflections, he looked over the top of the partition to make sure all the staff were present and occupied, paying particular attention to old Turner in the corner. At this moment Turner was hanging helplessly over a heap of window fittings. Mr Bunting watched him with a hardening eye. 'Putting 'em in the wrong boxes again,' he muttered. 'Putting 'em in the wrong boxes,' and he lowered himself off the bottom drawer, emitting irascible gruntings and snortings. Although Turner had spent all his life in the ironmongery trade he didn't yet know there were three kinds of fanlight openers. All Turner understood was hot-water fittings; all his life had been spent amongst hot-water fittings, and he had never had sufficient curiosity to make himself familiar with the goods on the next counter. When Mr Bunting asked him to fetch four quarters of short whites (his name for domestic pins), Turner stared as blankly as a first-day apprentice.

'I'm a bit upset,' quavered Turner, when rebuked. 'Don't like the news this morning.'

'We're all upset. That's no reason for putting the bronze iron fittings amongst the brass ones, is it?'

'I'm sorry, but we haven't heard from our boy for a long time. He's on a destroyer.'

'Oh!' said Mr Bunting. He had been about to tell Turner he must stop running out for afternoon papers, but hearing about his son on a destroyer prevented him doing so, at least for the moment. Instead, with a great show of patience, he took possession of the confused mass of window fittings and began to make orderly division: those that opened inwards, those that opened outwards and the patent ones that opened either way.

'Now do you understand?'

'Yes, Mr Bunting,' said Turner humbly. A poor, weak creature, Mr Bunting reflected, a man going downhill fast. One could feel sorry for him, but not without also feeling exasperated. He was naturally an exasperating fellow.

As though to confirm this thought of Mr Bunting's, Turner at once took advantage of his friendlier mood.

'I don't know what you think about some of these windows, Mr Bunting. There's a great big one right where I work. Suppose a bomb dropped – '

'A bomb! They haven't started dropping bombs yet. Too scared of getting a few of ours in return.'

A faint gleam, as of a thirst for reassurance, came into Turner's eyes. 'Do you think so, really?'

'You can bet on it. Besides, why should they drop one here? Lots of other places.'

'That's true,' said Turner, speaking as one who had given thought to this also. 'It's the glass splinters, you know. Sometimes when I'm working near the window I get a bit nervous.' He made this confession as a confidential matter, one that would not be believed unless admitted by himself.

'You save your nervousness till they get here,' advised Mr Bunting. 'It'll be soon enough then. In the meantime, keep your mind on these fanlight openers.'

Poor old Turner, he thought, as he returned to the cubby-hole in better spirits. There were two kinds of people who cheered you up in wartime: the nervous people who raised your spirits in an effort to lift theirs, and the calm and confident people, like Mr Bickerton, from whom you drew courage for yourself. Mr Bickerton never referred to the war except as it affected business. Then he referred to it in a business-like tone, keeping the war, as it were, in its proper place and perspective. He displayed neither anxiety nor complacency, nor emotion about it. Mr Bunting thought it possible he had no emotions. Short and square, brisk and formidable, his bald head gleamed with a fictitious benevolence, but his eye was bright and piercing. It was a commanding eye that picked you out from the farthest corner of the room. It was impossible to imagine Mr Bickerton as one of a conquered people, or ever being finally beaten, or even browbeaten. That eye, his whole presence, forbade it.

'He holds you with his glittering eye,' said Corder, who seemed to be under the impression he was an old mariner, a thing Mr Bunting thought unlikely. Though awed by his chief, Mr Bunting drew much confidence from their brief contacts.

Many times these days Mr Bunting took out his watch and sighed over the slow passage of hours. Never since the slump that followed the last war had he known such a falling-off in business. Often he sat in the cubby-hole drawing idly on the margin of his catalogues, listening for a step which, if it were Mr Bickerton's, caused him to turn a page and give his mind to its contents instantly. At intervals he sallied forth to give instructions, necessary and unnecessary, to prevent the shop from sinking into utter inertia. It was like stirring a twig in a stagnant pool. Inactivity settled on everything like a fine dust, the room yawned. But there was nothing he could do about it.

These spells of boredom were broken by the lunch hour when he joined Corder at McAndrew's Café. There was always the interest of the menu, and choices to be weighed, and Corder's newspaper, which arranged current events according to its own estimate of their importance, giving the day's news a touch of novelty. And there was Corder's conversation. There on the back of bill-heads they drew maps of strategical interest, Corder's green fountain pen flashing out to correct Mr Bunting's geography. Corder would illustrate the proper tactics by arranging cruet bottles and cutlery into squadrons round the coastline of the tablecloth, imperiously waving away the waitress if she came after the vinegar bottle at a critical moment in the action. Sometimes, and taking equal place with these larger questions, the plan would be of Corder's back garden, and Mr Bunting would instruct him in garden planning and the cultivation of vegetables.

In these discussions he figured very pleasantly as an expert, for Corder had never done any gardening and was beginning purely out of patriotism. His garden was, he admitted, an un-weeded garden; things rank and gross possessed it merely. A thorough double-trenching was what Mr Bunting recommended. 'Make the soil friable,' he said. 'Most important.'

They left McAndrew's reluctantly; it was an oasis in the dreary desert of the day. They returned to the boredom of the shop. Having had dustless shelves dusted, packing paper cut, and everything he could think of done and done again, till his assistants were on the verge of mutiny, and the ironmongery department prepared to deal at an instant's notice with a torrent of business, Mr Bunting hid himself in the cubby-hole. Whenever Mr Bickerton appeared he sprang up with an alacrity that he felt must sometimes look suspicious. Mr Bickerton, strangely enough, seemed always busy and full of plans. His present one was to expand the business on the wholesale side by supplying air raid equipment to local authorities. Therefore he consulted Mr Bunting on the constructional details of stirrup pumps and force pumps, nozzles, unions, and hose terminals, all of which were questions Mr Bunting could answer; no one better. It was the sort of discussion he enjoyed, and the consultations fortified him in the belief that, whoever was discharged through lack of business, it would not be himself.

As Mr Bickerton said, peacetime demands had fallen off and wartime demands not yet begun. There was, therefore, this bad patch, which, he knew full well, Mr Bunting must find trying. Grateful for this implied compliment, he was prompted to assist his chief at the climax of his exposition with the word 'hiatus', making, he was sure, an excellent impression.

After days like these he travelled home with his spirits at zero. He worried about the war, he worried about the firm, he had vague misgivings about certain members of the Cabinet. But however disheartened he felt, he always remembered to pull himself together as he reached home. He looked upon it as a duty. Pausing in the darkness at his gate, he looked up at the black shape of the house. It represented all that he possessed, and everything he loved, and the whole was now in jeopardy. Exactly how life was threatened, or to what extent, he did not know, but the shadow of the threat came upon him whenever he reached the one place on the earth he could call his own, upon which his life and all its simple hopes were centred. The world was launched on strange courses, and whither it would be driven no man could tell. There was no one in control of events now. Well enough did Mr Bunting understand that.

So he paused there, gathering together his courage and that cheerfulness which is the badge of courage: a middle-aged, unheroic Englishman in a bowler hat and worn blue suit, carrying a leatherette attaché case and a rumply umbrella.

It wasn't the first time he had faced an ordeal. He had passed through ordeals of many kinds before now, of family illness and near bereavement, financial loss, unemployment, and the frustration of the hopes he had cherished for his sons. And there had been other crises, the secret battles of his mind and heart, conflicts within himself. They had all been endured and surmounted, and so would this. Even if a bomb dropped on them all, they could crawl out of the wreckage and begin again somewhere else, if they were left alive. And if not, that would be the end. They might not even know of it. The thing was to keep your heart up and go on from day to day.

Mr Bunting had a modest enough opinion of his brain power, and even of his courage. But he had a tremendous belief in his ability to hang on.

He entered the lighted haven of Laburnum Villa like an added ray of light, self-consciously cheerful, his eyes able neither to express nor yet conceal his ingenuous affection. There were times when his manner bordered even on the jovial. That was how Mrs Bunting knew his really bad days.

Standing on the hearth, and greeting his family as though he hadn't seen them for a week, with an interested eye on the tea table, Mr Bunting diverted his thoughts to the compensations of life. He counted his blessings. The war couldn't take everything; at least it hadn't yet. He had the best of wives, three interesting children, a well-seasoned pipe, two bottles of 'Bonnie Prince Charlie' and his own fireside to sit at. Hitler, according to his reading, didn't possess a single one of these items, though they were the best things life could offer, and the sum total of all Mr Bunting worked for.

There was another thing he noticed as he turned on the wireless after tea; news didn't sound so bad the second time you heard it. The first time it rocked you on to your heels; then you recovered balance. At least you did if you'd got a proper British spirit. There was, after all, something in English complacency, as Corder had pointed out. It was a sort of armour for the nerves, an integu– ... He hadn't yet looked the word up in the *bijou*, but he knew what Corder meant. It was being armed so strong and honestly that threats passed by upon the idle wind, as in the case of Brutus.

He ran his eyes down the column of situations vacant, looking for something for Julie, whose vegetarian solicitor had joined the artillery. It would be difficult for a vegetarian in the army, he thought; probably teach him more sense. His eye alighted on a likely post in the food controller's office, thirty-five shillings a week and an opportunity of seeing how few people were too high-minded to accept bacon coupons.

Julie was sitting at the table writing one of her many applications, and Chris was reading the *Aeroplane*. When spoken to, he grunted in a preoccupied manner from behind that absorbing journal. The war had simplified life to the extent that he could deduce from Chris's presence that Monica was on duty at the control centre, having been enrolled by Mr Rollo. There were times when Mr Bunting wished Chris would not so assiduously read about flying; it was the only aspect of the war that interested him. A restlessness had come over Chris since Bert Rollo's leave, and an uneasiness of mind, betrayed by his odd silences over the newspapers and his still odder comments on the war. Some of his remarks suggested that he even thought his father didn't realise what the country was up against.

'They've got to be stopped, dad,' he would say. Chris never got beyond this statement, which he repeated from time to time as though appealing to Mr Bunting to see his point of view.

'I know that. But how?'

'In the air.'

'That's one place we've got to tackle 'em. But – '

'There aren't any "buts," dad. It's in the air we've got to beat 'em. If we don't, they'll come over here and blow places like Kilworth to blazes.'

'Aeroplanes ought never to have been invented. Gashly things!' The mere thought of flying, not merely himself, but of anybody flying, filled Mr Bunting with a faint, rather sickly dread. He thought of it as something unnatural, a trespassing into a forbidden element. However common it might be, however soundly based on science, it was bound to be extremely hazardous. A man trusted himself to a mere machine, went soaring up into the immense hazardous spaces from which the most trivial mechanical defect could instantly fling him in a terror-stricken spiral back to earth.

'Too late to say that now, dad. They've been invented, and Hitler's got stacks more of 'em than we have.'

Here Julie gave a stage sigh, leaned back in her chair, and resigned herself to wait for silence. The reason why so many of her applications failed, she had let it be understood, was that she was not allowed peace and quietness for their composition.

Mr Bunting bent encouragingly over her shoulder. He desired to drop the subject of aeroplanes and bombs and the magnitude of the Luftwaffe. 'What sort of a testimonial did he give you,' he inquired, and read the document in question with extreme satisfaction. 'That's the best testimonial I've seen for years,' he remarked, returning to re-read the finer phrases. 'Better than Ernest got at the town hall. Here, Chris.'

Julie snatched it away. 'Don't let him see it, dad. He'll only make a lot of sarcastic remarks.'

'No, I won't, Julie, honest. Let's see it.'

'You said the last read like an epitaph.'

'Epigram,' corrected Mr Bunting. 'Epitaphs is texts on gravestones.'

'Don't if you don't want to,' said Chris. He seemed kindly disposed tonight and disinclined to argue. Got something on his mind, perhaps difficulties about petrol. If Julie got another post it would help a bit, but Chris would really have to do something about the garage. So ran Mr Bunting's thoughts, following, he fancied, those of Chris. Now and then he looked up to find his son's glance resting on him pensively.

Suddenly Chris took his slippered feet off the couch, and with an air of decision said: 'I've fixed up with Mr Rollo about the garage. Old Rutherford 's going to run it.'

'Why *old* Rutherford?' thought Mr Bunting. He disliked this epithet exceedingly. Rutherford was only fifty-six.

'I thought of doing a bit to help the war.'

'Good idea, Chris. I've just seen the very thing in the papers. Experienced motor mechanics wanted for aeroplane 'struction. You got to apply. 'Course it would mean leaving home and going into lodgings.' He hung over this as a difficulty.

'Make 'planes! Golly, that's no good to me! I want to fly 'em!'

Something like a shaft of ice went slowly through Mr Bunting's heart. Chris looked at him cheerfully as ever, but very determined.

'You're going to join the RAF?' exclaimed Julie excitedly.

Chris nodded. 'I think I could make a pilot.'

Mr Bunting sat very still, unable to speak, his whole being jarred by the blow. He was filled with uncertainty about his duty in this issue. And there was pride, too, a bitter but overwhelming pride.

Across the room he saw his wife looking at her son. Not since her family had been babies had he seen that look on Mary's face. Then she went into the kitchen.

'Hrrm!' said Mr Bunting, very matter-of-fact, but he strained his ears towards the kitchen. No sound reached him, but he was intensely aware of his wife, apparently standing quite motionless in there.

'Course, it's not easy to get in as a pilot, is it?'

'I can go as a flying sergeant.'

'Oh, no, Chris,' urged Julie: 'be an officer.'

'No, just a plain, ordinary sergeant pilot. That's my fancy.'

'But you'll get wings? I say! How squish!'

With an air of not being noticed Mr Bunting went through into the kitchen. His wife was standing by the sink; their glances met and he put his arm around her shoulder. Swallowing something in his throat, he whispered: 'We mustn't try to stop him if he thinks it's his duty.'

'No!' softly, with a hint of tears, but much to his relief. There seemed little else to say.

'Don't let him see we're upset.'

'No. If other parents can, we can, George.'

'Yes – that's so.' He began to fumble with the supper dishes. He noticed Chris's raincoat hanging behind the kitchen door, its sleeves half in the armholes. He straightened them carefully and hung the coat on the stand. It had a careless hang, as though it had taken on some of Chris's more endearing qualities. He found his boots caked with mud that rotted the soles for want of scraping. Not one of them took care of their clothes, or ever put their shoes on trees. All these things Mr Bunting patiently attended to and said no word.

He was inclined to think Chris was not the type to get into the Air Force as a flier, not enough of a daredevil. He was a quiet boy really; even as a car driver he was steady.

Returning to the living room, he sat down and deliberately filled and lit his pipe before returning to the subject.

'I wouldn't be in too great a hurry, Christopher. Get everything settled with Mr Rollo.'

'But I've joined, dad. I've passed the doctor.'

Mr Bunting had expected this. He knew Chris's ways of old, but it was with relief he heard the definite announcement. When a thing was settled beyond recall one could make one's mind up to it.

'Won't Marvellous Monica be proud, walking out with a pilot?' mused Julie, whose share in Chris's glory would only be that of a sister.

'Oh, stow it!' he retorted, and returned his feet to the couch and reopened the *Aeroplane*, whilst his father watched him from across the hearth with a heart full of misgiving pride.

Later, Mr Bunting sat up alone. He had been round the house to make sure no bedroom lights were showing, and now he waited for Ernest. Meanwhile he filled his Pipe with 'Lighthouse,' his new tobacco. Only one and four ('Only!' he thought. 'Ye gods!'), and not a patch on 'Paradise,' but smokable if persevered with. One had to educate the palate and, incidentally, Mrs Bunting's nose. A woman who had associated her husband's presence with a particular aroma for thirty years is naturally averse to change.

Ernest was out with Evie; they got little time together. Evie was dispenser to Dr Earle and had been enrolled by Mr Rollo for special duty at the aid post. Between her duties there, her work in the surgery, and Ernest's long hours at the laundry, they had few opportunities of meeting. If Ernest irritated his father more than Chris and Julie, he also evoked more sympathy. He took life hard; too much thinking, too much arguing with himself, too much conscience, and too much psychology. Life was easier, Mr Bunting thought, if you cultivated simple ideas, and didn't make a life-and-death question of every principle. But Ernest was stubborn; one would never have believed a young man so delicately featured and obviously not strong could be so tenacious of an idea as Ernest was. It was simply a waste of time to argue with him, even if all you wanted was to get him to treat himself more kindly. He would always take the thorny road.

He came in now very quietly, with his shadowed smile. He looked tired. Whilst he took off his shoes Mr Bunting fetched in the supper tray and warmed up the cocoa. No point in mentioning Chris's affair, he thought; only give Ernest's brain something else to fasten on to. What the boy needed was to rest and relax.

'They seem to think the Germans might invade Holland,' said Ernest presently.

It was the first time he had admitted such a possibility. He had been apt to remind you that Germany had a non-aggression pact with Holland and that Hitler had recently confirmed it. To Ernest this disposed of a matter that was too straight for quibbling. People blamed Hitler for many things, but Ernest thought there must be facts behind the news that would explain many of his actions, if we were allowed to know them. As a man who had risen to eminence from obscurity, he naturally commanded Ernest's respect. But today the *Outlook* had spoken of an attack on Holland as a possibility. Seeing this in the *Outlook* had made a great impression on Ernest. It was by no means the same thing as reading a similar opinion in the *Siren*. The *Outlook* was his favourite journal and really quite advanced. If Hitler broke his pledge here the effect would be disastrous in every sense. There was a slight dimming of Ernest's belief that the *Führer* was always misrepresented.

'Evie and I have been looking round a few flats, dad.'

He stirred his cocoa and glanced at his father, thinking him slow of comprehension.

'The Government will be calling a lot more men up shortly.'

'But you won't have to go, Ernest. You're exempted through your job. No need to rush into anything.'

He had a feeling of having touched one of the sensitive springs that were Ernest's principles. 'I don't see why I should escape if others don't. Of course, I'd try to get non-combatant service, stretcher-bearing, or something. I wouldn't be any use for killing people.'

There followed a pause. Then Ernest said: 'Evie and I have decided to get married.'

'I see,' said Mr Bunting, receiving his second shock of the evening.

'We shall only be in the next road,' went on Ernest, beginning to explain his plans. There was a flat – only two rooms and a kitchenette – he produced his pocketbook, gave details of rent and rates, arrangements for hiring meters and cooker; his detail-ridden mind had a complete grasp of everything, and he put the whole up for his father's approval. But Mr Bunting scarcely heard the details.

He had jested often enough about the ideal home, but there was a touch of pathos about it now. Ernest's fine young dreams had dwindled to something that would scarce have satisfied his father.

'We all wish you well, my boy,' he said, putting a hand on his son's shoulder; 'and Evie, too. She's a good girl, and we're fond of her. Now get off to bed and don't worry about nothing.'

Mr Bunting sat by the fire, close to its dying embers. It was late, but he had no desire for sleep. He had a lot to think about, but he thought about it aimlessly. Emotion more than thoughts possessed him. He sat with his feet inside the fender, the faint glow of the fire lighting his full, gingerish cheeks, his cold pipe held in his thick fingers. The home was breaking up. After these many years he had reached the moment that had been inevitable from the start. His sons were going out into the world, his daughter in her turn would follow, and he and Mary would be left alone, old people at the fireside. It was the end of a stage in life's journey.

Yet he seemed to have got so little out of all these years. His memories of family life were contracted to a few vivid scenes and a host of things he had forgotten.

Your best hopes were like a tree you planted. You watered it and pruned it, and staked it against the storm. You waited eagerly for the first blossoms, and how their loveliness gladdened you, like the first almond blossoms of the spring! But the next time you passed the petals were already strewn upon the grass.

Mr Bunting rose and put out the light; the last ember in the grate winked and went out. Heavy-footed, he climbed the stairs to bed.

SEVEN

MR BUNTING TOOK a day off from Brockleys the day Ernest married Evie. Business had brightened a little, and he made elaborate preparations for his absence, almost on the scale of those that preceded his annual holiday. He nominated one of his assistants to act as deputy and, sitting on the cubby-hole stool with the honoured one before him, he uttered a few precepts for general guidance in all foreseeable emergencies. He also prepared a written list of instructions, and supplemented them by verbal warnings to various members of the staff, laying particular emphasis on those directed at old Turner. He was anxious that the firm should not suffer by this gratuitous day of liberty, the first almost of his entire service.

In granting leave of absence, Mr Bickerton had inquired if Ernest was in the forces.

'No, this boy ain't, sir. He's exempted, but my younger one's training to be an Air Force pilot,' answered Mr Bunting, and was aware of the warmth of Mr Bickerton's interest, knew he recognised a father's pride and instantly appraised him at higher value. Exceedingly pleasant! But pleasantest of all was Corder's unexpected gift. Corder had never seen Ernest or any of the Bunting children; he knew them in the way Mr Bunting knew Hamlet and Horatio, as recurrent subjects of his friend's familiar conversation. But he came into the cubby-hole bearing a brown-paper parcel containing, he said, a thing of naught save as the intention of the giver could enrich a gift so small, and Mr Bunting certainly understood it to be an avuncular token of esteem. Actually, as he discovered in the train, the parcel contained a silver entrée dish.

It was a quiet wedding. Evie had no relations near at hand, and the principal guest was Oskey, who gave her away. These arrangements pleased Mr Bunting, who disliked public occasions. He was pleased, too, by the clergyman who, surprisingly, seemed to know Ernest well, and by the organist, apparently a particular musical friend. The respect this person had for Ernest was plainly manifest, and made a tremendous impression on Mr Bunting, for the organist was no mere

69

boy, and no long-haired dreamer either, but a business-like looking person of his own age, who could be credited with judgment and common sense. Mr Bunting took pride in his son that day.

He sat in his pew, full-cheeked, rather breathless, dressed to the point of discomfort. The organ pealed above him, and every ancient stone seemed to vibrate to that glorious music. An old place, Kilworth Church, six hundred years old, they said; he believed the monks built it. Its shadows were more impressive than the finest scientific lighting of the new age. They seemed to quieten and console you, to solemnify life's trivial meaning and all your thoughts. The darkness you looked into seemed to be the darkness of past centuries, you fancied you could see dim figures hovering there as it might be knights and ladies, or the monks themselves. You were surrounded by the past's silent witness. Down the long centuries couples had been married here, on that very stone before the altar, gentle and simple, the true and the faithless; countless numbers of them. They passed before the mind's eye in their quaint costumes, an endless procession wending its way down the ages – all long since dead, dust, and forgotten.

And now Ernest and Evie.

They looked very young standing there, very inexperienced, waiting on the most important threshold of their lives. Ernest's youth was the most obvious and most touching thing about him at this moment; a mere boy he looked to his watching father.

A quietness fell; the elms rustled near the windows. Everybody waited. They had entered a dimension of life far removed from the humdrum of the working day, which had washed away from them like a receding tide. Their thoughts and feelings were strange even to themselves. Difficult to believe that within a day's journey of this home of ancient peace the war was being fought out with desperation and carnage inconceivable.

The emptiness of fear touched Mr Bunting. He remembered the shock of the morning's news. The Germans had broken through the French defences, there was a battle in progress, the 'Battle of the Gap'. Opening the paper this morning and seeing the positions indicated had given him the same sickly feeling he felt when he looked down from a height and knew himself within a step of peril.

At this moment hidden guns were flashing, tanks rumbling across fields, infantry crouching in hedge bottoms and abandoned houses. The most bitter fighting was in progress, even now as he sat here, unable to do anything but wait and hope and keep his nerve.

These were sad days. Throughout Europe couples were parting at the altar, their next meeting in every sense uncertain. In Germany, too, he supposed – even in Germany, that land of the fantastic creed. It seemed possible to Mr Bunting that a German father might be witnessing such a scene as this with the same troubled mind and heart as he had at this present moment.

He sighed deeply and moved in the pew. Mrs Bunting gave him a cautionary nudge, awakening him to the fact that he had sighed and moved several times during this waiting silence. These were, indeed, not fitting thoughts to bring to a wedding.

He was brought back to reality by the clergyman's voice and a tensing of the group around him. Monica and Julie, the bridesmaids, stood before the altar. It was the first time he had seen either of them bereft of the springy self-possession all young women seemed to have today. They had lost it now, if only momentarily, and gained renewed youth and innocence; they were just two overawed young girls. His eyes rested on Monica. He had always thought her a trifle 'band-boxy', too finished and too high of heel. She stood very still, holding her bouquet, her expressive eyes catching the light from the high windows above the altar. She was a beauty, certainly, and few strangers would spare a glance for Evie whilst Monica was near. But his eyes travelled beyond her to Evie with a particular tenderness. Evie wrapped herself round your heart slowly and gently, like the tendrils of a climbing plant, and could not be dislodged. Though Mr Bunting admired Monica for her picturesqueness, he thought Evie a darling.

Now there was the business of the ring, a feeling of nervousness, of climax, and the clergyman's pronouncement.

Then at a touch all solemnity vanished, the organ pealed out its song of joy. Everybody moved. They were through in the vestry, laughing and talking; they were out of the church into the churchyard and into the prosaic world of the street. There was a confusion about taxis, Mr Bunting bustling backwards and forwards giving contradictory orders, aware of confetti in his hat and his huge and gorgeous buttonhole. Then, through confusedly seen streets, crammed tightly into the most intimate contacts, back to Laburnum Villa, where Mrs Oskey had the lunch laid in a room that seemed over-flowing with people, everybody talking and nobody listening, and Evie and Ernest being congratulated as though they had come through some tremendous ordeal.

'My only regret,' said Mr Bunting, as he served the ham, 'is that Chris wasn't able to be with us.'

'And Bert,' put in Julie, unexpectedly.

'Yes, Bert, too. Sorry I forgot him.'

Oskey gave a rumbling assent to these sentiments. He had been staring at those corners of the Bunting garden not visible from his side of the fence, thus satisfying a long-standing curiosity. There was a clump of mallow – common mallow – a great sprouting weed, which Mr Bunting had left blooming in a border because he admired that particular shade of blue. Oskey's solemn eyes were lit with a veiled interior light, as of a man who puts a good laugh on deposit. Then, portentously solemn, he sat down. Throughout the proceedings he had conducted himself with a deliberate and elephantine correctness, threading his way through the ceremonies like a battleship on manoeuvres.

Having disposed of his tin hat and laid an enormous palm flatly on either knee he remarked that it was the best day's work he had ever done and hoped Ernest wouldn't live to bear him malice for it. This remark, which had been made to Oskey at his own wedding by his father-in-law, was received as a masterpiece of humour, Ernest and Evie blushing and Mr Bunting pausing with the carving knife to see how they took it.

'Lovely tomatoes, Mr Oskey,' he said, paying tribute to the grower of the salad.

'"Crimson Globe,"' Oskey told him. He was about to add a hint on their particular culture when Evie forestalled him.

'The bouquets were lovely. Do you mind if I send mine to the hospital?'

'Not at all, miss. I mean missus.' He reddened violently at the error.

'Oh, Mr Oskey! I never knew you were so witty,' exclaimed Julie, and had her foot promptly stamped on by Ernest.

'This is what I call a 'am,' declared Mr Bunting. 'Starving England, eh? Pity old Goebbels can't see it. Some for you, Julie?'

'No.'

'What! Not on Ernest's wedding day?'

'Leave her alone, George,' advised Mrs Bunting hastily.

Mr Bunting put down the carvers and reached for the corkscrew. He didn't wish the festivities to be marred by arguments about ham being dead pig. Everybody knew that, but nobody remembered when they were eating it – not if they had sense.

After the sweet came the port; it was pronounced excellent – Wishart's. Everybody began discussing port like connoisseurs. Sometimes it was too heavy or too syrupy, and sometimes it gave you a headache. But today it was just right; there was nothing like getting a good port. It even brought a smile to Oskey's lips. Now and then he ran a finger round the inside of his choke collar, giving Mr Bunting at long last the clue to his unnatural appearance.

Mr Bunting rose to propose the health of the bride and groom. As he did so he felt an internal discomfort, a sort of sea-sickness, which he ignored like a true Briton. He cleared his throat manfully.

'This has been a great occasion. Truly a great occasion. Hymeneal.' Here he put down his glass for safety. He had eaten a good many things that did not agree with him, and felt a strong desire for soda mints. All he could do was pull down his waistcoat, which he did with a firm hand, as though indicating that deeper disturbances must wait. During this pause there were cries of 'Hear! Hear! Order!' and Mrs Oskey suspended her labours to listen.

'Let all unto the marriage of true minds omit impediments.' Seeing a blank look on Oskey's face Mr Bunting added: 'As the poet said. We know, we all know, everybody knows – What's that row, Mary?' he demanded, with a sudden descent to irritability.

A direful wailing as of ten thousand dislocated circular saws drowned his question. Everybody froze into a listening attitude. 'What the – ' began Mr Bunting.

'Siren!' ejaculated Oskey. 'Air raid.' He reached for his tin hat. 'Into the shelters, everybody. Quietly now. No need to get the breeze up.'

'If I could get at those – ' began Mr Bunting, still in his speech-making attitude.

'You can talk in the shelter,' Oskey informed him. His tone was distinctly official.

They trooped out on to the lawn. There was general indignation at this necessity to break up the party, Mrs Bunting saying: 'Isn't it just like those Germans?' whilst Julie stared up into the clouds and said: 'Oh!' fiercely and venomously.

'You girls had better go into my shelter,' said Oskey. 'You can squeeze through here. Mind the shallots.'

He shepherded everybody calmly and officially to the prescribed places of safety. He was, in fact, altogether too calm and official for Mr Bunting's liking. It was obvious that he found pleasure in being able, for the first time, to put into practice all he had learnt about the duties of an air raid warden. Having seen everyone to cover he surveyed the sky, still empty of planes, and with a feeling of having outwitted the enemy he stalked off to duty at the wardens' post.

The bride and bridegroom and Mr and Mrs Bunting sat on the dugout bench, conscious of cramped space and a general earthy dampness. They were out of breath like people who have just caught a train and now wait for it to start. They listened, they looked out at the small patch of sky visible through the entrance. A nervous expectancy possessed them.

'Trologytes,' murmured Mr Bunting. 'That's what we are. Nothing but trologytes.'

'George!' exclaimed Mrs Bunting, evidently protesting against doubtful language.

'We're all right,' said Ernest, cheerfully.

'After all, we did get married, Mr Bunting,' said Evie, 'and have lunch too.'

'Yes,' he answered absently. If a bomb fell on the back of the shelter, the best thing would be for them to lean over, whereas if it fell on the front – His consideration of air raid tactics was interrupted by another and more urgent thought. He got up, went to the entrance, looked this way and that, and listened. For a second his eye rested on Ernest as though formulating a request. Then he made his decision.

'Shan't be a minute,' he called, and climbed up the steps into the open, experiencing an immediate feeling of being vulnerable and exposed. He darted across the lawn and into the house. There he paused. A sudden whoosh in the air made him draw his head in sharply, but it was only the wind rustling through his laburnum. There was still no sound overhead; you could count on about five minutes' warning, according to Oskey. His heart was thumping and his throat dry. He rinsed a cup, drank, and went looking for the gas masks.

They were not on the hall stand, not in the living room, not on the newel post. He searched feverishly, fumbling under coats and hats. For the first time since the war began the masks were lost, and at the very time they might be wanted.

He checked his sense of panic, and stood quite still. When others depended on you the thing was to think. Then he saw them suddenly through the opened front room door.

He was quite exhausted when he got back to the shelter. He sat panting on the bench.

Ernest smiled at him. Had he done something silly, he wondered, got scared without reason? Mr Bunting didn't care if they laughed at him. He'd got the gas masks.

'Dad!' exclaimed Ernest, and gripped his arm. A feeling that though Ernest might be amused he was also touched by his father's action was communicated through that warm grasp.

Suddenly Mrs Bunting started. 'Listen!'

A faint whizzing sound that loudened and rose in pitch to a long triumphant note like a trumpet call. They looked at one another for verification.

'The all clear.'

They came out of the dugout, stood once again in the open air and sunlight. Julie and Monica waved from the adjoining garden, and all looked at the sky.

'False alarm,' commented Mr Bunting. 'Somebody messing things up. Been no bombs at all.'

Nevertheless, everybody felt that the war had come a step nearer Laburnum Villa.

EIGHT

HOW QUICKLY A three-roomed flat can take on the appearance of an ideal home, Ernest learnt almost as soon as he was married. To Evie, the comfortless rooms they had inspected together were only so much raw material. Her imagination never ceased to play on them, and Ernest became handyman to her architect.

Until he married he had never driven in a screw in all his life, and he did not at first realise the necessity for preparatory action with the gimlet. He was often defeated by sheer natural ineptitude; he made blunders for which he would have blushed before his father, but which caused only hilarious laughter at the flat. All the lunch hours of Ernest's early married life were spent buying tools and screws and plugging apparatus, and consulting oilmen on the methods of staining floors; all his evenings in acquiring handicraft. The jobs which he had always avoided as messy, and consequently left to his father, had, he found, an interesting aspect. They developed certain faculties of the brain, as, for instance, the logical faculty, and development of the brain was one of Ernest's major preoccupations. It was an amazing thing that an intelligent man could fix a towel-rail without remembering the door had to open; but he learnt in time to take thought before driving in the nails. Often he believed everything was completed to perfection, only to learn from Evie that, before he could relax, there were still more possibilities of the flat to be exploited.

Cheerfully curtained and tastefully arranged, with the extravagance of just one Medici print above the fireplace, the flat became the brightest spot he had ever known. Much as he had valued his own home, homecoming had never been the chief event of the day till now. To enter the flat in Martin Street after a heavy day was to relax the mind even with the closing of the door behind him.

If Ernest at his fireside was a ship in port, the rest of his time was spent in a world where everything was hostile.

The less business the laundry handled the harder Ernest seemed to have to work, and often at things that were entirely unproductive.

He organised an air raid squad, provided shelters, sand-bagged where instructed, and held long discussions with the borough surveyor on using the laundry plant for decontaminating clothing in the event of gas attack. Ernest brought to all these conferences the passive co-operation of a mind to which gas attacks and air raids are sheer lunacy. Nor was his mood improved by the frequent presence at these discussions of an army officer, whose uniform was obtrusively decorated with pips and crowns and bits of metal. Ernest had an instinctive antagonism to uniform, he wondered how anybody could put it on without feeling self-conscious.

Showing these people round the works, and explaining the function of various machines, he would be met with the army officer's 'Quite!' or 'Definitely,' or, at least, if these words were uttered, they struck him with more force than any others. Ernest explained everything to Captain Smith one week, and was usually required to repeat his explanation to Captain Brown (who had never by any chance heard of Captain Smith) the next. He conducted these tourists round the Eagle Laundry with the contained professional patience of an Abbey guide. He desired only to satisfy and dispose of them, and return to business problems, which were ceaselessly multiplying. The struggle to get material was endless, the struggle to keep staff hopeless.

At his busiest moment his typist, speaking over a pile of unanswered correspondence, announced she was leaving him to become a land girl.

'Why a land girl?' he asked stiffly.

'I want to do my bit, you know.'

'Aren't you doing it here?'

'Oh, I don't want to carry on this sort of work in wartime. It's the first chance I've ever had to live on a farm.'

There was no point in further discussion, Ernest thought. She was efficient; she always remembered just those details he forgot, and it would be difficult to replace her. But she wanted adventure. Most of the men who joined the Forces wanted adventure, and he didn't blame them. But there was none for him; he was tied to his desk at the laundry.

To shorten the working day he frequently lunched in the office on sandwiches, always packed with a note from Evie which he read as an aperitif and as dessert. After eating, he spent some time reading Otto Reinberger's essays on *Life and Music*. This was the most wonderful book Ernest had ever read, a translation into prose of the spiritual qualities of Reinberger's music. It was Reinberger who first took him beyond the materialism of 'practical psychology,' and taught him to think of the soul. Up till now Ernest had never thought or spoken of the soul, or even heard it discussed, without embarrassment. It was one of the things one didn't mention in ordinary conversation. But Reinberger wrote of the soul as naturally as he did of the mind. There was, he said, one soul common to all humanity, and through it were made the communications of the creative artist. The core of the poet's message lay in those significances which only the soul apprehended. They were beyond words and thoughts; a recognition by man's immortal spirit of the things that were eternal.

Hitherto, Ernest had thought of creative artists in separate categories as poet, painter, and musician; different techniques divided them. Now he saw they were one brotherhood. They had nothing to do with technique. They were the missionaries of the unseen; they lived only in those minds where they awakened echoes. To be of this brotherhood in any sense, was to possess the crown of life, and to be emancipated from every fear that beset materialistic minds. One had to find access to the common soul through prayer or meditation, through art or nature or any form of beauty. From each of these paths man might gather a flower and, not hastening towards the future, nor leaning back upon the past, live in the 'eternal now,' and keep his garland unwithered.

Ernest often paused over this book, feeling his old signposts were being torn down and new and dimly seen ones erected. There was much he did not comprehend, much he accepted uncharacteristically, even when Reinberger made no appeal to reason. But he was cheered most of all by a fact accidental to the message and external to it. The book came out of Germany, had been written by a German, and circulated in Germany. There, as here, were men who reached out to newer conceptions of life in a richer, freer world.

One closed a book like this and opened a newspaper and felt one's heart sink at the contrast between what was possible and what was real. Never in human history, Ernest supposed, had crimes so monstrous in scope and wickedness defaced the human story. The invasion of Norway revealed a depth of turpitude that shocked him out of his earlier political beliefs. Every word of Berlin's cynical justifications seemed to proceed from minds so perverted as to be sub-human. One turned from the German Reinberger to the Germans of the Munich beer cellar, and knew it was not Reinberger his countrymen listened to. But all the still small voices were silenced now. Even here in Kilworth, with its forty churches, open hostility waited on such thoughts as Ernest clung to.

Such was the background of his mental life in the dark days when the German Army swept on its bloody course through France, and the word 'invasion,' like an echo from the history books, began to be heard on the lips of responsible men. Ernest talked little of the war, except to Evie, whose religious ideas were simple and, to him, extremely naive, giving him no comfort.

Sometimes in the evening she would bustle him into his hat and coat, and they would go along to Laburnum Villa for a little music. The cardinal defect in the flat was that there was no piano, nor space to put one.

Mr Bunting always welcomed them boisterously, rising from his chair with the paper hanging down before him like an apron, and saying in a voice of astonishment: 'Why, it's Ernest and Evie!' as though he had met them on the front at Brighton. He became very active, pushing chairs out of the way as though it was otherwise impossible for them to get inside. Then he would light the gas fire in the front room because 'it did the place good' to be warmed up now and then, and because the gas fire was a damaged Brockley 'Radiant' picked up for nothing, which hardly burnt any gas. He explained this on every occasion; but whether his intention was to put Ernest at ease, or to maintain consistency with his years long opposition to the expense of extra fires, no one could tell.

Whilst Ernest was playing he would take Evie round the garden, where there were developments or, at least, the promise of developments, and tell her she need never buy any lettuces; there would be any amount at Laburnum Villa when they began to come up. Oskey, whose lettuces had already come up, somewhat precociously, Mr Bunting thought (it was a miracle the frost hadn't got them), would be seen selecting a few of his very best, and uprooting them in the proper manner, preparatory to handing them over the fence. He did this out of regard for Evie but also, Mr Bunting suspected, to show what could be done with the right variety.

There was nothing Mr Bunting liked better than to escape from the war and listen to his wife and daughter-in-law discuss the technicality of 'turning the heel,' or report on experiments with recipes recommended by the Ministry of Food. To sit placidly smoking and listening to these discussions was to realise one had a home and a wife who was a jewel. If there was anything better in life, Mr Bunting wanted to know what it was. He supposed these Nazis and Fascists had homes – they must sleep somewhere – and it was a pity they couldn't stay in them peacefully, instead of dressing up and parading about and behaving like overgrown boy scouts of a particularly odious kind. It was a pity there weren't more people like himself, particularly on the Continent. The more Buntings, the fewer Hitlers, he considered.

These meditations were interrupted by the return of Ernest from the piano and the offer of a cigarette. These were the only cigarettes Mr Bunting indulged in, and he smoked them awkwardly, dropping ash upon his knees and remarking at frequent intervals that they were 'Jolly good, Ernest.' He usually contrived unobtrusively to obtain an assurance that the gas fire had been turned out.

A new relationship had sprung up between Ernest and his father, as though Mr Bunting now granted to his son increased status.

'What's a three-point landing, Ernest? Got to do with flying.'

Ernest thought a moment. 'I think it's the recognised way of landing a plane properly. I think that's it.'

'That's all right then. Chris says in his letter that he's made a three-point landing. I thought perhaps he's been trying to do some fancy business. I wrote and asked.'

He deposited the remains of his cigarette in the ashtray and wiped several threads of tobacco from his lips. It was clear he had been worried and was now relieved. 'I don't want him to get into any silly habits. Dangerous enough as it is.'

Despite his firm intention not to discuss the war he always drifted into a discussion of it. What he asked for was some reassurance, however flimsily grounded. To Ernest, who now saw him only at intervals, he looked older, and despite the eager bustle of his welcome, a man lonely and troubled at heart. The *Siren* failed entirely to comfort Mr Bunting these days. Great disasters were coming upon the country, and the future might be even worse; he saw it dark and threatening.

'I can't understand the Germans getting into France like this. Why don't we stop 'em? We always have before. They're getting a bit too close, Ernest. If they get as far as Calais the game's up properly.'

But Mr Bunting couldn't believe the Germans would ever get to Calais. It looked a long way on his war map from where they were even now.

'What's this blitzkrieg idea, Ernest?'

'It means lightning war.'

'Is that what it means?' It seemed a funny thing to call it. But he investigated the subject no further; a word had contented him.

He saw them to the door, watched them vanish in the darkness, and waited for the clicking of the gate. They were quite out of sight then.

'I'll just have a last pipe, Mary,' he said, when his wife and Julie prepared for bed. These last pipes by the fireside were the peaceful ends of Mr Bunting's days. There were times when a man wanted to be alone, and there were times when he wanted company. One's family never understood that, they intruded at the wrong moment. Sitting there in his slippers, secure from interruption, he reviewed the day and often the months and years that lay behind him, and thus kept his mind off the future.

Sometimes a patrolling aircraft flew low over the town. He heard its rising note in the distance, followed its course till it passed overhead, all the ornaments on the mantelshelf chattering as if with fright, heard it die away into the distance. Then he would look out at the kitchen door and watch the silently moving searchlight beams creep about the sky searching for the insect-like evasive speck.

'Might be a German,' he thought. Ernest said they flew over Kilworth sometimes. Scouting about, Ernest thought. Might be one of ours; might even be Chris. In any case, it was somebody up there, some young man sitting muffled in a cockpit on his eerie flight between two worlds.

Often whilst sitting up like this he would be seized on a sudden with a dread of his self-sought solitude, and hasten upstairs quickly for the comfort of lying down beside his wife. Then, for a time, he would listen wakefully, conscious of every external sound, whilst the day's dead thoughts stirred in his brain as a dog stirs fallen leaves before settling down to sleep. Hitler, Ribbentrop, Goering, Hitler – round and round and to and fro, endlessly, wearyingly, these names echoed and re-echoed. Somewhere, sleeping or waking, these evil men were living and visible at this very hour. Mr Bunting turned over and very resolutely determined not to think of them. He would think only of his own affairs. Concentrate. His lettuces, for instance, why hadn't they come up? Too much fertiliser, Oskey said, or not enough. He gave his mind entirely to his three-square yards of lettuce bed, and presently he fell asleep.

NINE

THOUGH POST TIME was always trying for a man with a son in the Air Force, Mr Bunting was not prepared for the shock he received from an official communication the following morning. He had a deep-rooted antipathy to all official communications; they were usually incomprehensible and always ill-timed, being among the pinpricks of the morning. As a rule he tore them open, exclaiming: 'More red tape,' and tossed them aside as things that could wait. This one, however, bore the incredible heading: 'If the invader comes.'

Mr Bunting read this with his first impatient glance, then focused his eyes steadily upon it. The letters did not dissolve into something sane and credible; they remained as official and intractable as an income tax demand note. He walked to the window and read the whole leaflet through in silence.

'Well, what next!' exclaimed Mrs Bunting, when he explained the contents.

'It says you've to stay put.'

'What! If the Germans come?'

'That's what it says.' He could make no illuminating comment. It was too simple for comprehension. A German, a parachutist was predicted as most probable, descended in one's back garden. You looked out of the window, recognised this advance guard of the Nazis, and you stayed put.

It occurred to Mr Bunting that the German might not allow you to stay put. What then had you to do, hide in the dugout? His moustache bristled at the idea. Entirely un-British.

He went out into the garden and searched for Oskey, finding him in his seedling bed. His first impression was that Oskey could not have received one of these Government circulars, for he was calmly watering autumn cabbages from his rain-water butt. All Oskey's actions were infused with technique; one got an impression of the watering can being held at the right height and angle, sprinkling in the approved manner, not sloshing water like an amateur.

'That's the stuff to promote root growth. Don't cake the ground, like tap water.' He seemed to think Mr Bunting had approached the fence to pick up a few useful tips, and, lest the limitations of his mental powers should prevent him from doing so, Oskey added an explanatory footnote to the effect that rainwater was more in accordance with nature than that supplied from the artesian wells of the Kilworth Water Company.

'Have you got one of these this morning? What do you make of it?'

Oskey compared the paper in Mr Bunting's hand with the one he had read at breakfast time, and concluded they were identical.

'All I wish is that I could get into the Home Guard instead of the air raid wardens. Have a go at the blighters.'

'But what are we supposed to do?'

'What it says. Stay put. Unless you're in civil defence.'

'Why can't the Government dish us out with a few hand-grenades!'

'Because they would make you a *franc-tireur*.'

'I don't see that it would,' said Mr Bunting, having waited in vain for a hint of this word's definition. It sounded foreign to him. Oskey had probably picked it up in a newspaper article.

'If you want to know the real danger to this country it's the fifth-columnists. They're roundin' 'em up in thousands. Fact, you never know who you're talking to these days.'

There was a slight pause after this remark, a questioning pause, during which Mr Bunting's eye hardened with affront. Then Oskey approached the fence closer, and dropped his voice to the confidential. Mr Bunting realised he, at least, was not one of the suspect.

'There are a few people round here that we ought to keep our eye on. Old Saunders at "Mandalay," for instance.'

'Colonel Saunders! Why, he's in charge of the volunteers.'

'Ah!' said Oskey, 'that's the artful part of it. Where did he spend his holidays last year? Can you tell me that?' Seeing that Mr Bunting couldn't, he added the damning word, 'Munich'.

'There's nothing wrong with the colonel,' declared Mr Bunting loyally. 'One of the best.' He was going to mention the Virginia creeper he had from him, but realised this was not evidence.

'If he ain't all right he ought to be shot. Shot without trial. That's what I'd do. Shoot the lot of 'em.'

Never had Mr Bunting seen Oskey so interested in the war, or, at least, in getting people shot. But he had often declared this was the only fitting end for Colonel Saunders, who won prizes with cucumbers which Oskey knew, and was prepared to swear in the witness box, Saunders could not possibly have grown himself.

It could hardly be said that this conversation greatly enlightened Mr Bunting on the practical difficulties of staying put; but he advised the wife to read the leaflet carefully during the day.

Three minutes late, his mind and his body in a flurry, he set off to the station with Julie, now in the Food Office at Bardolph's Green. There seemed to be more soldiers about than ever, more army lorries, more of those odd-shaped vehicles he had learnt to know as Bren gun carriers. One witnessed this activity with a mixture of disquiet and reassurance; if things were desperate, they were being taken in hand. At Kilworth's most important crossroads, engineers were erecting a blockhouse.

'Well, I *don't* know,' Mr Bunting exclaimed, pushing back his bowler from the red furrow on his brow that marked its habitual resting-place, and immediately bringing it forward again.

'I've a jolly good mind to join the ATS,' said Julie.

'You're going to stay in the Food Office,' he said firmly. He objected to young women leaving home to live in camps for reasons he was not prepared to discuss with a girl of Julie's age. It was true he did not like her being in the Bardolph Green Food Office either, but the danger there was an entirely different one; it was close to a bomb-filling factory. This news had given him quite a shock when first he heard it.

But Brockleys waited for him, square and massive, looking very much as it did the morning he came to beg on as an errand boy forty-five years ago. The buildings round it had changed out of all recognition, but a few superficial alterations had sufficed for Brockleys. It had the sober, solid look of a Victorian survival, its façade expressed integrity and endurance and twenty shillings in the pound. Under the strain of war the old standards of quality were vanishing, though, and sadly he saw them passing. They would never come back. They hadn't after the last war. How often did you see a bit of genuine leather these days? Goods had been getting tinnier and tinnier ever since he was taken off errand-running and brought into the shop. The class of goods he'd handled in his earlier days would make young salesmen stare today.

But Brockleys was still Brockleys, last outwork of old-time standards, even though quality was a relative term to men with memories like his.

Everybody in the train seemed to have volunteered for something except himself. They were mostly in the Home Guard, learning to shoot and throw home-made bombs, methodically preparing to kill every German who might get to England. They seemed to Mr Bunting in some ways more formidable even than the young soldiers who fought under orders light-heartedly, but who knew their country only as boys. These older men were preparing grimly to defend things they had cherished all their lives and meant to stick to. They would kill without compunction.

But they were all youngish men to Mr Bunting, not one of them more than fifty. He was sixty, and Mr Rollo had enrolled him as requested, but only on the 'reserve'. What else could he volunteer for?

That was a question indeed. He paused over it in the opening of his letters, and became aware of a rattling of the knob of the cubby-hole door, and a rubbing and a humming, explained only by the recent incursion into Brockleys of female cleaners.

'No need to polish the doorknob,' he said, opening the door and addressing a small, active figure in apron and cap. 'Quite unnecessary.'

'That's all right, Mr Bunting. I like to see things bright and shiny. Cheers you up.'

Surprise at being addressed by name being plainly registered on his features, the apron and cap said in a tone of bright confidence. 'I'm Mrs Musgrave. You know, Charlie's mother.'

'Really?' said Mr Bunting, and wondered who Charlie could be.

Not Charlie from the store cellar, into whom he had sought to instil ambition?

'Yes, that's 'im. 'E's in the army. Went into the infantry.'

'Really,' said Mr Bunting, slitting open an envelope by way of a hint. He had a foreboding that this bright-eyed little woman was going to button-hole him every morning from now on.

'He's in a platoon.'

'Jolly good. But don't polish the knob, makes a row.'

'I shan't be a minute,' Mrs Musgrave soothed him, and the knob rattled louder than ever. Mr Bunting waited, resignedly enduring another of the minor afflictions of the war.

Sending a sigh after her as she went, he looked over the partition to count the staff. There were few enough of them nowadays, but old Turner was there. He always waited for Mr Bunting's rollcall, making a sort of propitiatory bob as the managerial eye rested on him. Turner was never late; it was one of his widely advertised principles, prompt to come and prompt to go. His watery eyes met Mr Bunting's in daily confirmation of his one undeniable merit.

If business was now improving it was nevertheless becoming more trying. In the first months of the war there had been goods but no orders, now there were orders but no goods. Much of the purely peacetime stuff had been packed away; the cream-making machines and toasters, all the silly gadgets one had to demonstrate at the counter, and glad Mr Bunting was to see the last of them. More substantially, all the house-fitting stuff was out of demand: brackets, piping, all builders' fittings, no good now that housebuilding had ceased. You now realised how large was the category of the non-essential.

But if you wanted something that was essential you couldn't get it. You couldn't get a Watkin stove for love or money. There was a man in Elgin who had ordered Watkin stoves weeks ago, and had written so often about them that Mr Bunting bristled at the sight of his envelopes.

There was a time when to receive a telegram made his heart stand still, but he got them every day now. The cubby-hole was the focal point of two streams of telegraphic communication: customers demanding delivery, manufacturers protesting that delivery was impossible, Mr Bunting wedged helplessly between these irreconcilables. He greeted every yellow envelope with ejaculations, glaring with a ferocity that would have cowed any office boy but Mr Bickerton's.

His days were made up of a series of small crises, difficulties overcome by urgent telephoning and consultations with the chief, and spurts and rushes followed by empty periods during which his assistants showed a tendency to relax. In all his experience he had never had to contend with such a sorry crowd as these substitute assistants. One might at least expect them to have sufficient sense to keep a few articles on the counter to make a show of being busy when Mr Bickerton came in. It wasn't the sort of thing a manager could actually suggest, but he'd always done it when he was an assistant. But no; when they had been goaded and pushed to perspiration point to collect and crate an urgent order, they relaxed. They relaxed visibly and obviously like haymakers under a hedge at noon. When his head appeared above the partition they started self-consciously, their looks protesting the eternal fallacy of ironmongery assistants that there was nothing to do. Long experience had taught Mr Bunting that it was precisely at such moments one might expect the boss, whose eye immediately alighted on some neglected trifle. It had been so in old John's time, and so it was in Mr Bickerton's. But the heads never came in when the staff was busy.

He was particularly severe in the mornings, and only slightly mellower after lunch. The truth was, he got tired, and his stomach became unsettled. He had recourse more and more to soda mints and to the stock book, which represented a maturer variation of the intelligent assistant's spare goods on the counter. Turning its pages he rested his legs and his conscience, for no manager can be blamed if his staff take advantage of his absorption on legitimate functions of control.

He was sitting there when he heard a light step and, pushing open the cubby-hole door, beheld a lady. No other word could have described her, and Mr Bunting had an instinct for quality. She was elderly, with a small sweet face and greying hair, and was standing just inside the swing doors with rather a lost air. Her glance came to rest on him by that instinct which guides a shy woman to pick out the right person to help her in a difficulty.

'I wonder if you could direct me to my husband's office?'

Mr Bunting inclined his head.

'I'm Mrs Bickerton.'

'Ah!' he said, and his glance became full of interest; he glowed with gallantry. Not only would he direct her, he would escort her thither. But, as he turned to lead her on, in that precise instant of greatest self-importance, in came Turner from the street, four inches of *Standard* visible beneath his coat. Not only that, but he went to his counter and blatantly opened the double page, and put his nose inside.

At this glaring and ill-timed exhibition of indiscipline Mr Bunting made a half turn in the direction of Turner, thought better of it, and proceeded to lead the way upstairs. But he was very preoccupied. He fumbled at doors and tripped over steps, and betrayed every sign of being a shaken man. He took the contretemps downstairs very seriously, it was an affront to his position as manager; and, though Mr Bunting did not as a rule give much thought to his dignity, he could remember it on particular occasions. Besides, you never knew what a woman might think it her wifely duty to pass on to her husband.

He returned to the salesroom, his lips compressed, his jaw hard. Never in all his years of managership had such a thing happened, never had anything happened at such an unpropitious moment. An assistant reading newspapers in the shop, openly brandishing newspapers, not caring who saw him, in particular not caring if the manager saw him. Ah, but it was his own fault. Time and time again he'd meant to caution Turner, and had weakly put off cautioning him, being afraid to make a fuss. It could be put off no longer, not another instant. His steps quickened, as though he hastened after lost opportunity.

And there was Turner, rigid with interest, leaning over the wide-open *Standard* on the counter, lost to everything but war news. Mr Bunting did not so much advance, as swoop upon him. He snatched the paper out of Turner's hands and crumpled it into an unreadable mass with furious twistings and squeezings, his cheeks flaming.

Turner looked up dazedly, like a roughly awakened sleeper, his watery eyes blinked and the muscles of his throat quivered. But these frailties had no longer power to soften Mr Bunting's righteous rage.

'You blasted fool! Ain't you got no sense? Don't you know where you are?'

No answer from Turner. Only a shrinking as from an invisible blow, and a movement of his hands to the counter's edge for support.

'Can't you wait till you get home to read the paper?' Then, more loudly still: 'CAN'T you?'

Still no answer from Turner. He looked at Mr Bunting as through a cloud, seeing him dimly. But Mr Bunting saw him clearly enough, and did not hide his contempt.

'What are you good for anyway? You mess everything up. You don't know your job. But when it comes to this – reading papers.' He raised his voice again, infuriated at the stupidity of Turner's face. 'What do you do it for, eh?'

Mr Bunting was panting, but Turner had nothing to say; at least, nothing very audible though his lips were moving. Leaning towards him Mr Bunting caught the words, 'The *Badger*'.

'*Badger*?' he exclaimed wildly. 'Badger! What are you talking about? Gone barmy!'

'The destroyer *Badger*,' said Turner huskily. 'My boy's ship. In the papers.'

Mr Bunting stood stock still, aware of a throbbing in his head, the result of passion, like the beating on an anvil in a silent world. For a few seconds all his faculties were suspended; then he became once more aware of Turner, of the pale eyes blinking with a moisture beyond the ordinary, of the tremulous lips moving soundless as a fish. He stooped for the crumpled paper on the floor and spread it out upon the counter. It seemed not to matter who saw now.

Turner pointed. 'See, Mr Bunting. It's lost – it's – '

Mr Bunting bent his head over the paper, not seeing it. His cheeks were hot. Shame, remorse, and a sense of irretrievable wrong shook him. He could not raise his eyes to Turner's face; nor was it necessary, for he heard rather than saw Turner collapsing like an empty sack behind the counter.

With help he got him propped on a stool, and dispatched the boy to McAndrew's for a jug of tea. For a while he hovered helplessly on the fringe of those attending on the stricken man.

Later, he sat miserably in the cubby-hole. How often he had let faults go unchecked because he didn't want to make a fuss, and because it was easier to pretend he hadn't noticed, or for other self-indulgent reasons! Here was the one occasion when he should have made allowances, and yet he had shouted and bullied and he knew – no use denying it – he enjoyed shouting at Turner, enjoyed showing his authority, when he should have been showing a bit of ordinary kindness. There was hardly anything Mr Bunting set more store on in people than simple kindness; it was better than being clever or polished or anything that came by art, it was the real man beneath all other things. Yet he had failed in that fundamental quality – even in wartime.

It was no use one-half of his brain reminding him he couldn't possibly have known what was in the paper. He had known that Turner had a son on a destroyer; and that Turner was what Corder called one of the weaker brethren. He had known enough to act differently from this.

Mr Bunting sat very humbled and ashamed, thinking these thoughts in illogical succession, his elbows on the desk, his knuckles between his teeth, a prey to conscience. For he had a tender conscience and he had 'principles'. He could not have explained what they were, but they went deep into his system.

Sitting there, he made a vow with himself never to forget that when people were difficult and cranky it might easily be because of private grief arising from the war. This wordless and unformulated resolve cheered him a little. 'Fall to rise,' he murmured. 'Battled – fight better.' That was the spirit. It was no good brooding. He picked up his papers.

Mr Bickerton had ordered a minor stock-taking, having some idea of discovering how far he could expend the firm's resources in stocking up for civil defence and ARP contracts. It was a lot of trouble for everybody, and quite unnecessary, Mr Bunting thought.

His own stock he could estimate from records as near as made no matter. He suspected Mr Bickerton of finding work for the managers just as the managers did for the assistants.

So he sat adding up endless columns of figures, climbing from rung to rung like a labourer with a hod of bricks, becoming more and more giddy as he reached the top. He spread out his summary sheets, made his entries carefully in the right places, losing his blotter frequently amongst this multitude of documents, balancing one column against the other or, if he failed to do so, putting on his old bristling look as though accusing his figures of having wandered from their rightful stations. It was not work he enjoyed, but it required the whole of his attention, and so effaced the memory of his episode with Turner.

Corder's voice came to him suddenly, at his very ear, quiet and urgent.

'Siren's gone, George. We're all in the cellar. Didn't you hear it?'

'Eh? Siren?'

'To the hypogeum,' said Corder, beckoning.

Mr Bunting came out into the vacant salesroom. Every assistant had gone below, so had they all from the carpet department. Apparently someone had noticed he was not there, and Corder had returned to fetch him.

'Well! I never heard it!' exclaimed Mr Bunting with astonishment, as he followed Corder down the stairs. His failure to hear the siren struck him more forcibly than anything else at the moment.

Corder gave him a sidelong smile. 'Can't hear in these cubby-holes, eh?'

''Speck that's it, Joe. Been concentrating.'

Everybody was in the cellar, all the departmental managers, all the assistants, even Mr and Mrs Bickerton. The sight of her embarrassed Mr Bunting slightly; then he remembered. He could easily erase this fault now; a word to the chief about Turner's son would be sufficient.

They were a small, embarrassed crowd; no one speaking very loudly. The juniors whispered together in a corner and made quiet horseplay; the office boy sucked ink off his fingers, and the older men sat about on crates. Mrs Bickerton had a chair – where it had come from Mr Bunting had no idea – and her husband stood beside her, his hands clasped behind him, preoccupied, as though he deplored this waste of time. A waste of time it certainly was, Mr Bunting thought. All business suspended no doubt throughout the city.

'Is this the start of old Hitler's blitzkrieg, Joe?'

'I don't hear a thing. Yes, I do,' and he strained towards the window above the sink. 'Blest pair of sirens! It's the all clear.'

They all trooped upstairs again, Mr Bunting rising from his crate with an irritable 'Tchah.' Why couldn't they make sure before they sounded the siren, instead of getting the breeze up? He sat down at his desk, collected his papers, and tried to collect his thoughts also.

The figures looked more formidable than ever. He essayed two or three ascents, became confused, and put down his pen. He couldn't face them.

It occurred to him he might take these additions home to Ernest, who never tired of proving that four and three in one column were the same as five and two somewhere else. He got endless satisfaction out of these anticipated trivial coincidences. Yes, Ernest could do it easily – except, of course, that one should never take business papers out of the office.

'Blast the siren,' he muttered. It had come right in the middle of his tallest column. This was twice he'd had the warning and no bombs. 'Wait till I hear 'em dropping before I move another time,' he thought, obstinately.

What he needed most of all at the moment was a smoke, but the clock told him he must wait half an hour for that. 'What a day!' he murmured. 'What a day!' He sat on idly and unhappily, whilst the clock ticked round to the hour of release.

TEN

THE FIRST THING Mr Bunting saw as he entered the hall that same evening was an airman's hat and overcoat hanging on the stand. Chris unexpectedly home on leave. Immediate excitement gripped him. Without putting down his umbrella or attaché case, he pushed open the living room door and there saw Chris himself, standing on the rug. A new Chris, tauter, keener, but still a boy, and touchingly like the old one. On his breast were the silver wings of the RAF.

Blinking a little, either from the light or from emotion, Mr Bunting came forward, put a hand on either arm of his son, and gripped him tightly. It was almost an embrace. His heart was deeply moved, and he gave a great 'Hrrmp' to clear his throat, exclaiming: 'Well, Christopher! I *am* glad to see you. I am prop'ly.'

'It's good to see you, dad.'

Mr Bunting broke away to find Chris looking him smilingly up and down. He often had doubts about his children's affection for him, wondered how deep and real it was, but here was as simple and heartfelt a welcome as he could ever wish for.

Having got over the ejaculatory phase of greeting, they sat down together and Mr Bunting looked his son over. From the kitchen came a clatter of pans and dishes, on a scale reminiscent of the great family occasion of Christmas. Mrs Bunting, though taken by surprise, was making an effort worthy of the day. He and Chris sat apart from, and above, this feminine activity, though pleasantly conscious it was proceeding. Just two days, Chris said he had; passed all his tests, and posted to an operational squadron.

Mr Bunting rested his eyes on him, thinking of all the things Chris must have done since last he saw him; flown miles into the air away from the homely earth, through cloud into the remote and blue inane and – come down safely. An amazing thing, really amazing, and none the less so for being a daily happening. Mr Bunting could remember the days when scorching on a push-bike had been considered the limit of foolhardiness.

It was evident that Chris thought no more of these flights than of a spin in the Conway. But Mr Bunting could not think so. He was, in fact, relieved to know for certain that, at the moment anyway, Chris was safely on the ground, and not in peril in the air.

'An operational squadron, eh?' he said, not quite grasping Chris's meaning.

'Yes, and I shan't be half glad either.'

'That's all right then,' said Mr Bunting, satisfied.

Julie looked in from the kitchen. 'I suppose you'll be taking Monica out this evening?'

'Do you mean Marvellous?' inquired Chris mildly.

Julie flushed. 'No – but are you?'

'Can't. She's away from home till tomorrow. Had to send her a wire.'

'I'll go out with you, if you like.'

'Chris don't want to go out. Hardly got here.'

'Only just round to Mavis's, daddy. Got to return a book I borrowed.'

'I thought you were going out to buy a dog,' said Mr Bunting, puzzled by this change of plans. 'You've been talking about nothing but black Aberdeens for weeks. Didn't you write to Bert for the address of a dog man?'

'I say, have you been writing to Bert?' asked Chris. 'Gosh! He's got something to think of out in France besides dogs. The army's retreating at the rate of forty miles a day.'

'He sent me an answer all the same. But the dog can wait. We'll just go as far as Mavis's.'

'Gosh! You have a cheek to write to Bert,' said Chris, reflecting on his young sister's nerve. 'Why, I could have told you – '

'Now, now! Let's have no quarrelling,' put in Mr Bunting. Whereupon Chris and Julie turned upon him, insisting that they were not quarrelling; wouldn't dream of quarrelling whilst Chris was on leave. The heat of these protestations quite drowned Mr Bunting. As he pointed out, when they allowed him to be heard, it seemed reasonable that if the dog could wait, the book could wait also; the house was full of borrowed books, always had been, he was continually drawing attention to it.

'Oh, daddy, stop grumbling! You're spoiling Chris's leave,' protested Julie, reducing him finally to silent but aggrieved reflection. He was the last person – and they ought to know it – to start any unpleasantness. He was only trying to be reasonable. If Chris wanted to go round to Mavis's, then let him go round. Mr Bunting was upset by this small incident.

Left alone, he discussed plans for the evening with his wife.

'I'll pop round and bring Ernest and Evie up for supper. All have an evening together.'

He had felt dog-tired when he reached home, but he was now completely revived. He took his torch and his walking-stick for probing unfamiliar kerbs, and set out for Martin Street.

Mr Bunting always enjoyed a visit to the flat, and often went there to talk over the war with Ernest. He rarely left without being fortified with a dram of whisky, a drink in whose virtues Evie firmly believed, if taken on the right occasions. Sensibly used, whisky was not an extravagance, according to Evie, and she ought to know, having been a doctor's dispenser. This opinion of hers, and several similar ones, were much quoted at Laburnum Villa where Evie was accused of spoiling him.

For the second time Ernest had been put on the reserved list, and Mr Bunting was thankful. One son away was enough, and Ernest would only have got into trouble in the army. Judged by ordinary standards Ernest had queer ideas. Once he took it into his head that certain things were wrong, nothing would make him abate his criticisms. He was, in a manner of speaking, the sort of man who enjoys being shot at dawn for his beliefs; it was the most emphatic way of showing what they meant to him. Ernest could never be a conscientious objector, it was too easy. Whatever he believed in he had to work and suffer for. Still, his ideas about the war were changing. Mr Bunting didn't fully grasp the change; hadn't fully grasped the original ideas, except to know they were unpractical.

This unpracticality of Ernest's ideas was the chief ground of argument at the flat.

'You cannot hold a fire in your hand by thinking of the frosty Corsicans,' Mr Bunting used to say, quoting, as near as he could,

Shakespeare, or one of Corder's poets. You had to take the world as you found it, and form your ideas on that, not delude yourself into thinking you could act as though the world would operate according to your theories. If everybody believed what Ernest believed he granted there would be no wars, but it happened that everybody didn't so believe. In particular, the Germans didn't, or, at least, not the Nazis. And you couldn't afford to be soft-handed with such people. From long experience Mr Bunting knew there was a type of man with whom it was a waste of time to argue.

'If Hitler had got a crack on the head the first time he began making a nuisance of himself at street corners there would never have been any Nazis,' he used to say. 'It's as easy as that – in the beginning. Now it's going to take a million armed men.'

But he was not going to argue this evening; things had got beyond the stage when the war was a starting-point for theoretical discussion. Ernest, who saw all things in a sort of glow, worried enough about the war; had he possessed his father's capacity for seeing them starkly in the daylight he would have worried more. Deep in his bones Mr Bunting felt a dread that the entire British Army was now trapped in France, nothing facing his countrymen but massacre or mass surrender. As he tapped his way along the pavements in the dark, his face wore a look more scared than any he would have shown by day. Disaster unparalleled now loomed up imminent and inevitable. Beyond that he could not see.

One had to find some escape from these nightmares. And it was Chris's leave! Having rung the bell, he stood on the step as an actor might in the wings, brightening his features before an entrance.

Ernest and Evie were at tea, a small standard lamp on the table casting pleasant lights and shadows. The evening paper lay folded on the couch, its blaring headlines visible. In his own home Ernest looked more mature. Mr Bunting had a glimpse of him in his mind's eye as he would be at forty and after. What sort of a world would there be then? he wondered.

Sitting in the easy chair – it was not really easy, too new to be that to Mr Bunting – he gave the news about Chris, and his invitation. He even suggested Ernest might come up and play the piano.

'Fugues?' asked Ernest, with the tiniest smile.

'I got my rubber ear plugs. Should have had 'em years ago, Evie. Now I can shut out all these German noises – not just air raids.'

He balanced his teacup on his knee. These small jokes soon evaporated and the war came creeping in.

'Your pal who wrote those opuses – Otto – he's got it in the neck now.'

'Not Reinberger?'

'That's him. It's in the papers.'

Ernest stared at him, pausing; then rose from the table and picked up the newspaper. He turned it over page by page, running up and down the columns and stiffening over an inconspicuous paragraph.

'He's dead. Died three weeks after being put in a concentration camp at Dachau.'

He looked up, but saw that to them the news meant nothing.

'In three weeks!' he said, almost to himself. 'Dead – in three weeks.'

He sat down again. The paper dropped to the floor beside his chair. He was shocked. 'Reinberger!' he murmured. 'What can they have done to him?'

'Don't take on so, darling. We can't alter these things.'

Ernest looked at her: 'Oh, Evie! That man was one of the hopes of Europe.'

Mr Bunting exchanged glances with her, and shook his head. Just then he felt more sorry for Evie than for Ernest, and it was Evie whom he approached and touched on the shoulder. 'Come up home. Let's forget the rotten war. I want Chris to enjoy himself.'

Ernest hardly spoke during the walk to Cumberland Avenue. It was Reinberger, not Chris, who filled his thoughts. It was a pity Ernest took life so hard, and all through bothering his head about things that, as far as Mr Bunting could see, couldn't affect him one way or the other. This Reinberger, for instance, who was he? Nothing but a blasted Hun.

Ernest couldn't help it, he supposed; one had to make allowances. Mr Bunting sighed; he had received one bitter lesson about that today from Turner.

Still, it was Chris's leave and this was not the proper atmosphere. Once in his own house he strove for the proper atmosphere to be created.

Chris and Julie were back home. Mrs Bunting had put the supper ready on trays and made the almost unprecedented admission that the rest of her jobs could wait. This in itself was an enormous contribution to the evening. Mr Bunting helped Evie off with her coat, with much gallantry and fuss, smiling into those hazel-green eyes which always seemed to sparkle at him with particular liking.

Then Ernest, casting off his introspective mood, and remembering Evie's advice, played some jolly tunes on the piano, even including, for his father's especial benefit, the *Lily of Laguna*, which Mr Bunting sang lusciously, a glass of port in his hand, his first solo in the family circle for many years.

The talk, too, was cheerful, a confidence of the quieter kind emanating from Chris. The fighting forces apparently were not appalled by headlines. They were right on their toes and eager for a scrap. Chris said little about the Air Force, but what he did say tremendously impressed Mr Bunting. It was so matter-of-fact.

'I heard,' he said, adding his spark of optimism, 'that some of the bombs the Huns dropped at Scapa were dated nineteen thirty-nine. The ones we're using are nineteen thirty-two, a chap told me.'

'Do you mean old ones, daddy?'

'That ain't the point,' and he told them what the point was. Something perfectly obvious, though he hadn't seen it himself at first. The Germans couldn't have many bombs if they were using them straight out of the factory. Whereas we had years' and years' accumulation to start on.

It sounded hopeful, an instance of the British not being quite so slow as they sometimes pretended to be. When Mr Bunting was not girding at the Government's slowness, he was amusedly reflecting that much of it was put on. Mrs Bunting, in particular, remarked it would be a good thing if the Germans ran out of bombs altogether.

'But what do they date 'em with, daddy?' asked Julie.

'Rubber stamp,' said Ernest; which remark, though unnecessarily sarcastic, was at least a sign that Ernest was himself.

The evening ended with a tremendous supper, including everything Chris liked best, which, by a happy chance, included everything Mr Bunting liked best also. In spite of the heaviness of repletion Mr Bunting insisted on the port circulating even to the dregs. 'Lo, the grape!' he said. 'Omar Khayyém. Fill 'em up!'

Long did Mr Bunting remember this evening of good fellowship and laughter stolen from the tragically darkening hours. It was almost the only old-fashioned evening he did remember except the ones at Christmas. It was something good out of the war.

He went into Chris's bedroom to say goodnight and found him sitting with his knees up in the bed, and rather startlingly smoking the bulldog.

'Come and sit down,' invited Chris, unconscious of offence. He patted the eiderdown. 'Take a pew and light up.'

Mr Bunting sat down, not entirely easy in his mind. He was willing enough to overlook this bedroom pipe-smoking on a special occasion, but what if Mrs Bunting's nose detected it? He would be blamed for it, not Chris; it would be unjustly suggested that he had encouraged him. He charged his pipe from Chris's pouch, aware of the enormity of the whole proceeding.

'Not bad tobacco,' he said. It seemed an amazing thing to be smoking Chris's tobacco in Chris's bedroom; it would have been incredible three months ago. The war brought astounding changes.

'Put your feet on a chair, and let's have a look at you. You've no idea how I've looked forward to coming home.'

'You like it in the Air Force, Chris?'

'Rather! It's the life. By the way – ' and here Chris paused to deposit a spot of ash in one of the dressing-table ornaments! 'If I do happen to have a crash you'll hear at Brockleys – not here. Only upset mother.'

'I'll remember. Let's hope it won't happen.'

'I'm not worrying. It's just in case, see?'

'I understand.'

Between talking and smoking and falling into silences, Mr Bunting regarded his son with affection. Chris alone of the family had the full cheek and grey eyes of the Buntings. Ernest and Julie were dark and slim, imaginative and highly strung, inclined to fads and fancies that Chris never thought of. He was as free from isms and ologies as his father, but more tolerant of them in other people. His ideas were different from his father's, because he was younger, but his mental outlook was the same. The others heard Mr Bunting with impatience, but Chris listened to him with an open mind, and corrected him in the friendliest spirit as an equal. He had always got on well with Chris; had been the greatest friend of his boyhood, his companion at cricket matches and his chief authority on every subject. Those had been happy days of fatherhood; and if the phase had passed as Chris grew up might they not grow into it again? This midnight talk in his bedroom, the forbidden tobacco, and the mild sense of adventure that surrounded it, seemed to be drawing them together. The war would be over some day, and he would have a kindred spirit for the companionship of his age.

There was something else behind his thoughts, something he wanted to say, but was afraid might sound silly, so he kept it to the last, till the moment he rose to go. After all, young men were young men, they forgot things; it was best to give a friendly warning.

'There's one thing I've noticed about aeroplane accidents,' he said, adopting a very casual tone. 'A lot of them seem to be caused by chaps stalling their engines. It's a thing you want to be careful of when you're flying, Chris – not stalling your engine.' He gave Chris a look in which a desire not to appear ridiculous mingled with a graver anxiety.

'I'll watch it, dad. I don't want to break my neck. Got Monica to think of.'

''Course,' said Mr Bunting. He felt a pang, however. 'Good night, Christopher.'

Mr Bunting carefully knocked his pipe out into the dressing-table ornament. A dirty, obnoxious habit. Mary would make an awful fuss; he was amazed at his hardihood. But Chris, no doubt, would be excused.

He pushed open the bedroom door and listened; Mrs Bunting was fast asleep. He went in softly.

ELEVEN

RARELY HAD MR Bunting known a summer so lovely as this of nineteen forty. Glimpsed from the train the fields round Kilworth were wind-rippled spaces, greener and lusher than ever he remembered. And how unsettling to the heart is a hedge in blossom! London was dusted over with gold; its green corners were pools of shadow inviting the perspiring citizen to forget his desk and counter, and become a child of earth. But it was an absent gaze that Mr Bunting turned on all this beauty; it moved him with a great sadness as though every tree and flower, and every piping bird, were but echoes and mementoes of a world about to vanish.

Nearer and nearer the German Army rolled its heavy wheels, not to be stayed. The impregnable bastions of the last war were already trampled. From Dunkirk there had been an eleventh-hour ferrying of almost an entire army – among them young Rollo. He was reported by his father, with strange lack of emotion, to have communicated his deliverance in a two-line post card. When seen he had proved unnaturally silent and remote. Conjured thus briefly into remembrance young Rollo vanished from thought, one human speck swallowed by a nightmare background, for all men's thoughts were now on France.

Down the coast of that unhappy country from the Channel ports to the Atlantic seaboard point after point was taken by the enemy. Things that authority had warned Mr Bunting must never be allowed to happen had happened, and they were only a beginning. France was tottering; could find, it seemed, no strong hand and no firm voice to rally her. All was confusion over there; the last hour's news staled even in the telling.

These events Mr Bunting tried to get into focus and judge soberly. Facts had to be faced and he tried to face them with such a realism as keeps its nerves till life's foundations crack between one's feet. He imagined there might be some tremendous counterstroke that would catch the overstrained enemy at a moment of imbalance, and hurl him back. He imagined all manner of things as he bent over his war map, his under-lip thrust out slightly. But there was one thing he did not imagine – capitulation, for his was not a mind that could easily accommodate itself to the prospect of defeat. The French surrender came to him with a shock beyond anything in his whole life's experience. He heard of it with a sickness of the heart which, he felt, would lay its mark on him for all his days.

As the news bulletin ended he switched off the wireless and, with a stunned mind, stood at his French window looking down the garden. It was a still June evening, his roses shone in their beauty and beyond the bright red roofs, and over the wooded hills the sun was sinking slowly as though reluctant to leave a land so lovely. But Mr Bunting's thoughts were not stirred, his mind was frozen. Nothing moved within him except his heart, which seemed to expand and contract, as though it were an independent living thing lodged in his breast. He looked at his wife and daughter, methodically laying supper. Didn't they understand? Was he the only one with thoughts and feelings? He sat down with them, but could not eat, though he drank copiously and immediately felt sick. For a moment or two he wondered whether he were ill. But he knew he was not ill.

After the sketchy meal he went out into the garden. Oskey was crouching over a fine bed of cauliflowers, picking off caterpillars. It seemed an amazing thing to be doing at a time like this. But there he was, lifting one leaf after another and grunting, whether with annoyance at finding caterpillars or disappointment at not finding them it was impossible to tell. He looked up as though aware of Mr Bunting's presence, but only in a secondary degree.

'Heard the news, Oskey? The French have let us down.'

'So they say. Don't surprise me neither. Queer lot the French.'

Mr Bunting had often heard how queer the French were. Oskey had observed them closely when he was on service in the last war. He conveyed an impression of himself sitting in corner seats of estaminets, lugubriously drinking, and staring at a race of men who could nowhere produce the counterpart of his sagacious self.

'Too excitable,' he said, giving the essence of his conclusion. 'I heard the Germans took Abbeville with only six men on motor bikes. Town as big as Kilworth.'

'It isn't possible.'

'No?' retorted Oskey, laconically, and straightened his back and surveyed his cauliflowers. It was not clearly evident whether he was still thinking of the war or of his gardening problems, or how one might affect the other.

Then he leaned his arms on the fence and his voice sank to a husky undertone. He looked very sallow in the fading light. Missed a lot of sleep through being so much on duty at the wardens' post, Mr Bunting fancied.

'Between you and me, o' man, we're up against it. Jerry's a good enough fighter when he's got all the guns and men to back him up. That's what he likes, see? He's not too good on an uphill job. But this ain't an uphill job now.'

He appeared to be about to repeat this statement in elaborate paraphrase, as he did all his statements, having a firm conviction that Mr Bunting never grasped anything the first time he heard it.

'What do you think'll happen now?

'Ar!' said Oskey, beginning to clean his fork with a scraping instrument and concentrating meanwhile on this task alone. 'That's what I can't tell you, o' man. But we know where we are now – that's one thing. Only ourselves to rely on.'

They hung over the fence for a while talking in undertones. Hungry for a human voice, Mr Bunting was loath to leave Oskey. There were virtues in him hitherto not noticed, a steadiness and a calmness of mind that grew out of his defects as much as his qualities. For Oskey had much pig-headedness and no imagination; and he was incapable of being impressed.

'The war ain't over yet, not by a long chalk, whatever Hitler thinks,' he said. 'The Jerrys cracked up at the winning post last time. They can't stand up to punishment. It's hanging on what counts.'

These words Mr Bunting took away with him as he recrossed the dark and dewy lawn. Whether they were words of resolution or complacency, he could not decide. He still felt the shock of the day's events, and a thirst for news that was never satisfied. Turning the knobs of his wireless set, he was instantly assailed by the peculiarly unpleasant inflections of Hamburg. He listened, and the emptiness and weariness that had invaded him were displaced by a faint anger and disgust, even a sort of incredulity that official Germany should think him susceptible to such bogy talk as this. It was all old stuff; he'd heard it in the last war from the Kaiser. The renegade voice had a quality of over-emphasis, like an actor not sure of himself; his intonation robbed his message of effect. Mr Bunting listened, bending over the receiver, with an instinct that here was something with which it was impossible to come to terms.

He was quieter these days; no one could read the papers without being sobered. But he was calmer also. When you stood alone there could be no more desertions and betrayals. Those were the really upsetting things. One thing above all others angered him: to find his thoughts returning to the last war. Four years of misery and a million dead, and all for what? To get these same people, these Germans, beaten and settled. And within twenty-five years they were more of a menace even than they'd been before; even able to think of invading us. Over this Mr Bunting grew heated in his talks with Ernest, escaping from the realities of the hour to an inquiry in which he demanded to know why the country had been allowed to come to this. 'What have our leaders been thinking of? Some of 'em ought to be put on trial when this is over.'

'It's no good talking like that, dad. It only takes the heart out of you. We've got to think of the present and the future.'

'I know,' said Mr Bunting. He tried to keep his mind off the last war. It had been a victory thrown away, chiefly, as he thought, by people with ideas like Ernest's. But he didn't bring that up. Everyone must pull together.

He came back from larger questions to smaller ones. 'Have a whisky, Ernest. No good letting the Nazis get it.'

If the Germans landed on the Essex coast they could be in Kilworth within two hours. It seemed incredible, but one had to face it. Wherever the Germans went they looted and plundered – everybody knew they were just Huns – so it was no good leaving them the whisky, nor the eggs Mrs Bunting had laid down in water-glass, nor anything else – unless you could first sprinkle it with arsenic. Mr Bunting's inventive faculties were maliciously active;

there was nothing he was not prepared to do to kill Germans. Ernest was convinced that if there should be an invasion his father would certainly get himself shot for some needless small defiance.

'We've got something worth fighting for in this country,' declared Mr Bunting, drinking.

The things Mr Bunting was prepared to fight for, as far as Ernest could see, were chiefly his own possessions and what he thought of vaguely as his 'liberties'. They represented a good deal, but Ernest's thoughts went much farther. To him, the war had become a struggle between two opposing ways of life. Frontier lines didn't divide the supporters of either side; they could be found in any country. It was a civil war amongst the human family. It had begun in Germany as a civil war, the regime against the liberal-minded, and it was a civil war still. It was not being fought for territory, but for the power to direct human destiny; to say whether the Reinbergers should be allowed to speak openly as free men, or be silenced in concentration camps. Not to understand that was to cast away the inspiration of victory.

But everybody he knew regarded it entirely as a matter of killing Germans.

Mr Eagle's recipe for victory was simple: 'Bomb the lot! That's the way to treat the Huns. They'll soon squeal. Bomb 'em! Bomb 'em to blazes'.

This doctrine he preached continually in Ernest's hearing, for he had never forgiven Ernest's cranky ideas. He thought him soft and not much better than a conchy.

Eagle's patriotism was of the ancient order; running a laundry was the last and mildest of his adventures. He had served in Africa with Roberts, and had travelled far and lived violently, Ernest knew, in his early manhood. He had, he said, seen the Union Jack flying in a few wild corners of the earth and, so far as his dealings lay with yellow men and black men, and every variety of damned foreigner, he had taken care it was respected. Those who lacked the guts to stand up for their country were disenfranchised of his good opinion and fair game for his wit.

He would frequently come out of his own office into Ernest's before he left for home, and sit with his gnarled hands crossed on the top of his walking-stick watching with malicious amusement how Ernest reacted to his remarks.

'I've known lots of Germans,' he said, ignoring his manager's preoccupation with accounts. 'Those that weren't bullies were creepers. Thank God we've got plenty of young fellows anxious to have a go at 'em. You wouldn't be sitting safely here if we hadn't.'

'Nor you,' said Ernest, without looking up.

'Me? Why, bless my soul, my boy, I'm seventy-six. Did my bit of service fifty years ago. What do you expect me to do?'

'Stop urging young men to do things you won't have to do yourself. At least you can't accuse me of that.'

'Of course, *you* wouldn't bomb Germans.'

'No.'

'I thought not. Rather see 'em come over here and rule the country. You'd change your ideas quick enough if that happened.'

Ernest put down his pen. Except that he had turned a shade paler his manner was that of a patient man who decided at last that he must arise and swat a buzzing blue-fly.

'Mr Eagle, my ideas are my own affair; they don't concern you. But I can tell you this, they haven't changed. Not unless becoming more convinced of them is change. The best thing you can do is give me a month's notice.'

'Eh? What's that?'

'Do you think I enjoy being tied to a desk in times like these? There are plenty of things I can do. I can join the army as a stretcher-bearer. Or go on a mine-sweeper. But I'm fastened here, and it's you who fastened me. You got me put on the reserved list, and it's only you can take me off again.'

'Are you serious?'

'Never more so. Please write my notice.'

Mr Eagle leaned forward on his stick. It occurred to him he had been taken very seriously by this serious young man; had got a more violent reaction than he expected.

'Now, look here, Ernest, you know you can't go. How can a stranger manage a place like this, with all the old plant we've got?

Business would go to pieces. And don't forget – your father's got money in it.'

'We weren't talking about money. Will you, or won't you?'

'I can't. You know darn well I can't.' Ernest's air of determination had taken him aback. 'I was only having a tilt at your ideas.'

Ernest looked at him for a long second, his dark eye alight. 'I see,' he said, softly and reflectively. 'I'm having a tilt at yours now. What's your answer?'

Mr Eagle rose, his old joints creaking. He knew the folly of goading a quiet man too far, and began to retract. 'I could never understand you, Ernest,' he remarked, by way of digression. 'You know exactly how the laundry's fixed, yet because I say a word out of place you take offence all in a minute and want to walk out. Well!' He seemed to leave Ernest to draw some conclusion favourable to his own point of view.

'Perhaps you'll understand me a bit better in future.'

'Well – I apologise. Let's leave it at that.'

'That wasn't what I asked for!'

'You're not going to be released,' shouted Mr Eagle, reddening like a turkey cock. Almost immediately his anger evaporated, as though even that were too much for his strength, and in a pleading tone he said: 'You wouldn't walk out and leave me with all this, Ernest, would you? Look at my hands! I can hardly hold a pen.'

'All right,' said Ernest, returning to his papers.

Outside, Mr Eagle took out his enormous white handkerchief and blew his nose as some relief. For several days he lived in fear that the subject might be reopened. But Ernest never again referred to it. His old respectful demeanour returned, and his small kindnesses on which the old man so much depended. Ever afterwards Mr Eagle approached him with caution.

In the field behind the laundry was a newly built machine-gun post, its evil slits of eyes peering down the road; behind it the upward pointing muzzle of an anti-aircraft gun. Looking out of his office window at odd moments during this lovely summer Ernest's eyes, ranging over tree-tops, would come to rest on these objects to remind him, he thought sardonically, that he was living in the twentieth century. One worked under guard as savage tribes used to gather harvest. In the evening he went to the aid post to wait for bombs to be hurled on Kilworth from the sky. Thus far had man progressed beyond his primitive ancestors, whose only fear had been the arrow that flew by day.

What he most disliked about his duties at the aid post was the shocking waste of time. It was a waste of life. After tea he took Evie to Laburnum Villa, and called for her again as he went home. During the interim he sat in the post with his fellow volunteers. They smoked, or talked desultorily, or stared out into the sunlit street; in short, did nothing, which was exactly what Ernest never could do. He must be practising the piano to improve his playing, or reading a serious book to improve his mind, or planning improvements for the laundry – at all events, doing something.

There had been one stray bomb that caused an urgent summons to the aid post. Descending from the ambulance, Ernest found himself at a house where the tiles had been clawed from the roof and cascaded into the street. The front fence had been blasted into nothing, and every window shattered. Stepping over a door blown flat into the hall, he found a man sitting in the living room on a made-up bed, amidst plaster dust and broken glass, shivering with pain and shock. Much to Ernest's surprise, none of these sights sickened him. He attended to the victim's shattered arm, immediately becoming interested in it as a task and painstakingly completing it. What struck him most about the bomb-dropping was its senselessness, and the equal senselessness of the victim who endured his suffering stoically, gasping out only one passionate demand – for reprisals against someone equally innocent. It made Ernest feel he was an actor in a vast, crazy circus.

Evie, he knew, prayed for him on these occasions; she prayed that his life might be preserved amidst all dangers. The knowledge that she offered up this prayer for him every day filled him with a tenderness that struck him through the heart. For to him her faith was childlike and simple, at once above him and beneath him. He could not believe that God would save one man out of so many because of a prayer.

She was often listless these days. On Sunday mornings she rested, directing his domestic exertions from the bed. She missed the bells; in Martin Street they sounded clear and silvery, like village bells, Evie said. They reminded her of peaceful Sundays in the lost village in the fens, where she had spent her girlhood. Throughout the length and breadth of England no chime of bells was heard now.

'You won't hear them again till after the war, darling. Not unless the parachutists come.'

'And then what are we supposed to do?'

Ernest shrugged. 'Don't know. I only hope I'm here, not at the laundry.'

'I don't believe God will allow a wicked man like Hitler to rule the world, do you?'

Ernest set the tray beside the bed. 'No, dear.' But he spoke as though answering a child.

'You've forgotten the milk, Ernest.'

'Oh, dash!' he exclaimed, and moved towards the kitchen. He could never understand why he was forgetful at home when he was so business-like at the office. He rarely forgot anything at the office, and always came across other people's mistakes with an intake of the breath.

'And the spoon.'

'I feel sure I put out a spoon,' he said, coming back to the tray and focusing his abstracted gaze upon it. But there was no spoon there.

Searching for the milk in the larder, on the shelves, on the step outside, Ernest thought of Evie's complete trust in the things God would not allow to happen. It was a trust as simple and unquestioning as a child's trust in his human father. He never interrupted her with a reminder of the things God had allowed to happen already. Evie's serenity and her patience under the strain of war were due almost entirely to her belief that ends lay in the hand of God. God's will would triumph in the end. Ernest could never have used a phrase like that; but it occurred to him, as he paused at a loss in the kitchen, that the same words could be used as an expression of his own faith. Truth and justice were eternal; all things of the spirit were eternal.

Their power and range surpassed all material forces, so that a simple song could raise more armies than all the press gangs of history. There was nothing of which Ernest was more certain than that man's aspirations were the most enduring things of life.

He found himself standing in the larder, and remembered he was supposed to be looking for something. 'Milk and spoon,' he murmured frowning in concentration, and immediately saw them on the draining board where he had put them out.

He had learnt, these months, to value his weekends, and his father's nostalgia for weekends no longer struck him as amusing. He greatly missed the piano, but he could sit with his eyes closed and run through a Beethoven sonata in his mind, playing it more perfectly in imagination than ever he could in reality, and hearing it just as well. There was the wireless, too, and if Evie were busy in the kitchenette he would sometimes go so far as to turn it on and imagine he was conducting the orchestra. He had heard somewhere of a Russian professor who did the same thing with gramophone records, only the professor first put on his dress suit. Once he knocked the shade off the lamp whilst urging on the violins in a final presto, causing Evie to come in with a breathless: 'How on earth did that happen?' Whereupon Ernest stared and slowly coloured. It was only by degrees and with amazement he discovered that his foibles in some mysterious way endeared him to her.

Calling for Evie at Laburnum Villa, one evening after duty, he found young Rollo sitting stiffly in Mr Bunting's chair, apparently conscious of being a self-invited guest, and embarrassed by the size of his army boots. Whenever he found these twin monsters sprawling across the hearth he drew them up and disposed them under his chair in various positions. He was more ruddy than ever, and taller and heavier; he looked like an enlisted policeman. As Ernest entered he explained that, having found himself in Cumberland Avenue, he had 'just looked in'. He seemed anxious to make this clear lest Ernest should think his presence odd; he had already given the same explanation several times to Evie and to Mr Bunting since he sat down. Immediately he heard sounds of supper being prepared, he collected his feet and rose heavily on them with the intention of 'hitting the trail'. But he was easily persuaded to draw up to the table.

Bert confirmed that he had returned home via Dunkirk. When pressed for a first-hand account of this affair, he said, after some consideration, that it had been a pretty tough set-up. The war appeared to have reached a stage when he no longer understood it. He had sailed to Norway, but had seen that country only dimly through the morning mist as the troopship put about to bring him home again. He had been to France, and had been brought from thence at great hazard through a hail of bombs. He resented being the subject of these evacuations; most of all he resented having to leave his tank behind him. At the moment he had no tank at all; hardly any tanks existed.

'So the Germans got old "Daffodil",' mused Mr Bunting, wondering how much income tax it represented.

'Yeah. Three Jerrys and an officer got into her and drove her off. I watched 'em out of a bit of orchard.'

'You mean, you just stood there and watched them?' demanded Julie.

'Yeah. They hadn't gone above twenty yards before she blew up.'

Mrs Bunting paused with the teapot in her hand. 'Oh, I say! How lucky for you, Bert!' It was clear he had narrowly escaped being killed. The Buntings looked at him with a new interest.

'Bert, you blighter!' exclaimed Julie. 'I bet you put a Rollo tank-buster in it.'

His face brightened. 'You said it – ' He was going to add 'baby', but bit back this expression out of respect for Mrs Bunting.

'Do you think they'll land here, Bert?' inquired Mr Bunting, in the most casual tone at his command.

'They might *land*,' said Bert, giving significant emphasis to this last word. 'That's where we'll get the bite on 'em.'

'That's one way of looking at it,' agreed Mr Bunting. 'But let's have no more war talk. You go and have a tune, Ernest, whilst I gather Evie some vegetables.'

Bert found himself alone with a remote-looking Julie. He unbuttoned his pocket, took out his wallet, and from the wallet extracted a portrait of himself. He glanced at it for reassurance, then held it towards her with some pride. 'Got it taken since I got my second stripe. See! Like it?'

'It's very nice,' said Julie, examining it over the sock she was knitting.

He pushed it an inch nearer her hand. 'It's okay, if you'd like to have it.'

'That's very kind of you, Bert. But will you have enough to go round?'

He gave her a dubious look, but her rounded eyes disarmed suspicion. She didn't mean anything; just her way, he guessed.

'That's okay. I can always get more printed.'

'Oh, of course!' said Julie, suddenly enlightened. 'But don't do that for me. Perhaps – if you have one left over.'

'This *is* one I've got left – ' He broke off. Surely he must be losing his touch, continually saying the wrong thing. Taking the situation in hand he approached it from a different angle. 'Did you get a dog from that chap I told you?'

'Not yet. Later.' Julie did not wish to discuss the dog. Bert's friend, the dog man, had been very crude in his explanation of why the puppies were not yet available. There seemed to be no refined way of putting certain facts about dogs.

'I wish Chris were here,' sighed Bert presently. Conversation hung fire even more decidedly after that; justifiably on her side, Julie thought.

'Chris is a swell guy. In the Air Force too! I guess he put it across me that time. I never thought of the Air Force; only tanks.' Naturally he expected Julie to be willing to talk about Chris. But all she said was: 'Knit one, knit two together.' Whereat he raised his head only to discover these words were not addressed to him. She was concentrating entirely on her needles.

In came Mr Bunting with his best cabbage and cauliflower. He picked up the photograph with interest.

'This for us, Bert?' and he examined it critically, looking from Bert to his portrait and making a point-by-point comparison. 'Jolly good! Lifelike,' he commented finally. 'I'll put it up here on the mantelpiece. Get a frame for it some time when you're passing Woolworth's, Julie.'

'I'll try to remember, daddy.'

Bert rose. He did not like the way Julie's thoughts seemed to have come back to the photograph with a jerk, as though it had passed completely out of her mind. He wished now he had given it to Molly Parrott instead of to the Buntings. Still, there it was on the mantelshelf, and it looked swell; he was obliged to admit it; the stripes visible, but not too much; it was a point you had to be careful about.

'Well,' he said, hesitating from one foot to the other, but plainly starting to get under way.

'Best of luck,' said Mr Bunting, opening the hall door and speeding him with a handshake. 'Been nice to see you.'

'Goodbye, Bert!' said Julie softly. Her eyes dwelt on him darkly and thoughtfully, and with obvious interest. They seemed to flash to him some message of which he had not the key. He couldn't make her out, couldn't make her out at all; one of these artistic temperaments, he dared aver. She looked slim and pretty doing the sock, but rather distant, like somebody seen through the wrong end of a telescope.

Mr Bunting relaxed visibly when Bert had gone. To him young Rollo always seemed to fill the entire room, and he was tactless; would stand with his hand on the doorknob all night if you didn't bustle him off.

'Time you stopped playing, Ernest, and took Evie home,' he said, going into the front room. 'Must look after your missus. We may all have a lot to go through yet.'

They made a little group under the dimmed hall light, putting on coats and hats, and bidding farewell. Not one of them believed anything dreadful was likely to happen to their circle; but there was a touch of uncertainty behind every wartime parting. Ernest felt his father's hands, roughened with years of handling metal, squeeze his own slim fingers with a warmth beyond that of ceremony, and felt a pang shoot through him. For his father so obviously worried about Chris in the Air Force and Julie near the bomb factory, and was often seen pulling at his cold pipe in abstracted silence. Whether he worried about himself no one could tell. Kilworth was relatively safe, but Mr Bunting went every day to the city, where anything might happen.

TWELVE

MR BUNTING HAD waited so long for the blitzkrieg to burst about him that he had months ago decided it was just another empty threat. But there came a morning when everybody in the railway carriage rose at his ejaculation to crowd round the window. There, close to the line, the familiar expanse of London's roofs was gashed open; bare, broken rafters pointed to the sky, walls were down, and the passengers saw, amidst heaps of bricks and splintered timbers, the wrecked interiors of what yesterday had been homes. Every tawdry bit of decoration, every intimate arrangement was pitilessly exposed. From these ruins rose the smoke of extinguished fires, and farther away hung other clouds of smoke from causes not visible. This patch of desolation passed in a swift panorama as the train slid on, and for the rest of the journey Mr Bunting remained at the window anxiously observant. But there were no further signs of devastation amongst the lineside property; nor beyond, where towers and spires and chimneys rose out of the sea of roofs and gables that stretched into infinity. He reached the terminus reassured by the immensity of London.

He noticed, as he arrived at Brockleys, one broken window on the upper floor, the result, he surmised, of some coincidental accident. He had seen a shattered shop front down the street, the glass already swept into the gutter, but there were no shattered windows anywhere near Brockleys. Only this one, towards which he stared thoughtfully, placing it at last as the landing window of the glassware room. He made inquiries of the porter.

'Yes, Mr Bunting. Got broke in last night's raid.'

'What a peculiar thing!' he remarked, struck by the odd effect of bombs which broke distant windows without harming nearer ones. Effect of blast, he supposed. He went across to Corder with the news. Brockleys had a window smashed in the air raid!

'A window!' retorted Corder with derision. 'I've been dodging bombs all night. Dropped a ton of 'em down our way.'

'Not really!' he exclaimed, for he knew Corder was inclined to exaggerate. 'Not a ton, surely?'

'The blast of war was in my ears all night. But did I imitate the action of the tiger? No; the mole, George, the mole. I took cover.'

'Nasty thing, blast,' observed Mr Bunting. A man should protect his ears, he thought; use his ear plugs.

'Anybody killed?'

Corder nodded. 'They're not called Huns for nothing.'

The emotions Mr Bunting felt in the train found expression. 'We've got to hit back, Joe.'

'True, and we've got to stop the swine coming over here. We ought to send more fighters up. Grapple in the central blue!'

'Yes,' he said, and thought of the times he had looked up from his kitchen door into the starlit sky, seen the cloud masses driven before the rising storm and thought how horrible it was to send any boy up there alone into that spectral moonlight. But he said: 'Yes, that's what we got to do, Joe. No other way.'

With a sudden gust of anger, he exclaimed: 'I'd 'sterminate the entire race of Germans. What have they ever done except make wars and upsets and mess everything up? The rotten swine.'

'I know! I know! That's how we all feel,' said Corder, using the calming tone Mr Bunting had used on innumerable occasions to innumerable people since the war began. Anger and indignation didn't do any good. The thing was – to do whatever one had to do and keep one's head and temper.

Listening to Corder's experiences of the night, Mr Bunting wondered how he would bear himself in an air raid, with dead and dying people around him and maybe children trapped under debris shrieking for help. He had once seen a motor accident, had turned a bend of the road in the Conway and come across a group of people clustered round a policeman and an overturned car. There had been a huge claw mark in the surface of the road, and at its end a mangled cycle and a weeping woman sitting on the grass. Edging past this spectacle, he had seen, lying on the verge, the figure of a man with his hat covering his face, his boots, which Mr Bunting saw first, stretched towards the road. There had been a stillness about the figure that moved his hair upon his scalp and chilled him to the pit of his stomach, so that his hands shook on the wheel. It had taken him several days to recover from the shock of that one moment. But it was nothing to an air raid.

There had been hundreds killed in Stepney; bodies flung on to the roofs of churches. He had heard the most terrible things. Heard, too, the most amazing stories of the inhabitants' behaviour. Stepney was by no means cowed this morning; it was defiant, angry, even cheerful, anything but cowed. Such people must be vastly different from himself, he thought; it amazed him how anyone could stick it.

'Ah, well!' he murmured, brushing these thoughts away and turning into the cubby-hole. Brooding wouldn't help and there was always work to be done. It was a blessing in every sense that business was brightening. The shorter he was of staff, the easier it was to keep them busy. Compensations – those were the things to look for in life – the bright side. They smiled at him at home when he repeated these out-of-date expressions, and told him he got his ideas from mottoes on the calendar. Such words might sound empty and trite in ordinary times but not when you were up against it. Often he had cheered and fortified his desponding heart merely by repeating a 'motto'. That was one advantage of not being a highbrow.

He gave his mind to the batch of letters sent down from the main office and discovered a compensation at once. The 'Watkin' stoves, ordered months ago, and demanded by McCall, of Elgin, with ceaseless iteration ever since, were now in process of delivery. Eight – not twelve – why McCall wanted twelve he could not imagine, unless he were thawing out the whole of Elgin – and all eight he should have at once to reward his pertinacity. It would be a job for Turner; he could at least count up to eight in stoves, thought Mr Bunting, as he went out to give instructions.

There was an unusual buzz of talk in the salesroom this morning. He caught the words. 'Did I hear it? I felt the bits fly past my earhole. I wasn't thirty yards – '

'Now, now, that's enough!' he interrupted, disdaining interest in this hair-breadth escape. 'Forget about the Germans and 'tend to business.' His manner was brusque, implying that air raids were mere incidents not worth discussing.

There was a handful of orders this morning, and a steady stream of customers. For some months things had been drifting back to normal, and he hoped the blitzkrieg wouldn't spoil it. It was odd the demands that cropped up even in times like these. People would have things, war or no war, if they had the money. Only this morning he sold some patent stair-rod fixings to a woman from a district where the bombs had fallen. It had been a foolish purchase, and for a moment he stared at the woman blankly. But he served her, not without a certain admiration for her act of faith.

During the lunch hour he climbed to the roof of Brockleys with Corder, and looked over the city. Smoke was still rising here and there, but the landscape was unchanged. In the street, crowds and traffic were as usual. It had been a blow at a giant; severe, but not too severe to be shaken off. Away to the north there was the suggestion of a larger fire; Corder said it was Mossley way, but to Mr Bunting it was near Bardolph Green, close to Julie and the bomb-filling factory.

Bombs would explode even with a slow heat, he supposed, and a single spark would touch off the explosive. He had heard of explosions happening hours after burnt-out bombers had crashed.

'Nobody's safe now, Joe.'

'No; and mark my words, we're only at the green leaf, George, the prologue to the swelling act;' a quite unnecessary piece of pessimism, Mr Bunting considered.

Re-entering the salesroom, he came across an assistant repacking tools after a sale, and his eye fell upon some cheap screwdrivers, relics of Ventnor's search for new lines. 'Made in Germany,' was stamped on the steel. 'Steel!' he thought, contemptuously, picking one up and running his nail along the blade. Some German workman had handled this thing, 'finished' it in Germany, and perhaps gone home from work to don a brown shirt and shout 'Heil Hitler,' and dream his silly dream of conquest. Or perhaps a decent German. Mr Bunting entertained the thought of a decent German, but not for long or with much conviction. Their steel, their finish, and their decency were alike imitation. *Ersatz*.

'Shove these out of sight. Tie 'em up and pitch 'em on the top shelf.'

That was the stuff such shady men as Ventnor favoured, and thought they could build a business on. He shouldn't wonder if Ventnor were a fifth-columnist; he was fundamentally unsound. The one surviving trace of him was the sign 'Sales Floor' just inside the entrance. As though anyone coming into a shop and seeing counters and goods on shelves wouldn't know he was in a salesroom. There had been another sign of Ventnor's which always struck him as particularly daft, and which he had removed immediately he succeeded Holroyd and sent off with the paper salvage. It faced the customer as he went out, and inquired if he had forgotten anything. What could be sillier? If a chap had forgotten anything, then he had forgotten it, in Mr Bunting's opinion; no point in asking him.

Memories of old battles with Ventnor passed through his mind as he ambulated from point to point, bearing in his hand a piece of board on which an order paper was fixed with a drawing pin. On the board he made entries from time to time, drawing a black line under each one as a sign of having satisfactorily got it down. Behind his memories, like a ground bass to a melody, was the thought that Ventnor had vanished, and George Bunting remained. The cosmos had a moral basis. Compensations! Ah! Life was full of compensations, the best of all being that honest, sound material told in the end. Quality was decisive. No bit of honest Sheffield steel was ever thrown on the shelf anywhere to rust; it remained true and trustworthy under every strain; it imparted virtue to the craftsman's hand. The German screwdriver had been eloquent to Mr Bunting; 'foreign' had always been his other name for shoddy.

He was in a cheerful mood, he was eupeptic; this was a day when the clock moved nicely. He always reproved his young assistants when he caught them looking at the clock; and there was a legend that boys who watched the clock at Brockleys never grew up to become departmental managers. But being himself the manager, he could see it through a joint in the partition of the cubby-hole where he now took his seat and began rummaging amongst old papers. Holroyd had turned out a lot of Mr Bunting's papers, probably with the intention of burning them, but had considerately not done so. Unearthing these from the bottom drawer, he came across one or two of his old diaries. He had been for years an industrious keeper of diaries. He never remembered reading any of them afterwards; his sole pleasure had been to make the entries. But it was possible now to learn that on the first of May nineteen twenty he planted a twopenny packet of Tom Thumb lettuce, and that on the fourteenth it rained and he forgot his umbrella. Thus solemnly perusing these trivialities, Mr Bunting turned the faded pages to pass the time, and recapture what he could of the atmosphere of the years when he was still a moderately young man. The references to his children interested him most of all; there was an entry in nineteen twenty-six which was so moving that he hung over it with a thrill, as though he found himself in the atmosphere of those far-off days.

'Bought Chris a wooden horse; 4s. 11d.'

'Well!' he exclaimed, and took out his handkerchief and dusted the end of his nose. He had a good mind to take the diary home to Mary. Chris had been just six years old when that was written, and Mr Bunting could see him at this moment as plain as paint. A wooden horse! He had an aeroplane now.

'Telegram!' piped the office boy, coming right into the cubby-hole and observing what was going on in a manner Mr Bunting always thought impertinent. His eye dwelt on the office boy balefully; he had never known whether his perpetual grin was natural or wilfully put on as cheek.

'Just what I expected,' he muttered, reading the telegram. McCall, of Elgin, demanded to know when, if ever, he could expect his stoves. Turner was at this moment packing the stoves. True, McCall, of Elgin, could not be expected to know this, but his tone was excessively peremptory, surpassing the inevitable and unavoidable peremptoriness of telegrams by a good margin, Mr Bunting thought.

'Mr Bickerton says will you send a wire when they're on their way; but I can't take it 'cos I'm busy copying letters.'

Mr Bunting nodded, not deigning to honour this precocious youth with speech, and jerked his thumb towards the door.

Moistening his pencil, he began to compose an answer to McCall. He desired to propitiate his customer and to offer him a hint of explanation; but the only message which accomplished these ends successfully and yet made sense would, he found, cost Brockleys three shillings to dispatch. Mr Bunting's habits of economy extended to the firm's expenditure with the same force as to his own, and he grew more and more impatient with each version of the telegram. Still, he persevered with substitutions and excisions, with an increasing wonder that he found this simple thing so difficult. He was thus engaged when there was a terrific crash which shook Brockleys from floor to ceiling. Desk and stool quivered under him and the partition rattled like paper. Torn across by this explosion he heard the wailing of the siren and almost instantly two further detonations which shook the building with such violence that he felt the floor sag and strain beneath his feet.

Scared, he dashed out into the shop, and, glancing to right and left, made his way towards the cellar. Every person on the premises was hurrying thither. He heard the hollow clatter of feet on the wooden stairs above and the heavy clatter on the cellar steps below. Mr Bunting's urge was to run, but he did not quite run. The bombs had dropped, he remembered that. But he was out of breath by the time he reached the basement.

Sitting down heavily on a box he glanced up at the ceiling. Doubtless you were safer in the cellar, but not entirely safe. If there were a direct hit your plight was worse; you were buried under tons of debris. He felt uneasy and glanced at his companions, trying to mask his fears.

'What's that row now, Joe?'

'It's guns – anti-aircraft. There's a lot of planes up. Some of ours, I fancy.'

'Good!' he said, and thought of Chris. His squadron was one of those defending London; there was every probability he was overhead at this moment, engaged in a life-and-death fight with the enemy, perhaps his first. One knew so little; you could get nothing out of these boys; they had a tradition of not talking.

Mentally he urged Chris on, dwelling with pride on what he knew of him. Though not reckless, Chris wasn't easily ruffled or excited. If he was up there now Mr Bunting could imagine him, his lips smiling, his brow wrinkled with intentness on the job. He was a single-minded young fellow, capable of stalking his selected antagonist patiently and persistently, then pouncing at the right moment. Perhaps out of a bit of cloud, Mr Bunting thought. Sort of spontaneously.

'Good,' repeated Mr Bunting, conscious of his heart beats. 'I hope we get 'em, get the blooming lot of 'em.'

'Hallo! Ancient Mariner's got his wife with him.'

Mr and Mrs Bickerton had come downstairs quietly, as though, since the general scurry of the staff, the raiders had passed over. Calmly the chief took in the company with his blue eyes and inquired:

'You managers got all your people here?'

Being assured of this in half a dozen voices, he clasped his hands behind him and waited aloofly, as though this hiding in cellars affronted his dignity, but in no way made him forget it. Mrs Bickerton sat on the chair, her small feet crossed on the concrete, her gloved hands folded in her lap. She was still a pretty woman, without actually smiling her eyes held the suggestion of a smile, as though she found her fellow mortals pleasant. Like her husband, she had the gift of repose and waited without strain.

Minutes passed with a dragging silent tension.

'Soon have the all clear.' said someone, breaking a silence in which the only sound was the occasional rumble of a vehicle and the dripping of the tap. Mr Bunting, relieved of strain, looked about him with a sentimental interest. After Brockleys took him back he had worked for nearly two years in this cellar, and during that time it had taken on a familiar, even a homely, look. Now he saw it, ill-lighted, musty, and cluttered up with stock, none of which he considered to be satisfactorily arranged. His favourite corner where he used to write his notes and drink illicit tea looked a dingy, draughty spot when he compared it with the cubby-hole upstairs. He wondered how he had stuck it. Two years! It was marvellous how time flew past.

Suddenly, there came the hurtling crescendo of a bomb, a gasp of silence, and a shattering explosion. There was a stir in the cellar, and somebody muttered: 'That was close'. Amidst the sudden movement Mr Bickerton turned swiftly to his wife who had slipped sideways on the chair, her face hidden. Gently he supported her and raised her head.

'I'm afraid she's fainted. Can someone get water?'

Turner, who was sitting near the sink, hesitated, then got up frailly and held Mr Bunting's old cup beneath the tap. But his hand shook, so that the cup knocked against the metal with a sound like chattering teeth. A burst of gunfire rattled the window.

'I can smell something. Gas!' he cried, ducking in a panic. A feeling of anger rose in the cellar, a murmur of disapproval – and something of uncertainty. In this tense moment Mr Bunting rose.

'That's *gunpowder*, you – ' It was difficult to control his feelings. 'Sit down,' he said sternly, and took the cup from Turner's hands. With a calmness he was far from feeling he turned on the water. He was determined his hand should not shake; nor did it. Steadily he held the cup till it was filled, bending his mind and will solely on this task. But, looking through the basement window, he saw the warehouse opposite disintegrate before his eyes. Its front wall rose as one mass on its foundation and blew to pieces like a building of toy bricks. Into the air ascended an immense cloud of smoke and dust, through which Mr Bunting could see debris falling with a peculiarly slow alighting motion. In the aftermath of this concussion all the bulk of Brockleys swelled and shrunk as with a violent breath, and he had a sudden terror that the window would be blown into his face.

But he reached Mrs Bickerton with the cup of water. There was a little fumbling, and he turned it round to offer her the handle.

'We broke the saucer,' he explained.

She drank, smiling her thanks at him whitely.

'That's better!' he said, with almost fatherly encouragement. 'That's the spirit!'

'Thank you,' said the Ancient Mariner; and his voice had for a moment a human ring that made it unfamiliar. He took the empty cup from his wife, and after looking here and there put it down on the nearest box.

Quietness fell once more upon the cellar, and Mr Bickerton took up his familiar stance, hands clasped behind him, his eye running thoughtfully along the girders overhead, as though he were estimating the possibilities of collapse. There was a thud, and a flake of plaster, like a snowflake, fell from the ceiling; but it was a distant thud and soon the sound of gunfire ceased and the drone of engines faded.

'Exeunt first and second murderers,' murmured Corder.

They sat on, feeling the chill of the cellar; there was a growing restlessness, and a collective uncertainty as to whether they should remain below or return upstairs. But nobody moved until the all clear rang out at last, cheerful and defiant, like a trumpet call to the survivors.

They trooped upstairs. Mr Bunting re-seated himself at his desk, picked up the telegram to McCall and found it hopelessly inadequate. He went across to Corder.

'Doctor this up for me, Joe. Can't think today.'

With a few slashing strokes of his green fountain pen Corder lopped the rambling phrases. Mr Bunting read through the resulting sentences with admiration, for a word, however long, is but a single word to the Post Office, and they can only charge it at a penny.

He went to see how Turner was progressing with the packing, and found him bewildered and defeated.

'I can't get them off tonight, sir.'

Mr Bunting stiffened at sight of this hopeless fellow. 'Why not?'

'Look at the time. We've been over an hour in the shelter.'

'They're going tonight,' replied Mr Bunting on his mettle. 'I'm not leaving the shop till I see 'em off and you aren't either. Eight stoves and accessories.'

He walked away, his under-lip protruding. Not get 'em off tonight on account of the Huns? 'Not blasted likely,' he muttered.

He had just time to dispatch his telegram and to fortify himself with a strong cup of tea at McAndrew's before proceeding circuitously, past roped-off streets and along glass-strewn pavements, to catch a late train home.

THIRTEEN

THESE WERE THE days when Mr Bunting leaned towards the carriage window every morning as his train approached the city and looked out at the battered face of old London. He knew it as well almost as his own. Every cottage and yard on the railway side, every factory and warehouse – he knew it all, down to the details of chimney pots and garden sheds and curtains. This familiar foreground he scanned morning after morning, and the wider sky-line, too. When he recognised its nobler landmarks still standing his heart lightened, for, to him, there was no place like London. He would not have exchanged one of its dingy east-end churches for the showiest cathedral in Europe. There were buildings of all kinds in which he took a pride. But he knew he now saw them as survivors during a lull in the battle, and he eyed them with affection, for tomorrow they might not be there.

Where the night's smoke was clearing he saw, or speculated about, what was missing: irreplaceable history, or homely streets. Though by no means model dwellings, the little shabby houses had character and atmosphere absent from the standardised new estates. They represented Mr Bunting's London, the London of his childhood. Looking at their ruins he thought of the families who had there endured the terrors of the night.

Still, London was immense, too immense for destruction; its mass was scarcely changed, it was an enduring city.

It was when he left the station and walked towards Brockleys that he saw things at closer quarters, felt the heat of smoking fires, and suffered the shock of finding some familiar building gone for ever. Through the devastation he walked, stepping over hoses, skirting the edge of craters, threading his way past grimed and bloodshot firemen, single-mindedly pursuing his own particular business. There were gruesome sights too, sensed rather than seen, tarpaulins stretched over what he knew were human forms. Once a lock of a girl's hair fluttered brightly as the wind ruffled her crude shroud. He bit his lip, and looked away.

All the warnings of past years, all the unheeded prophecies, were now the facts of the moment, a nightmare made true and visible. Through it strode Mr Bunting, to do business in ironmongery, one of the million little men Hitler failed to understand, his chief emotion a resolute, slow anger as of one who marks the tally against a day of retribution. Grief and pity fed the slow fire of his passion, and made him silent.

His wife and Ernest showed great solicitude towards him these days. Mrs Bunting would have been glad for him to retire and stay at home, but feared to suggest what had obviously not occurred to him. Neither did he suggest that Julie should find work in safer Kilworth, though his first thoughts when he heard the siren screaming were of her nearness to the bomb factory. She came home a little white and shaken these days; but when asked if an attack had been made on Bardolph Green she only replied that the cross-eyed Nazi pilots couldn't hit anything they aimed at. Hadn't the sense to see, Mr Bunting reflected, that it was precisely this fact that made her position dangerous.

He worried about her pallor; he ceaselessly urged her to drink beef tea or something more nourishing than a silly vegetarian diet. 'Must have proteins,' he insisted, ''sential for everybody. Life-giving.' He kept on repeating this creed till Julie flew at him with unexpected passion.

'Leave me alone, dad. I'm all right. Let me eat what I want to.'

He was quite taken aback. Just like Ernest, he thought. Get an idea, stick to it through thick and thin, in spite of reason and advice, and go on sticking to it till it killed you. It was a trait from his wife's side of the family, sheer obstinacy; he had no patience with it.

Still, there was no point in making her unhappy; she was only a young girl, and young girls had to be taken care of more than boys; the midnight shocks were bad for them.

The Germans, not content with disturbing Mr Bunting's days, began to disturb his nights also. Frequently he was awakened by Mrs Bunting exclaiming: 'The siren!' and sitting up in bed he would faintly hear it, a muted note, as though it were much more than half a mile away. The things were not loud enough, in his opinion; would never awaken a normal sleeper. There had been some Government red tape about sirens, he supposed; relying on civil servants instead of going to a practical man. The result was that Mary lay awake half the night listening in case she missed it. To its wailings all three would come downstairs and poke the fire up, or sit round the Brockley 'Radiant'. He had long ago decided not to go into the garden shelter at night until an actual raid began, and to make this escape swift and easy had painted white lines across the lawn and set white posts near the dugout. At first, they held themselves in instant readiness, torches and gas masks on the table, coats and mufflers close at hand, and even the kitchen door unlocked. But as time went on they relaxed more, Mrs Bunting dozed on the couch and Julie often fell asleep on a stool, her head against her father's knee. He alone remained alert out of a sense of duty, following the sound of every aircraft, sometimes tensing as they drew near so that Julie opened her eyes and sleepily murmured: 'Has he bopped his droms yet, daddy? Has he bopped his droms!' Which silly way of talking (an echo, no doubt, of the Bardolph Green Food Office) moved him only to answer consolingly: 'They're a long way off, dearie. Go to sleep.' Once these words of Mr Bunting's were immediately followed by a humming through the air and a sharp metallic ping upon the garage roof. Whereupon Mrs Bunting sat upright and said accusingly:

'That wasn't a long way off!'

'Only a splinter off the ack-ack.'

'I'm not so sure. I don't think you hear the things.'

'Course I hear 'em!' he retorted, nettled. 'Go to sleep. What's a splinter?'

Watching the clock in the long blanks of silence and grudging every irrecoverable minute, Mr Bunting learned to long for sleep. In normal times one went to bed as a sort of routine, to pass the time till morning; but now, when night after night he sat in his chair, drowsy, yawning, and bleary-eyed, he thought of sleep as a blessing and a luxury. He longed to be able to lie down anywhere on anything and know with certainty that he would not be disturbed by warnings nor awakened by the house collapsing on him. Even the name of sleep had a poetical and lulling sound; it embalmed you in the still midnight, as the poet said.

To the tea which concluded these sittings he dedicated the bottle of 'Bonnie Prince Charlie', a teaspoonful to each cup, carrying all three into the bedrooms on a tray. As with the siren, so with the alarm clock, it was Mrs Bunting who heard it and aroused him. Only by blinking drowsily into its face and almost staring it out of countenance could he persuade himself that it had truthfully announced another day.

One event overtopped the interest of the blitzkrieg: Chris's forthcoming second leave. In preparation for this event Mrs Bunting 'went through' his bedroom, and beginning there she inaugurated a spring-cleaning operation which gradually enlarged itself until the entire house smelled of furniture polish. If there was one smell Mr Bunting abominated above all others, it was the smell of furniture polish. When that was in the air he knew, as sure as fate, that whatever chair he sat on would inevitably be the next for dusting. The whole procedure he regarded as a ceremonial rite, and one the war rendered more than ever unnecessary. What was the point, he demanded, of spring-cleaning a house that might be bombed? Chris, he declared, wouldn't want his bedroom cleaned, wouldn't even know it had been cleaned. He might suspect something had been afoot if his private belongings were hidden in holes and corners instead of being where he preferred to keep them but not, as it were, *prima facie*. His was a voice crying in the wilderness. Mrs Bunting ignored all protests, looking past rather than at him, a woman preoccupied with inanimate objects, temporarily deaf and fully resolute in her purpose.

But the cleaning was finished at last, in spite of both Mr Bunting and the *Führer*, and the days of waiting were accomplished. As the train drew into Kilworth on the day of Chris's arrival, fortunately a Saturday, Mr Bunting's sole thought was that he would already be at home. For once he decided to take a bus, but as he passed through the station barrier he saw Bert Rollo.

'I just happened to be down this way with the car, so I thought as Chris is home I'd give you a lift, Mr Bunting,' he explained.

Thus invited, Mr Bunting entered the Corton-David, which immediately leapt forward, its double-noted horn giving a plangent warning to less stately vehicles to make way, for here came Corporal Rollo of the Tanks.

Bert confided that he had saved his spot of leave for the sole purpose of meeting Chris. His conversation was not easily followed by any one not a patron of the talkies, but Mr Bunting understood his commanding officer had given him a 'break'. This commanding officer was a guy you had to hand it to; he was asbestos. Nevertheless, he was a *good guy* (if you got it), and Bert admired him. There was just a tincture of a suggestion that this admiration was mutual and very warm on the commanding officer's side, who had therefore fixed it for Bert with great goodwill and, as Mr Bunting gathered, with much 'okaying' on both sides of the orderly room table.

'Seen the *Kilworth Gazette*, Mr Bunting?'

'Not till I get home. Why?'

'I wondered,' said Bert darkly, and leaned back, steering with two negligent fingers. His manner suggested that even a Corton-David was but a toy to one who habitually drove tanks. He accelerated, he braked, he swerved, he darted through traffic like threading a needle. Mr Bunting was constrained to lift his attaché case upon his knee, and lean his abdomen upon it, finding frontal support as necessary as the upholstery behind him.

'Got a new tank?' he inquired, with slight sarcasm.

'Got the very latest. Hadn't cooled off before I took it over. And can it move?'

To this purely rhetorical question he gave no answer, but some recollections of the new tank's capacity for moving stirred an impulse, and he trod even more violently on the accelerator.

'Steady! Steady!' exclaimed Mr Bunting, with a fierce look.

'That's okay; we're home.' The Corton-David drifted demurely to the gate of Laburnum Villa, and came to rest as gently as a feather.

Thank God for that! thought Mr Bunting. 'Where's Chris?' he demanded, bustling in.

'Hallo, daddy. Gone out with Monica. Gone to the Rollos.'

'Gone out!' His face fell, and he put his attaché case on the nearest chair with the blankness of sudden disappointment.

'Mrs Rollo asked him for lunch, and Monica's coming here for tea.'

'I see!' He thought it most inconsiderate of Mrs Rollo.

'I can run you down in the car, Mr Bunting. Always got plenty of eats. What say?'

'Oh, no! No, thank you.' He shied from this suggestion. But if Bert had known where Chris was, why hadn't he mentioned it? Probably because he lacked sense. Still, Chris could get the Rollo visit over, come home for tea, and spend the rest of the day with his own family. There was that in it.

'Perhaps Bert would like to come for tea,' said Mrs Bunting.

'Sure I will. Glad to, I'll be right back.'

'A peculiar young man,' observed Mr Bunting, after Bert had gone. 'Seems sort of queer to me.' He couldn't think why Mary had invited him. Chris and Monica wouldn't want a brother hanging round. Between Monica and everybody it seemed likely he would hardly get a chance with Chris.

'Seen the *Kilworth Gazette*, daddy?' asked Julie, handing him that paper opened and folded to display a photograph. 'Bert's been awarded the DCM. Didn't you notice his ribbon?'

'No,' said Mr Bunting, taking the paper. 'For gallantry in the field,' he read. Corporal Rollo of Kilworth. It was the identical photograph they had on the mantelpiece.

'Well!' he exclaimed, in astonishment; 'young Bert Rollo!'

'So you see he's got a few good points as well, daddy.'

'He's certainly got pluck. But I don't like him saying "We're home". He don't live here.' Mr Bunting's thoughts were still tinged with a general feeling of grievance and disappointment.

There was nothing now but to wait for teatime, and meanwhile to remove himself from the turmoil of the preparations. Throughout his married life the arrival of every visitor had been preceded by this turmoil and fuss, as though Mary didn't have the house so neat and clean at all times that the queen herself could have come into it. But there was no altering his wife; not that he particularly wanted to – except in a few minor details where she was most stubborn.

132

He went out into the garden and eyed it indulgently, noting what was thriving rather than the blank patches, as an angler looks longest at the more fruitful pools. Things were doing well this year; not so well as Oskey's, but for the first time in his life Mr Bunting had raised cucumbers. It was true that the best one had been inadvertently truncated by Julie during a bit of negligent hoeing, but the rest of them were still alive, and that was the first thing Mr Bunting noticed about any of his vegetables. Even his tomatoes, though not actually thriving, were still alive and there was a number of belatedly developed green knobs. There were bits you had to pinch off; as a rule Oskey leaned over the fence and performed this office for him, saying it was easier to do the job himself than teach Mr Bunting how to identify the side shoots.

He did what little he deemed necessary to the garden at the moment. During the week, when he had no time, he noticed a great many jobs requiring his attention, but when the weekend arrived and he had the time, few of these jobs seemed necessary, or, at least, they were not urgent. Watering was the safest thing, it rarely killed anything, and today he contented himself with taking Oskey's advice and merely watering. When he returned indoors to wash and change, Mrs Bunting suggested he might also shave.

He turned sharply. 'Why shave?'

'Monica's coming.'

'I shaved this morning,' he said obstinately. 'Once a day's enough.' Shave indeed! He thought. But, having washed, he decided he might as well run the razor just once over the point of his chin; and it was during this operation that he heard Julie going in and out of the kitchen singing some silly words to a tune of her own:

Marvellous Monica's coming for tea!
Marvellous Monica's coming for tea!'

to which he listened, the delicate operation of shaving suspended, for Mr Bunting used a Brockley Standard razor, not a bit of tin in a so-called 'safety'. He put this instrument down and continued lathering his face, going right up to his ears (it was just as easy once you had started) and listening and thinking what idiotic things his children did. That was what you got for paying for expensive education. Julie was coming upstairs now, singing these daft, not to say unkindly, words, adding a final and outrageous verse:

'Marvellous Monica's coming for tea!
And also 'evingly Evie.'

This was too much. He put down the lather brush, tore the bathroom door open, and shouted: 'That's quite enough. What on earth are you thinking about to say such things about Evie? Monica, too, for that matter. I'm surprised at you.'

Julie's lips pursed into a soundless whistle of surprise. 'Oh, daddy-oodlums, is 'oo angry?' she cooed, and took a blob of lather from his cheeks with her fingertip and put it on the end of his nose; another blob she placed on his forehead, and was proceeding to make him into a 'nice spotty Damnation terrier', when he awoke to the enormity of these indignities, and, taking her firmly by the wrists, compelled her to desist.

'Oh, daddy! You've no idea how funny you look!' she exclaimed, and escaped to her bedroom convulsed with laughter, his disconcerted stare following her. Through the door came the same tune with indistinguishable words interspersed with laughter.

'Nerves. Reaction, I expeck,' he thought, and wiped away the blobs with an impatient movement of the towel. Even after waiting all this time he cut himself at the first touch. 'Blast! Oh, blast it!' he shouted in a fury. He would not shave. He immersed his face in the bowl, splashing recklessly, and wiped and examined his chin.

'Perhaps I'd better,' he thought, and began again, a sorely tried man. 'Furniture polish,' he muttered, returning to the root of all the dissension in the house with extreme sarcasm. 'Lot of rot!'

He was on his way downstairs at the moment Chris arrived with Monica. He hastened, stumbling over the lower steps in his eagerness to give Chris his hand. But this was not a moment for a proper greeting. Monica was there, and in the presence of this spectacular beauty, Mr Bunting felt awkward, a daw beside a goldfinch. Very coolly, very prettily, she greeted him, her eyes just faintly warming as they met his, her every hair shining in its proper place, her cheeks delicately and downily shaded. An exceedingly well finished young lady, even her eyelashes stood out separately each one in a way that invited his close and fascinated scrutiny. But the total effect of her was to snap off Mr Bunting's eagerness, and make him polite and even a trifle formal. It was a pity he couldn't get to know Monica better. She was a nice girl, and a good girl, too, he told himself, as though in this he commended her for having overcome the handicap of exceptional good looks.

To his relief Julie welcomed her warmly; there were smiles and kisses, and gossip all the way upstairs where the visitor went to put her hat and coat upon the bed. Julie herself looked rather well turned out this afternoon, and Mr Bunting was pleased to notice she had lost her pallor of the last few days. She was, in fact, somewhat too radiantly pink when she went into conference with Monica upstairs, though not quite as inartistically and obviously so when she came down again.

The hubbub of their voices receded up the stairs, and he was free at last to have a word with Chris. Precisely at that moment Bert arrived. Mr Bunting had hoped that something would prevent him, but here he was, more than ever confident that all the world was glad to see him. There arose a hubbub of a manly, even military kind, Chris and Rollo talking pithily and slangily in service language or American, throwing half sentences at one another, whilst Mr Bunting stood aside, a person of no consequence, understanding little of their conversation except that it tacitly excluded him. It seemed that he was never going to have a chance even to say 'How do?' to Chris, and that Chris didn't mind, didn't notice, even. Not in the least aware of his father eagerly waiting, he stood on the hearth in Mr Bunting's time-honoured place and attitude, smoking the bulldog, his eye watching the door for Monica's return.

Mr Bunting went into the kitchen to offer assistance with the tea but was extruded with asperity. Mary was nervous today because of the inadequacy of the butter ration. This particular difficulty, it seemed, was responsible for the scones not being up to standard. Mr Bunting snorted; he never remembered the scones being up to standard when they entertained visitors; it was either the quantity of baking powder, or the speed of the oven, or some other unfortunate circumstance, for which Mrs Bunting began to apologise as soon as she poured the tea out. Yet he never remembered eating one that didn't melt in his mouth like candy.

'Oh, blast!' he muttered, out of sympathy with the entire household. He wandered from the kitchen to the front room and stood before the window jingling his change. He could stand here an hour, he supposed, and nobody would miss him. He'd looked forward to Chris's leave, and now it found him in a thoroughly bad temper.

He took a soda mint from a tin in his waistcoat pocket and sucked it thoughtfully. Nothing had gone right all day; everybody had been obstinate and difficult, and none of them had shown him the least consideration.

'No good sulking,' he thought. But the edge had been taken off his appetite for the proceedings. The best thing was to pretend there was nothing wrong. He wandered back to the living room, his exit and his entrance both unnoticed, and was immediately asked to stand aside so Julie could bring in the tray. Today the leaves of the table were fully extended, and the best cloth stiffly laid upon it. Everybody was present except Ernest, who was on duty at the aid post. In wartime you never could get a full muster; there was always the absentee on duty. There was general commiseration with Ernest enduring the discomfort of the aid post; but Mr Bunting was cheered by the food, though he thought there was too much noise; it tended to give him a headache. Noise it was, not conversation; questions and interruptions, laughter without reason, and to excess, a regular row, in his opinion.

'Now that we're all here,' he said, as though calling the meeting to order, 'I feel sure we'd all like to welcome Chris and Bert back from their conflicts with the enemy.'

'Very well put, dad.'

It sounded well, Mr Bunting thought himself. Spontaneous. He brightened visibly. He wished he'd thought to get in a drop of port. He was about to follow his slight oratorical success with some borrowings from Mr Churchill, when Mrs Bunting, not understanding his pause was a reflective one, instructed him to serve the pie.

This word directed his attention to the table and the pie, one of Blenkinsop's he dared to swear, recognising the excellent crispy brownness of the crust.

'Bit of pie, Bert? Dead pig pie.'

'George!'

'That's what it is. Ask Julie.'

Julie's eyes were daggers for a moment; then she remembered the insouciant pose, and raised her brows at him coldly and superiorly. Mr Bunting's feeble attempts at humour frequently consisted of saying the very things he forbade everybody else to say.

'How's the war going, Chris?'

Chris had little to say about the war. If you asked a question he would answer briefly and barely. Yes, he was flying a Spitfire; yes, eight guns. He'd seen a few Germans, their Messerschmitts were quite decent; it got colder the higher you went. These questions he regarded as purely business matters; what really interested him was the films on show at Kilworth.

Failing with Chris, Mr Bunting turned to Bert, cut him a second helping of pie to follow his prodigious first one, and inquired what he had called his new tank.

'I hope you remembered to give it a name with a sting in it,' said Julie. 'Like the "Wasp". I'd call it – let me see, what would I call it?' And she puckered her brows. Nothing resulting from this except a look of puzzled charm, she escaped into lucidity by saying: 'I suppose you've already named it.'

It was evident from Bert's confusion that he had not forgotten their criticism of his choice of 'Daffodil'. All the Buntings seemed to be waiting for the new tank's name, as though assuming he had some thought of pleasing them when he christened it. Mrs Bunting came to his rescue.

'Don't you tell them, Bert. We don't want any arguments.'

'That's right,' agreed Mr Bunting. '"What's in a name?" as the poet said.' He tried to remember what came next, failed, and resumed mastication.

'Nice to have you all here. You too, Evie.' He met her hazel-green eyes, dark and sparkling eyes, that always invited him to look right into them. 'Pity Ernest isn't here. Stops us having a bit of music.'

'Monica and I thought of going down to the Odeon tonight,' put in Chris a trifle hastily.

A constriction affected Mr Bunting's throat, arising, as he told himself, out of sheer selfishness. But he would have liked just five minutes with Chris. He longed for it with a longing that was unreasonable and juvenile, even silly, he knew. He had an absurd feeling that he hadn't met Chris yet, had made no satisfying contact with him. Still, what was more natural than that Chris should want to go out with Monica? She, rather than his parents, was in the forefront of his life now. Chris was doubtless unaware that his father had these absurd emotions.

'Course, enjoy yourselves,' he said, and thought of Bert. Chris and Monica wouldn't want Bert hanging round; but Bert had no tact. That was the most obvious thing about him, except his appetite, which was enormous. Mr Bunting had, in fact, observed everything Bert ate, not in any inhospitable spirit, but with the attention one naturally gives to any intrinsically interesting phenomenon.

He lit the pipe that followed every meal, and considered methods of disposing of Bert, now standing beside him on the rug, and occupying about three-quarters of its space. Strategy was required; hold him here till Chris and Monica got a start. Might show him the garden, lead him, as it were, up the garden in the fully classical sense.

'I guess I'll pop outside and have a word with Miss Bunting.'

Mr Bunting glanced up in sudden perplexity; then his face cleared. 'You mean Julie? She's in the garden. Ask her to show you round.' Most hospitably he opened the door and gently pushed him out.

Julie was in the garden gathering roses, a picturesque occupation in which she was completely absorbed. She chose her bouquet thoughtfully, composing its colours with an artist's care, and not disdaining to lean over the fence to add a necessary effect from Oskey's nearer bushes. Bert had long since put her down as a girl of artistic temperament, and this further evidence of it caused a diffidence to fall upon him, and a fear of interrupting processes beyond his comprehension. He was considerably surprised therefore when, without raising her head, she met him with the question: 'Bert, what did you call your new tank?'

The probing curiosity of women! How often had he encountered it, like a needle jabbed into a fellow at the moment of his friendliest approach.

'Did you call it "Vindictive", or did you name it after an animal or a bird of prey, like "Vulture" or "Parrot"?'

'Oh, forget it!'

She looked at him over the bouquet, a charming pose. 'Come on, Bert, tell me.'

'Well, it's this way,' he began, and prepared to defend himself by advance explanation. Finding this altogether too complicated he let it go and, with what was a reckless burst of confidence, said: 'It's called "Julie".'

She straightened her back: 'I see! Not "Repulsive" – just "Julie".'

'Listen! You got me wrong.'

'How many Julies do you know?'

Bert felt himself blushing, but he got the words out at last: 'Only you.'

'Um!' she said, and put two rose stems side by side in her palm and, with one of the sudden changes of mood that so nonplussed him, said: 'That was extremely nice of you, Bert. I'm honoured. I'm surprised as well, but still I'm honoured.'

'That's okay!' he said generously, and feeling himself on safer ground, assumed an easier pose. He took out his pipe, a new one that still tasted more of wood than of tobacco, and lit it. Remembering it induced in him a desire to spit, he put it back again. He should have got a bulldog like Chris's, with a patent filtering gadget in the stem.

'What about a run in the Corton-David?'

'I'd love to. But not just now.'

'When then?'

She shrugged. 'Oh – some other time, maybe.'

They walked across the lawn and to the front of the house. He had a feeling that he was being shown off the premises. Hardly friendly, he thought, in view of what he'd told her – unless she was offended. Chris and Monica had left, so there was nothing to stay for, anyway. Of course, there was always Molly Parrott, she 'adored' being driven in the Corton David. She adored a great many things that Bert found expensive; was, in fact, as he had known for a long time now, a fickle little gold-digger.

Julie came to the gate, leaned over it, and looked up the road. It was the sort of moment favourable to confidential conversation. Bert leaned on the gate also; there was something in the atmosphere between them. Then, a touch of eagerness came into her manner.

'Look, Bert, your friend the dog man.'

There he was, in cloth cap and leggings, most obviously the dog man. Under his arm was a jet-black puppy, its head wagging from side to side like a china mandarin, its tiny muzzle sniffing up and down and round the dog man's elbow, its stumpy forelegs pawing the air. Altogether a lively and tender creature, lovable at first sight and in the distance.

A pleasurable prescience filled Julie. She raised on to her toes and watched the dog man reading the name on every gate with the deliberate scrutiny of one determined to deliver his puppy to the right address.

'I'd better be going,' said Bert, moving his army boots a few inches.

'No, don't go. It's a Scottie. I'm certain it's for me. He's bringing it here.'

Bert appeared to be certain also; his embarrassment betrayed him. At that moment she thought him something of a darling – a great, hefty, inarticulate darling. His desire to escape without being thanked made him so much more a darling that it was almost on her lips to tell him so.

The dog man proved he had some rudiments of courtesy by touching his cap as he recognised Julie.

'Here you are, miss. Grip 'im; grip 'im tight. He's wick as an eel.'

'Oh, Bert! It's just the sweetest thing,' she exclaimed, struggling with the black bunch of liveliness. 'Stand still, pet. Let me see what your label says.'

'For Julie.' Simply that, without added sentiment. Still hopeful, she turned the label over and read its further message: 'With love from Chris!'

For a moment there was a let-down in her emotional pitch; a silent, but open admission of surprise. 'From Chris,' she repeated, and recovered her natural sprightliness by a gallant effort.

'Now isn't that perfectly sweet of him? I only mentioned a dog to him once, and the first thing he does when he comes on leave is to get me just what I wanted. Isn't it just like him, Bert? I must take it to show daddy!'

With a wave of her hand she left him; forgot all about fixing up the run in the Corton-David. She was interested in the puppy, too intensely interested in it, Bert thought; he considered a lot of this interest was put on. He'd been left flat many times before but never for a puppy.

How the devil was he to know she was so stuck on having a puppy?

He went back to his first impression of her, for first impressions somehow get built up into delusions until you never saw a girl as she was, but hypnotised yourself into a silly belief she was somebody quite different. And what had been his first impression of Julie Bunting? That she was only a kid; she hadn't yet worn out her last school blazer; she gardened in it. Not old enough to realise she wasn't the only pebble on the beach.

Besides, when it came to *style* – Thinking of style naturally made him think of Molly Parrott. Whatever her faults, Molly had style and dash so that chaps asked where on earth he found her. And she knew how to appreciate a fellow who'd been on active service and got two stripes up and a DCM.

He lit his pipe, but as he held the match against the bowl some words floated back to him. 'Bird of prey – vulture or parrot. Yeah, I get it. Wise-cracking, eh!' He stood there motionless, whilst the match burnt down, and had to be dropped suddenly with manly expletives.

'Thinks I'm dumb, eh?' he murmured, and walked glumly up the road licking his scorched thumb.

FOURTEEN

CHRIS'S PREFERENCE FOR wearing his civilian clothes on leave disappointed Julie, but greatly pleased Mr Bunting. Uniform was a reminder, every time he saw it, that his son was bound over to the military authorities. There were many considerations that must outweigh the value of his life to them. Chris's life was now a counter to be paid, if need be, towards the price of victory. But you were not perpetually reminded of this when you saw him in his blazer and flannel trousers; then he was just himself. Though he had been chasing Germans up and down the sky last week, he very pleasantly volunteered this week to plant out the curly kale. No baby-killing Nazi pilot, Mr Bunting thought, would condescend to do a job like that on leave, or do anything except play the hero and swagger in his uniform. It was uniform, uniform all the time in Germany; they simply loved it. Not one of their leaders had ever possessed a suit of civvies, if their photographs were anything to go by.

The eagerness he had felt, his disappointment at Chris's apparent unresponsiveness, soon wore off, looked a little foolish even in retrospect, though not entirely so. Mr Bunting could not persuade himself that anything which sprang sincerely from the heart could really be foolish. But he and Chris returned to the level of their old relationship and, whenever Chris was free of engagements with Monica, he sought the company of his father. Nothing particular was said, but their talks were satisfying. The warm anticipation with which Mr Bunting came home from business was clouded only by the thought that seven days don't last for ever, and that Chris must soon go back to the dreadful business of machine-gunning in the air.

On his last evening, after Mrs Bunting and Julie had said good night, father and son sat up together.

'Just ten minutes, mother,' Chris said; but no sooner had the door closed than he sprang up and produced bottled stout from behind the wireless set, and a corkscrew, and with a truly conspiratorial air, bade his father fetch glasses.

'Shan't be home for a bit. Let's have a jaw together.'

'Stout, eh?' said Mr Bunting. He rarely drank stout. It didn't occur to him to ask for it; besides, it was more expensive than beer.

'Jolly good stuff, Chris. Got tonic prop'ties.'

'Helps you to sleep if you've had a jolt.'

This was Chris's first reference to jolts received whilst flying, and he did not dwell on it. Instead, he put his feet on the opposite chair, leaned back, and smiled at his father.

'I've had a jolly time.'

'Really, Chris?' said Mr Bunting. All the week he had been worried by a fear that Chris must be finding things dull.

'Yes, I've thoroughly enjoyed myself.'

'Be a good thing when you're home for good, Chris. All 'preciate one another a bit more.'

'We've got to lick the Jerrys first.'

'That's what we've got to do, Christopher.'

Mr Bunting smoked thoughtfully. He couldn't help thinking how like Chris was to himself, how much more like he would become as he grew older. He would carry on the line of Buntings, those decent ordinary chaps the world was so in need of. But, of course, the thing just now was to beat Hitler.

'Going to be a big job,' he said, thinking aloud. He had lately known moments when he felt he couldn't go on facing it. Devastation and ruin had been his daily spectacle in London; there had been unnerving moments in trains and buses, and the strain of working with noises overhead. Besides, he missed his sleep. Beating the Germans was going to be a bigger job than last time, more to go through for everybody. But these thoughts were silent. He didn't always feel like that, only now and then when he was tired. The men in the Air Force were a light-hearted crowd, and Mr Bunting was never one to spoil a good heart.

'One up now,' said Chris, listening to the drone of an engine. 'Hope Moaning Minnie doesn't sound, and bring mother downstairs.' His desire seemed to be to make this drinking and smoking together a sort of secret session.

The drone faded. They replenished their glasses, and leaned back looking at one another.

'I got a Dornier the other day. Came out of a bit of cloud, and there he was, right in my gun sights. So I gave him a packet.'

'Did he come down?'

'They baled out. I saw the pilot afterwards. He runs a garage like the "Snappy" somewhere in the Rhineland. Invited me to go and see him after the war.'

Mr Bunting considered this. 'Might be interesting. Think you'll go?'

'Gosh! I'm not so stuck on Germans as all that.'

'No. Cheeky of him to ask you. Best thing is to have nothing to do with 'em. What sort of a chap was he, Chris?'

'Seemed all right. Wanted a shave badly. He didn't need a haircut though.'

'Proper square-head, eh? I been thinking a good bit about when you come back after the war. I been putting a bit of money on one side for you, Chris. 'Taint much; just what I can afford, see? I thought we could improve the garage, help you to branch out a bit. I want you to have a proper chance in your own business when you come home. Not this flying, see?'

'That's good of you, dad, but I don't want to take things.'

Mr Bunting leaned forward, anxiously. ''Tisn't taking things, Chris. I *want* to do it. The war won't last for ever.'

'No. There'll be an after-the-war again, won't there, dad?'

'Course there will, Chris,' said Mr Bunting, hearteningly. 'It's just something we've got to live through.'

Chris gave him a reflective, even a wistful smile. Mr Bunting's words seemed to hang between them as though printed on the air. Then he took his feet off the chair and stood up briskly.

'You're right, dad. And now, let's go to bed.'

It was a needless lack of consideration that required Chris to leave for duty on Saturday morning, Mr Bunting thought, for it emptied his weekend of interest. This gap he filled with miscellaneous pottering, his mind full of his son. There was nothing Chris had said or done too trivial for Mr Bunting to run over in his mind, and dwell on as he might upon a favourite song. Every burnt-out cigarette in the ash tray was a memento that awakened echoes of some casual word. And when, after searching for his trowel, he found it rusting amongst the newly planted kale, he scraped it clean, thinking 'Just like Chris,' as though this trait of leaving things about was altogether an attractive failing.

The leave-taking had been informal, Mr Bunting and Julie hastening off to catch their train whilst Chris was still at breakfast. Monica was driving him to Carberry Junction to share the long wait with him there, and so prolong the parting. Life at Laburnum Villa slipped back into its groove.

Standing in his garage on Sunday morning Mr Bunting wondered why it had not occurred to him to license the car for Chris; Chris had, in fact, inquired whether it was licensed. But it had not occurred to Mr Bunting in advance. He meant to remedy this regrettable omission in time for his next leave.

The Conway was old and battered, which was perhaps why, when Mr Bunting looked at it, he thought: 'Been a jolly good car, done good service,' and he switched on the ignition and pulled the starter. Nothing happened beyond a lifeless sound under the bonnet, which he presently lifted to peer inside. Then he flushed the carburettor and swung the handle; patiently at first, presently with exasperation, for flushing the carburettor was as far as Mr Bunting's technique in these matters went. Still the Conway would not start, which was strange, for he had always boasted of its capacity for easy starting, and had frequently watched men sweating in attempts to start more expensive cars with a feeling that there was, after all, a great advantage in owning a Conway.

So he rested to recover breath, and put from him the temptation to leave the car alone. It was not actually the business of the moment; he had come into the garage to get the fertiliser. That, however, was not Mr Bunting's way; his way was to accept practical difficulties as a challenge, and overcome them. He could hardly ever leave a practical difficulty alone. Besides, he had an instinct that the trouble lay in the carburettor, and the carburettor of a Conway is child's play to dismantle. The Conway owners' booklet said so.

Therefore, with a collection of fine screwdrivers and the official booklet of instructions, Mr Bunting started on the carburettor, and the garage became silent. So silent that Mrs Bunting presently looked in to inquire if he was all right, and was brusquely ordered to go away. With deepening incomprehension and diminishing confidence, he followed the instructions, increasingly aware of a suggestion in the writer's tone that although he was preparing the booklet as a job of work, actually everybody knew that the necessity of going to these extreme lengths never happened with a Conway. He explained how to dismantle the carburettor, but was silent about what was to be done to it afterwards. Apparently, you simply reassembled it and put it back. Mr Bunting knew that such pointless processes often mysteriously overcame defects in cars, and were beyond explanation. But he felt annoyed with the writer of the Conway booklet, and for some minutes forgot the carburettor and explored further pages, staring stonily.

But when he came to the crux of the problem, which was to reassemble and refix the carburettor, it was dismissed in a bored way as being done by reversing the process just described. It was also suggested that the carburettor should not be interfered with except by those reliable fellows, the authorised Conway agents.

At this Mr Bunting hurled a shameful epithet at the writer, who had now become unashamedly flippant and superior. One of the directors' sons from Eton, Mr Bunting surmised; public school.

Nevertheless, he doggedly got on his knees again, thrust out his under-lip, and with the resolution of repressed anger refixed the carburettor. The entire messy and protracted business arose from a generous impulse and, not unnaturally, he expected his generous impulses to make him feel happy and serene, not lead him to an anger and the utterance of oaths barely short of blasphemy.

Even now the Conway wouldn't start, and Mr Bunting gave it an offended stare. It seemed to have taken on the infuriatingly stolid look of inanimate objects, that can drive you to the pitch of frenzy, but to which you can do nothing in retaliation. He cursed it in passionate undertones.

It was then he saw Monica. She came through the green and white gate, a wistful, introspective Monica, who brightened undisguisedly at sight of him and paused; then turned aside from the house, and came to join him in the garage. She wouldn't have done that, he knew, if she hadn't been saddened with thoughts of Chris.

Mr Bunting's faith in the power of trivialities to comfort and protect the heart was immense, and he greeted her with the information that he had been having a little trouble with the car. A little trouble, he called it, for he had sufficient faith in the Conway to know that was all it could be, especially to any member of the Rollo family.

'I suppose Chris immobilised it. Took out the rotor,' and she pulled off her gloves and peered at the engine. She looked rather like Mrs Bunting examining her sewing machine, except that she proceeded more by scientific method and less by feminine instinct. 'Won't start without the rotor,' she smiled.

'Course not!' he agreed, feeling foolish at not knowing what the rotor was. There was something you took out to foil the parachutists, he knew; but he had always intended to do something much more drastic to the Conway if parachutists arrived.

'Chris put it in a cigarette tin,' she said, looking round. 'Here it is, and this is how you fix it.'

With a momentary revelation of pink silk above a shapely knee she slipped into the driving seat. The Conway purred contentedly, like a kitten at last given what it craved for. It was some relief to know he had at least not irreparably damaged the carburettor. He always appeared at a disadvantage before this girl; she must think him dull, old-fashioned, and out of date.

Now she turned upon him the full beauty of her smile.

'I know I'm an ass with cars,' he admitted.

'Oh, no!' she exclaimed, as though realising her smile had been misinterpreted, and they talked cars for a time with a feeling that Chris was waiting on the fringe of all this gossip. Then, with a swift digression to the confidential, he asked:

'See him off last night?'

'I went with him right down to Surrey.'

'Really?'

'Yes.'

There was a pause which Mr Bunting's mind automatically filled with a calculation of the distance between Kilworth and any part of Surrey. A misgiving touched him.

'Oh!' he said, not knowing what to think.

'I only left him this morning. He went straight up on patrol.' Her words died away in a bitten sob.

Something caught at Mr Bunting's heart, a simple question looked out of his widened grey eyes. It was answered by the glance that met him steadily; not shameless, but unashamed.

'My dear!' he muttered huskily, and put his arm round her shoulder. He did not know what to say, but cleared his throat manfully. 'There's lots of things in life. You and Chris – you got to be patient.'

He broke off, his words blown away like smoke. Monica looked at him from behind a wisp of handkerchief with which she dabbed her brightened eyes. Then, suddenly, she reached up and put her arms about his neck, hugging him tightly. He heard her whisper in his ear: 'You're a darling, Mr Bunting; everybody ought to love you.' She pressed her lips warmly and tightly against his cheek for an instant and then was gone.

He stood in the garage his fingers gently touching a spot that burned and tingled. These young lovers! Life was hard on them in wartime; it was not for him to be hard also. But he was distressed, afraid, shaken beyond measure.

FIFTEEN

MR BUNTING'S TRAIN, after stopping and whistling uncertainly outside its London terminus, drew in warily and halted. He descended, and finding himself not at his usual platform, stared about at first to get his bearings, and then stared again because the scene compelled his horrified attention. Above him, great gaps in the station roof revealed the sky; before him, waiting room and offices were flattened out under their collapsed roofing; in his path loops of fire hose straggled like hissing serpents. A locomotive lay with its nose in a crater like a burrowing animal, its under parts showing. How they would ever extricate it he could not imagine. Since Saturday the familiar scene had changed into a spectacle of ruin that took his breath. This was what happened when the Hun found his objective, or hit it by chance. The havoc appalled him, for Mr Bunting abhorred waste and destruction of any kind, even on the domestic scale he abhorred it. Here had been held a true German orgy.

Becoming aware he was standing still, and betraying what he most wanted to hide, his sense of shock, he walked on.

'Thousands of quids' worth,' ran his thoughts. 'Thousands!' He shut his lips very tightly. It was incongruous to find at the boundary of this devastated area a ticket collector regulating his own small section of a disordered world.

'The old station's caught it all right,' said a man at Mr Bunting's elbow, and he responded with a curt 'Seems so'. He was too shaken to talk about it. The man might begin to pour some poisonous pessimism into his mind not, at the moment, fully armoured to resist. Force of habit made him look up at the clock. It was still there and neither a minute fast nor slow; its expressionless face looked down impassively, as it must have done at the height of the bombardment when everything else was crashing in a hail of bombs. Its huge minute hand crept on with its customary jerk, as though the clock twitched him a friendly wink as he passed beneath.

Leaving the station he was cheered to see how much was left even of this London corner. The district was not completely wrecked, not even noticeably disorganised; much close at hand was quite untouched. The streets were brisk, the buses running; a girl, holding an impetuous terrier on a lead, went past him carrying a new-baked roll in tissue paper. There was even a certain cheerfulness, perhaps of relief, in the air. With their backs towards the station, a knot of taxi drivers were clustered round a newspaper reading, he supposed, about the war. There was something about them that reminded him of Oskey, an imperviousness to shock, and an incapacity to realise how serious were the things they witnessed. Their stolidity helped Mr Bunting to pull himself together, and he set his face towards Brockleys.

He found he could still buy his ounce of 'Lighthouse' round the corner from a tobacconist too busy sorting held-up newspapers to mention what had happened to the station. Mr Bunting didn't mention it, either; he never talked about air raid damage on principle. His confidence in his fellow countrymen was immense, but he also had a fear of depressing them.

Signs were not wanting that he was walking into another area of damage. An hotel displayed all its bedrooms, and a bank, already barricaded, was guarded by a single policeman. He hastened on in increasing suspense, straining for his first glimpse of Brockleys, and seeing it at last with the relief of one who learns the worst. His own ironmongery window had been blown into the street, Corder's was likewise shattered, the wind rippling the sheetings of its interior. Already the porter was clearing up the mess with a matter-of-factness which Mr Bunting found commendable. 'We've got boards in the cellar, if someone'll give me a hand with the nailing,' he said, breaking the concentration of his task.

Mr Bunting nodded, and went inside to make a tour of inspection. Brockleys had caught it; the war, which had been so much discussed there, had been brought right to them now. There was something in the thought of Brockleys being knocked about by Germans that to Mr Bunting surpassed all limits; he had no words for such an outrage. The back windows were shattered, Mr Bickerton's office partially wrecked, and there were articles thrown about in confusion, broken and soiled. But the cubby-hole, when he arrived there, was exactly as he left it on Saturday. Not a pen nor a book thrown down, not a speck of dust on the smoothly worn desktop. His catalogues, his memoranda, his diaries, everything was there quite undisturbed. He entered thankfully; amidst all the havoc he had at last found the refuge of the unchanged.

He blew out his cheeks and sat down. Almost as an afterthought he took off his hat and put it on the desk. He wanted a minute to relax. There was a note on the desk, the latest of many in Mrs Musgrave's handwriting. It referred, like all the previous ones, to Charlie's progress in the army. She was convinced that Mr Bunting was passionately interested in how Charlie was faring in the army, and particularly that he should not do anything silly, like volunteering to become a bomb thrower. Charlie, he learned, had now been taken into the quartermaster's stores, and wouldn't have to fight. It was the experience gained under Mr Bunting in the stores at Brockleys which had so fortunately saved him.

'Tchah!' he exclaimed, tearing the slip of paper viciously. He supposed that blasted woman would be here for days now, scrubbing and polishing and filling the air with smells like spring cleaning.

'Mr Bunting! Mr Bunting!' came Turner's voice shriller and more urgent than ever, and Turner stood before him, shaken, but trying to control himself under the Bunting eye.

'Come and see what's happened to my window!'

'Oh, damn!' he murmured, rising from his stool. Braced as he was against shock, Turner's splintered window moved him chiefly to one more interested observation of the vagaries of bomb blast. The windows at the rear of Brockleys had been blown inwards, not out into the street, as at the front. This it was that had affected Turner, for he worked between the window and the shelving. 'Look!' he said, and pointed to fragments of glass driven into the woodwork. He stood behind the counter demonstrating where various pieces of glass would have struck him had the raid occurred in working hours. They would have gone through him in an assortment of places, each one vital, according to where he chose to stand. He discovered one place where he would have received five huge splinters – had he been there when the bomb burst. As he remarked: 'It wouldn't be very nice, would it?' Gingerly, and with only half an ear for Turner, Mr Bunting attempted to dislodge a splinter with his fingers; then he tried pliers. He had to use all his strength to extract the sharp edges from the wood. Never before had he realised the terrific force behind these explosions, or that a man could be cut in half by fragments of a broken pane. As a practical demonstration it was most impressive.

The question was: what to do with Turner's window? Brockleys had plenty of glass, they dealt in it, and the window could be reinstated when they did the front ones. Turner hung on his decision. No use telling him, Mr Bunting supposed, that they never dropped 'em in the same place twice. That fallacy had been exploded. They dropped them everywhere and anywhere, which was understandable, for they were not aiming at anything more localised than national morale.

This word was not included in the *bijou* dictionary, whose compilers had not foreseen it would acquire so great a vogue, but Mr Bunting understood it from its contexts. The Germans believed most of all in attacking civilian morale, which to him seemed a plain indication of their own weak spot. Once a civilian like Turner saw the war entirely as it affected himself, the game was lost. But it was not Turner he thought of as he examined the window, but the Londoners who night after night endured the terror. In the evenings after business, he could escape from London, but they had to sleep in shelters and dugouts, or gregariously in tubes. How often he thought of them as he lay in bed, and felt almost ashamed of his safety in Kilworth as though he had left the front line to be held by women and children and old men. The thought of them driven into cellars and shelters oppressed him; he imagined them crouching there, knowing that even these refuges did not offer safety; safety was not to be had.

Even down at McAndrew's Café there had been tragedy. The waitress he and Corder claimed as their own, and called 'neat-handed Phyllis' (exactly why Mr Bunting had never understood), was no longer there. She had been dug out of the wreckage of her home. He remembered her, mousy-haired and pale, but with a sweet voice and an engaging smile. He used to think she could do with a month in the country. Now she was dead, killed in the blitz, another Londoner. When Mr Bunting heard it, his heart burned for the lost youth that could have made him an avenger.

'It's chiefly nights they come,' he told Turner, summarising these reflections but anxious to show kindness. 'I'll have it boarded if you like. Fix up a light for you to work by.'

As he turned from Turner's excessive gratitude, his eye fell on a collection of objects, imperfectly concealed by sacking. Tubular, sizeable objects, in familiar grey enamel. A thought that these articles could be flue connections came into his mind, and was dismissed as preposterous. He bent over them, nevertheless, and tugged away the sacking. The name 'Watkins' hit him squarely in the eye. Still perplexed, but with rising suspicion, he counted.

Eight! Eight flue connections. They must belong to the stoves dispatched to Elgin. His heart sank. Some catastrophic blundering had stultified all his efforts to hasten that consignment. What was the good of sending stoves without the parts to fix them? Mr Bunting's thoughts flew to McCall of Elgin, not a patient man, judged by his correspondence, nor even a polite one, but at this moment he had Mr Bunting's heartfelt sympathy. He pictured McCall unpacking his long-expected stoves, then leaping into the air with rage, a red-haired profane Highlander, justifiably incensed.

He pointed: 'You don't mean you sent the stoves and forgot the fittings?'

A movement of Turner's throat gave the answer. Under Mr Bunting's gaze he shrank into himself, tried to dwindle out of sight like a terrier that expects a whipping. His eyes pleaded dumbly like a terrier's eyes. Mr Bunting stared, too stupefied even to feel anger. To send the stoves without the fittings was bad enough, but to say no word afterwards, to play this silly boy's trick of covering the pipes with sacking to conceal the error, struck him as simply idiotic. It baffled him completely. He wondered whether Turner was losing his reason. Turner, in fact, was hopeless; Mr Bunting did not know what to do about him. If it would have done any good to rage, he would have raged, but Turner was past praying for. If a man was as old as he felt, Turner was eighty, nerve and vitality gone, his life troubled by a sick wife at home and a son drowned in the North Sea.

There was only one practical and useful thing to do.

'Get 'em off. Pack 'em and get 'em off.'

'Yes, Mr Bunting.'

Mr Bunting's sigh as he walked away went right down to his heart. Such gross incompetence was a reflection on the department and most of all on the manager. He wondered whether he should write to McCall, or even wire him. Stave off his wrath by blaming everything on the blitzkrieg. It would be true, wouldn't it? In a way it was the blitzkrieg.

'No!' he muttered and, without knowing why he did so, murmured the word 'Brockleys'. Brockleys, above all other houses, should be superior to the blitzkrieg. But there would be the devil to pay when Mr Bickerton found out.

He went upstairs and hung indecisively about the corridor of the main office, flattening his one wisp of hair and making sure from time to time about his waistcoat buttons. Mr Bickerton was visible through the half-open door of his private room, shaking brick dust off his papers, and superintending the removal of his furniture to another office. He was greatly irritated by the dust, and frequently took out his silk handkerchief and made passes down the front of his immaculate black waistcoat. Work was impossible for Mr Bickerton unless everything was as neat and orderly as a clinic. Nor could he find the papers he most wanted; there had been mysterious evanishments. Catching sight of Mr Bunting, he waved him inside, remarking, with a burst of confidence quite unusual, that unless he kept his eye on everything that damned office boy would, in future, explain all lost correspondence by reference to this incident of the blitz.

'It makes things very difficult. Could you, by any chance, remember what we quoted Wardles for those nozzle things?'

Out came Mr Bunting's distended pocketbook and shed its confetti shower of cuttings. 'Hose terminals,' he said, correcting his chief's nomenclature: 'Duckbills. I got 'em down somewhere.'

Mr Bickerton looked over his shoulder, impressed, not so much by the pocket-book, as by its confident production.

'Do you enter everything in here?'

'Most things. Got lots of these old books.'

Amidst a mass of detail, entered out of his natural love of making notes, Mr Bunting's finger indicated the necessary figures.

'Ah!' exclaimed Mr Bickerton with relief. He paused and regarded his surroundings with distaste. 'Let's go downstairs.'

The cubby-hole evoked his appreciative glance. He entered it as though he were coming indoors from a storm and sat down at Mr Bunting's desk as if he were drawing up to a fire. Now would be a good moment to break the news of Turner's blunder. McCall would certainly write a stinging letter, and there was nothing like inoculating a man with a little advance knowledge so that he simmered gently instead of exploding in an instant. But McCall might not wait to write, he might wire. Whenever he got into a temper he wired, and his messages were exclamatory and incoherent. If a really typical one arrived at Brockleys on top of the day's catastrophe, it would spell the end for Turner.

These thoughts revolved in Mr Bunting's mind as he watched Mr Bickerton writing at the cubby-hole desk, and becoming so speedily immersed in one problem after another that it became evident he had forgotten where he was. He took a batch of letters from his pocket and made notes and did calculations, paying no attention to Mr Bunting except once, when he looked up and said: 'Yes, Bunting. Want anything?' To which Mr Bunting replied: 'No, sir,' and took himself off hastily, feeling that he left the chief wondering what Bunting was doing hanging round his private room.

He was moody at lunch time, unable to decide whether he should try to beg Turner off in advance, or delay explanation until some message came from Elgin. Corder mistook his quietness for depression.

'Cheer up, George! London will rise again. Phoenix from the ashes. A better London – perhaps the London Wren planned.'

'Suppose so,' replied Mr Bunting, who had heard of Wren, but not, till now, of Phoenix.

'I believe the human race is at a turning point; on the threshold of a great march forward. It's true I believed in the last war, but there's more faith in the air today. A new world order. Not this Bolshie business – something Rooseveltian built on the English tradition. The common sense of most holding the fretful what-is-it in awe. Of course, nobody reads Tennyson now.'

Mr Bunting indulged in a long intake of breath, which indicated he was being very patient. 'Don't you start with a new order, Joe. Hitler's got one, so has my son Ernest. The old order wasn't so bad till we let the Germans mess things up again. The ordinary chap doesn't want any high-falutin new order. He wants a decent wage and a decent house, and a bit of time to do what he likes. He wants the good things in life made a bit cheaper! An Englishman hardly ever sees a bottle of whisky these days, and soon he won't be able to have a smoke. Takes him twenty years to pay for his house. But I never hear about these things in the new order. Yet they're just what helps the ordinary chap to keep going, the sugar in his cup of tea. It's the things we live on and enjoy that matter.'

'Sheer materialism!' exclaimed Corder. 'Water with berries in it. Caliban.'

He leaned forward, stabbing the air with his cigarette.

'Do you think Britain will ever be the same again? We've been in battle together. From the king to the coster at the corner; we've all taken a hammering. And everybody's trusted everybody else not to weaken. Do you think nothing's going to come out of all that?'

Not often had Mr Bunting seen Corder so much in earnest. As a rule he seemed not to be earnest about anything. His face had grown leaner of late, his gestures sharper. His house at Purley had been blown to pieces, with his treasured library of half-crown classics. He had been bombed out of his temporary home at Croydon, and had passed through experiences about which he would say nothing. He had grown paler and finer, and more vehemently fiery, his tension that of a compressed spring.

Now he leaned forward, and spoke as one who goes below the surface facts of life to the very pith and marrow of his faith, and finds words and intonation to move his hearer. 'Whoso sheds his blood with me this day shall be my brother,' he said, speaking with unusual passion. 'That's what I think of as I go about the streets of

London.'

Mr Bunting stirred his coffee and drank it off. To import such depth of feeling into a lunch-hour conversation gave him a curious discomfort. He could feel these things, but he could never talk about them; could never listen without composing his features as for a sermon or a grace. So after a fitting silence he looked at his watch and said: 'Time's up, Joe.'

They walked towards Brockleys, the siren screeching its warning above the din of traffic. A few pedestrians paused, staring into the sky, but most of them continued unperturbed. No one scurried underground for the siren now; it had been officially reprimanded, and put in place: it was only an 'alert'. But Corder cursed it with flowery epithets derived, Mr Bunting assumed, from the eternally applicable works of Shakespeare.

The shop recalled him to his personal problems. He had arranged with the office boy to side-track any wire from Elgin, and there, on the cubby-hole desk, lay a yellow envelope, the result of this collusion, proof that the office boy could be relied on in any arrangement that was illicit. Though by no means unexpected, it made Mr Bunting's pulse quicken as no telegram had done for months. He wondered whether Corder could descend from the abstractions of the new order and advise him on this homely matter of Turner and the flue connections. He doubted whether Corder's advice would be practical, even if it were comprehensible. Still, asking for advice isn't the same thing as taking it.

'Joe!' he called, and closing the cubby-hole door behind him, produced the telegram. 'I'm in a bit of a difficulty with this chap at Elgin. It's Turner. What do you think he's done this time?'

He proceeded to explain, going right back to the receipt of McCall's order in July, laying the foundation of his story firmly and in detail, and proceeding, with some unavoidable digressions and repetitions, to add further detail, tapping the yellow envelope on his palm meanwhile, and gazing fixedly at his friend, exhorting him to be patient; he was coming to the point in question.

'Why not open it and see what it says? Not all these limbs and outward flourishes.'

'I'm only telling you,' said Mr Bunting, hurt that Corder should think this momentous affair devoid of interest. 'If it's a cancellation, Joe, Turner will get the sack. We paid five pounds carriage on that lot,' and, sighing, he unfolded the tissue and read its message:

'Regret to inform you that Sergeant-Pilot C R Bunting...'

For a second Mr Bunting stared, petrified; then desk and partition lurched towards him, the clock in the distance and the ceiling overhead revolved dizzily, and all was shut out in a falling blackness.

He became aware of voices and faces, the faces near, the voices afar off, and of a peculiarly close impression of the legs of the cubby-hole desk and of a smell of dust in his nostrils.

He stirred; glanced from face to face, and felt a slight shame. 'I'm all right,' he said struggling. 'Be all right in a minute.'

'Take it easy, George. Boy's gone for a drink.'

'I'm all right,' said Mr Bunting, levering himself into a sitting position. He felt a saltiness on his upper lip, drew his hand across it, and realised his nose was bleeding. He tried to think what had happened, strove to gather his thoughts together. But nothing came except a sensation of dizziness, and he sank back defeated.

Then, without effort, the truth floated into his mind. It was Chris. He remembered: Chris was dead.

It came to him, a fact in all its bareness, like something he read over and over again without grasping its full meaning. It amazed him that he felt no terrible emotion, only this stunned feeling. Suddenly, he thought of his wife, and with a sobbing intake of his breath averted his face from those above him.

Corder took the jug and pushed everybody outside.

'Let me help you up, George.' With difficulty Corder got him on to the stool and propped him against the partition.

'Be all right in a minute, Joe,' repeated Mr Bunting. He wondered what had happened exactly to Chris; what the telegram had really said. He looked round for it, felt in his pockets helplessly, and abandoned the effort. All virtue seemed to have been drained out of him. Presently the fumes of hot tea encouraged him to drink, which he did slowly, pouring out a second cup with some spilling.

'I've got to tell the missus, Joe,' he said, and unashamedly broke into weeping. 'I don't know what to do.'

'Rest a bit, and then go home. That's the best thing.'

'There's some galvanised sheeting. Mr Bickerton said – '

'Never mind about that. Take it easy. We're all sorry, George.'

'Yes,' said Mr Bunting simply. Home seemed a long way off, at the end of an arduous and complicated journey. He drank off the rest of the tea, thinking of the difficulty of the journey as an ordeal that had to be endured sooner or later.

'I'll ring up Ernest to meet you at Kilworth station and to tell his mother.'

Mr Bunting bit his trembling lip. 'That bloody Hitler!' he burst out passionately, and Corder heard a confused vehement muttering behind a crumpled handkerchief.

For a time Mr Bunting became still again; Corder watched him anxiously but said no word. He was able to give his friend no other comfort than his presence. Presently, pale beneath his gingerishness, Mr Bunting rose. He understood he was free to go off duty; it was Mr Bickerton's express desire. This seemed to comfort him, for he had never asked the firm for favours, and to leave the shop at three o'clock was a departure from a lifetime's standards. Corder gave him his hat and coat, his attaché case, and his umbrella, and wiped the blood smear from his nostrils, Mr Bunting suffering these attentions passively like a child.

The closing of the cubby-hole door behind him seemed to mark the end of something; of what he did not know, but there was significance in it. He looked at the desk and stool as though they belonged to someone else, his past self, a man who until now had not known sorrow.

He walked through the salesroom averting his glance from those of other men. The porter held the door open for him and, as he turned towards the station, he met Turner with his new-bought *Standard*.

There was brightness in Turner's eyes, a jauntiness in his step. His timid spirit cared naught just now for any breach of discipline. Seeing Mr Bunting, he waved and came towards him.

'He's safe! He's all right. Look! It's in the papers.'

Mr Bunting felt his heart quicken at these incredible tidings. Turner was panting with excitement; his thin hands clutched at his lapels and shook and trembled.

'Safe! Thank God!' Turner panted. 'It's in the stop-press.'

Mr Bunting bent over the paper but he could read nothing. The news came to him in gasps from Turner.

'They've all been landed at a Scottish port. Picked up by a cruiser. Every man off the *Badger*.'

'I'm glad!' said Mr Bunting huskily, feeling something die within him. He struggled to add something to this, but Turner was no longer there, had gone on his gleeful way to Brockleys. Finding himself looking into nothing but the passing traffic, he walked on towards the station.

At Kilworth a figure detached itself from the group of people waiting at the barrier, and Ernest, looking pale and strained, came towards him. Mr Bunting had an impression of his face being closely scanned. They moved away a few yards and he got out his important question.

'Have you told mother?'

Ernest nodded. Mr Bunting's momentary feeling of relief at once gave way to deeper fears.

'How is she? How did she take it?'

Ernest did not answer at once but turned towards the street. They walked some way in silence, Mr Bunting's mind filling with forebodings till the unbearable suspense made him take Ernest roughly by the sleeve and compel him to halt and face him.

'I don't know how she took it, dad. She just stood and stared and – ' His voice broke and his features twitched.

'Steady, Ernest, steady. Don't do to weaken. We've got to think of your mother.'

'Yes,' said Ernest simply, and added: 'Evie's there.'

'Ah!' breathed Mr Bunting receiving the first bit of comfort these last hours had brought him. They walked on again. 'It's your mother we've got to think of,' he said as though repeating a watchword, and he glanced sideways at his son, who was walking with eyes lowered, his raincoat collar ruffled against his neck, looking unutterably depressed. Mr Bunting stifled a sigh. They seemed to keep on walking endlessly, as one does in a dream through an unreal world. Then all at once he found himself at the green and white gate, the moment of ordeal rushing towards him. With the slightest pause he pushed the gate open and went forward.

Evie met him in the doorway. Her glance, like Ernest's, seemed to pause upon and scrutinise his every feature.

'She's all right. She's been awfully brave.'

He nodded and watched her go down the path to join Ernest, then he went into the hall and dragged off his coat. Through the living room door he could see the table laid for tea. There was the familiar snowy cloth and the gleaming cups and the fire glowing brightly as it always was when he got home. But there was no sight nor sound of Mary.

'Mary!' he called; then louder, 'Mary!' Instinctively he turned towards the kitchen, and there he saw her, standing by the sink in her working dress and apron. There was something passive in her attitude, something weak and defenceless yet strong in fortitude, that touched him with a moment of vision. Patiently standing there in her workaday surroundings, with her roughened hands, and her pale ageing face, she seemed to typify the chief of war's victims throughout the ages, the mother of the slain. She might have been any mother in any country at war.

At the meeting of their eyes the tension snapped. Her hands moved with a pitiful gesture, and the next instant she was sobbing on his coat. He got her on to the battered old kitchen chair, and there for some minutes she wept without restraint, whilst he bent over her murmuring half-formed words and sentences. Presently she quietened, and raised her head and looked into his eyes.

'We got to go on living, dearie,' he said simply. 'Got to bear up. Best way we can.'

She seemed too preoccupied in her reading of his face to hear him, but took a corner of her apron and gently wiped a faint smear from his upper lip.

'Are you all right, George?'

'Me? Yes. I'm all right. Why?'

She looked at him doubtfully; he thought the tears were going to well into her eyes again. Then she said: 'You'll want your tea,' and got up, and with her habitual care brewed the tea and carried in the plates.

With some anxiety he watched her mechanically carrying out these duties, giving her mind to them, it seemed, with an effort. When she paused in the kitchen he turned his head and listened. But the comfort of his chair and the warmth of the fire induced an overwhelming weariness in him. He leaned forward, his chin in his hands, staring and thinking.

She touched him on the shoulder.

'I don't want anything,' he said, turning a bleak face.

'You'll need something to keep you going, dear.'

'Just a cup of tea, then.'

She hesitated, then put the cup into his hand, and brought him a plate and stood beside him till he began to eat and drink. As though this relieved her of some deep anxiety she smiled suddenly and with a lovely tenderness.

'It must have been dreadful for you, George.'

'It's not me,' he choked. 'It's you.'

Gently she shook her head. She knew that as wife and mother she must be the source of comfort. 'We've got to go through the dark days together. It helps when you've got somebody.'

He sat that evening by the fireside. His wife and Julie had gone to bed. The blow had fallen, and in that sense the worst was over. The slow recovery must set in now, and time's lenitive assuage the pain. 'Absalom!' he murmured. It always had to be Absalom, the best of his sons, the one most dearly loved. He had loved Chris. Had Chris known? He wondered. He thought of their last evening together, of their talk in the bedroom. Chris had surely thought something of his father. But he was thoughtless, only a boy, scarce reached twenty.

They said youth was the golden time of life, but as Mr Bunting sat there considering his own life all the best of it seemed to lie this side of twenty. His earlier self he thought of as quite another person; an identity so different from the middle-aged changeling he had become, so eager and so hopeful, that he could think of the boy he used to be almost with affection. But all the best of life lay on this side. The bread he had eaten with joy, the wine he had drunk with a merry heart, and the days he had lived joyfully with the wife he loved, all these lay this side of twenty. And Chris had surrendered them. For no New Order either; Chris had no more thought of New World Orders than his father had. He had died fighting to protect his home and family, and the few miles of England around Kilworth that he had learnt to love as a boy.

And now he was dead. Every thought returned and dissolved into that irrevocable fact. Never more would they hear him come whistling up the path.

SIXTEEN

MR BUNTING'S RETURN to business after Chris's death was an ordeal for which he had to brace himself, pausing outside the swing doors to rearm his spirit. But he walked through the salesroom to the cubby-hole apparently unnoticed. Corder, divining that all his need was to be left alone, had protected him from repetitions of the same ineffectual words. He plunged into his work, for business had to go on, and thinking of lesser things would help him to forget greater ones.

Leaning plumply against his desk on the first day of his return he went through his correspondence with his habitual care. But he grasped the meaning of written messages with difficulty; something escaped him, as a sound escapes the deaf however hard they strain. He was not yet his real self; his real self, he recalled, was amazingly quick in grasping what a customer wanted.

Frequently during these early days he found himself standing trancelike, some train of business thought having merged into a speculation as to how Mary got through the days alone. It was hard for her, ever in the same place, with all Chris's things about her. Recalling himself with a start, he would look over the partition at the clock, and finding it had not moved, compare it with his watch, not able to understand that these trances were but momentary. Then he would focus his attention doggedly upon his letters, reading them slowly and carefully till everything grew clear to him.

Almost the first person at the firm to speak to him directly was Mr Bickerton. He called at the cubby-hole before going to his office upstairs, and Mr Bunting received him with a conscious stiffening of moral fibre. Standing, he listened to his chief's words; they were sincere and kindly, they were everything that words could be, and what could anyone bring him now but unavailing words? Mr Bunting listened, enduring them patiently, his glance steadily adhering to his blotter till the chief ceased speaking. Then he looked up and said:

'Thank you, sir. 'Preciate it. Course, nobody knows what it means to lose a son till they lose one of their own. I don't expect them to, really. It's something his mother and me have to face, not losing heart, if you understand what I mean, sir.'

Had he known it, he was touched during these few minutes with true and natural dignity, as a man may wear laurels on one occasion in his lifetime.

'That's true,' said Mr Bickerton; 'we are the ones who know. We must carry on and not lose heart.'

He was gone. His words, echoing in Mr Bunting's mind, made at length a lucid pattern.

'Joe,' he began, crossing to the carpet room. 'Has the Ancient Mariner lost a boy in the war?'

'Yes; didn't you know? Quite early on. That's why his wife used to come to see him.'

Thoughtfully, Mr Bunting walked back to his desk. Thinking over the past months, he could not remember any day when Mr Bickerton had appeared at Brockleys looking one whit different from his normal self; immaculate, precise, terse, and searching as an admiral. The blow had struck him with an inward wound, his pride had covered up the scars. He was like one of those old Stoics or Spartans (Mr Bunting's history was confused) or those aristocrats who examined the headman's axe without a shiver. 'Old school tie, I suppose,' he murmured, uttering these words for the first time without scorn. There were some strange people about, tough; they amazed him, he could never rise to such heights himself. He knew truly that he had little courage.

From a hook in the partition hung his gas mask, the only one at Brockleys. Though its presence marked his distrust of Hitler, Mr Bunting was, in a general way, no longer intensely interested in gas masks. His civilian gas mask hung there because he had been given another one at home.

After Chris's death his first act had been to ask Mr Rollo to enrol him for more active duties. He was quietly insistent; he brushed aside the argument that Kilworth was a safe area. There was a gap in the ranks and, so far as lay in his power, he meant to fill it. He was now a sort of clerk and telephonist at the control centre, with a special kind of gas mask in a sacking bag and a tin hat like Oskey's, though not so ostentatiously carried about. He sat there three evenings every week and came home early morning to snatch a short sleep, except when night alerts delayed him.

Mrs Bunting tried to dissuade him from enrolling at the centre. It was, she argued, too much for him, he would be going past his strength. But Julie gave her mother private counsel.

'Let him if he wants to. I know how he feels – as though he's not being used enough. I'm joining the ambulance drivers! I'm fed up just working in the Food Office and knitting.'

'You know what father says.'

Julie sighed. Mr Bunting was opposed to her following him into the ARP service. 'Can't leave mother alone in the house night after night, dearie,' he said.

'Just knitting!' exclaimed Julie. 'I'd like to knit a halter for Adolf, the *schmutzig* old *drecksack*.'

'Julie!'

''Tisn't swearing, mother – it's German.'

'It doesn't sound very ladylike to me.'

'Course it isn't, darling. I learnt it in case I meet any parachuters.'

What Mr Bunting's thoughts were during the days that followed Chris's death none of his family really knew. In times of trouble he always retired into himself. One could feel he was recovering slowly, was sorting out his thoughts, making mental adjustments, and coming to terms with the new situation. That he had joined civil defence because Chris had been killed in the war Mrs Bunting understood; she gathered enough, too, of his motives to understand he wanted to help finish what Chris had begun. A great deal of Mr Bunting's loyalty was transferred to his son. If Chris had died, his death must not prove in vain. Out of half sentences and gruntulous hintings, she pieced together this much of her husband's way of thinking. She watched him anxiously when he was not aware of her.

He had often paused in his gardening operations to look beyond his own small plot and survey the landscape as a whole. Though London-born he had grown attached to Essex as he grew older. Kilworth was set in beautiful country and he had learned to love it. That was patriotism, he supposed; loving one's country, its soil and trees, the smell and taste of it, wanting to preserve it and pass it on. Barging into somebody else's country wasn't patriotism. They could never have got Chris to volunteer for that, only to defend his own. Sometimes he watched the sparrows feeding at his birdtable with a sense of comradeship beyond his powers of definition, becoming intensely interested in them for several minutes. Sometimes he would cease working abruptly, feeling that some wraith or essence of Chris was near him. There were moments when Chris seemed very close; wherever his eye fell, there a memory stirred. All these sensations came to him simply because Chris's death was recent. He understood that; for he well knew how completely as time goes on the dead become forgotten. To Ernest at sixty – what would Chris be? No more than a legend, a figure dimly seen amongst the bright memories of youth.

At such moments, when all the doors of his mind were open, grief would enter; with a strained face he would go into the garden shed and sitting on an upturned box lose himself in a fit of sobbing. Presently he would emerge again, and be seen bending over his more hopeful plants, pricking the earth with a trowel or pressing it around their roots, his face hidden. When Julie or her mother spoke to him, he looked up with red-rimmed eyes which besought them not to notice. Everybody was very good to him, he thought.

Oskey went so far as to dig up his entire crop of potatoes. Mr Bunting had been taking them up as wanted, one root at a time. Going out one Saturday to consider what he ought to do about this task, postponed for lack of energy, he found Oskey dexterously lifting the last root, and it was observable that his fork had not speared a single tuber.

'Whether you like it or not, Bunting, they're all up. What's the sense of leaving spuds to rot in wartime?' He leaned on his fork, like Gideon upon his spear, to count his fallen enemies. 'Not a bad lot considering the soil don't suit King Edwards.'

'They're a jolly good lot,' said Mr Bunting, who, after all, had grown them. His eye ran over the rows of disinterred potatoes. He was amazed at the prodigious numbers; it was a crop unprecedented at Laburnum Villa.

'What's the matter?' said Oskey. 'Looking if there's one missing? 'Cos they're all up, not one left in for once. Potatoes, with you, Bunting, are like horseradish. Once you plant 'em, you never get rid of 'em. But none of these'll come up next year.'

Oskey scraped his fork with a workmanlike air of having for once settled the potato question. He would not next season be offended by seeing odd potato plants struggling to rebirth amongst his neighbour's peas and beans. Unlike Mr Bunting, he could never appreciate these fortuitous resurrections nor see them as a sort of bonus.

'Thank you, Oskey. Very decent of you.' They hung side by side whilst Mr Bunting lit his pipe and wondered whether the proper scientific thing with freshly dug potatoes was to let them lie to dry and harden, or to store them in a clamp whilst they were moist. He imagined Oskey was waiting for some indication that he intended doing the wrong thing so that he could give correction. At the moment, the expert's eye was travelling up and down the Bunting garden. Here and there it came to rest and grew puzzled; then moved on as though the brain behind it had solved another riddle.

Oskey moved his heavy feet and cleared his throat. He was in process of leaving.

'Don't forget to plant out your broccoli, it's overdue. Eighteen inches apart, with a bit of bonemeal.'

'I'll remember. Got some very decent broccoli.'

'You'd have done better with Cobden's King,' remarked Oskey. What Mr Bunting had planted he did not know, but it was obviously not Cobden's King. 'I always plant Cobden's King myself. It's the best variety for heavy loam.'

All Oskey's kindnesses were purposely heavy-handed, as though he had an instinct that this made it easier for his neighbour to accept them. In fact, too much consideration of his feelings seemed to Mr Bunting to underline the fact that he was a man oppressed with sorrow. He in no way wished to appear ungracious, but he disliked the modulated voice in which certain people addressed him, and the too punctilious attention to his wants on every hand. It was all well meant, and he could not defend his antagonism to it, but the dislike was there. He felt people were anxious to help him to 'bear up' in his troubles when he was quite prepared to bear up and keep a stout heart in his lonely way. He had taken a knock, it was true, but he was not broken. Behind the physical shock he felt a strengthened spirit, a determination to carry on, that nothing now could weaken. At home he had to dissipate what was to him an overwhelming solicitude by being matter-of-fact and even occasionally grumpy. That was the best thing. Once you gave way you were lost. It only needed a word, an intonation, to break down Mrs Bunting's guard; she lived continually on the edge of tears.

When they were lying together in the dark he could be tender and she gave her grief its rein, but at other times it was better to keep his tone carefully normal, and do what he could to help her with odd jobs. But he observed her closely and with anxiety. She had grown much more faded, she went about with a set countenance, one straggle of hair across her brow brushed aside again and again with a patient ineffectiveness. When he spoke there was often a pause before she answered, as though she did not immediately hear him. Then she would turn, and, like the brave running up of a flag, he would get her smile.

The air raid warning punctuated domestic life so frequently now that the words 'The warning' were no longer shouted from room to room, but were passed on as conversationally as changes in the weather. But the siren irritated Mr Bunting a good deal; it was a voice that timed its howlings for most inconvenient moments. He could hardly put his feet on the fender without hearing it, and it never failed to catch him in the bath or to interrupt the most interesting talks on the wireless. Frequently he declined to believe the siren had sounded, not having heard it himself, even when he put his head out of the window. Frequently, too, he would forget the siren in his reading, and would hear Julie call from the staircase window.

'He's bopped a drom. Did you hear a bop, daddy?'

Whereupon Mr Bunting would breathe in and out in a sizzling fashion, and be on the point of rebuking his daughter for mutilating the king's English, till he remembered this was not at the moment of the first importance.

'Come away from the window.'

'I'm doing a bit of spotting. Listen! Can you hear our chaps after him?'

'How the dickens can I read?' demanded Mr Bunting, lowering the paper to his knees, and staring at his wife.

'He's dropping 'em in the fields. Got the breeze up, the big twerp.'

'That girl's language, George. You'll have to speak to her.'

'Me speak to her? I like that!' His snort had an ironic note. When he wasn't accused of being 'always on to Julie' he was accused of not sufficiently correcting her. It was better, he thought, for her to be light-hearted even if she were also a trifle silly. Grim and gay, was what Winston said; got it out of Shakespeare probably, Mr Bunting thought. Certain of the Premier's words rang in his ears. 'Never had so much been owed by so many to so few.' Chris was one of those few. He had fallen in no frontier skirmish, but in a moment of destiny. When grief passed, pride remained.

And there was still Ernest. Very sincerely did Mr Bunting try to understand and grow closer to his remaining son. Ernest was still exempt from military service. Whether that was something to be glad or sorry for, Mr Bunting did not know. The boy was doing what the authorities required of him, but he tried to pass on to him something out of his troubled meditations. For the admonitions of a father matured in the mind like wine in a dark cellar; one thought they were forgotten, but they ripened silently in some corner of the brain and came home to a man's bosom, with full potency, only years after they were spoken. That was how his own father's words came back to him, and so his might come back to Ernest.

All this talk of war aims and new orders, and brave new worlds to be, were to Mr Bunting no more than echoes of older promises broken and forgotten. However man moved forward, his place would still be on this earth; there would be no world of gods feasting on nectar and ambrosia. Man must break the clod, sow, reap, and store, must plan and build, buy and sell. His tools, his food, his needs, his joys and sufferings till the world wore out, would be what they now were and had been always. Pursuing dreams and fancies, men like Ernest forgot the foundations they must build on, even the things for which a little while before they had fought with bitter courage and suffered to defend. In the hope that what he said might someday be remembered, Mr Bunting addressed his son with quiet but passionate conviction.

'All these ideas, Ernest, they're all right, I speck, and I don't condemn them. But they're not the things that matter most. The 'sential thing is to see it don't happen again. To see that these Germans don't ever have the power to make it happen again. These young Nazis, Ernest, they'll all be men twenty years from now. What do you think they're going to be like? Give 'em what you call a square deal and you'll live to see your sons in khaki.'

'But, dad, we've got to come to some sort of terms with these people someday. We live on the same earth together. There must be some decent Germans.'

'Yes,' admitted Mr Bunting, in no way deflected from his reasoning. 'You'll find all the decent Germans at the top after this war, like they were after the last. You won't be able to find a Nazi anywhere. And when you've kissed and made friends, lent 'em your money, and cut down your armaments, you'll wake up to find the decent Germans have disappeared, and the same old Huns have got in power again. Us older men have seen it happen, but we shan't be here to warn you then.'

Ernest was silent, conscious of his father's deep sincerity and of his anxiety to be heeded.

He went on, not looking directly at Ernest but with a glance that wandered introspectively from point to point as it did when he was very serious.

'I think sometimes that even after this the Germans'll try again if we don't watch 'em. There's millions of youngsters over there had their minds poisoned under Hitler. And it's you idealists that get taken advantage of. I'm not against the things you believe in; I'd like to see the country made a better place to live in. But, first of all, make it safe, and take no chances.'

'Yes,' said Ernest, and for a moment pondered his father's words. There were bound to be difficulties with post-war Germany, eradicating the false philosophy and lies. The prevention of another war depended, surely, on doing that very thing.

'We can't go on fighting them for ever, dad. If we're going to have peace in Europe we've got to work for it from the moment we put down our arms. That's the mistake we made last time.'

'Not altogether,' said Mr Bunting. 'That wasn't the mistake. The mistake was that we forgot all we'd learnt in four years about the Germans. We not only put down our arms. We threw them away.'

SEVENTEEN

ERNEST AND EVIE sat side by side on two stools under the stairs. Her head lay against his shoulder, and he would have thought she slept, for it was past midnight, except that now and then he felt the tensing of her body as she listened, straining beyond the capacity of human hearing, for the approach of the loaded bombers. From time to time, through a chink in the letterbox, came a white flash. Then she started and he calmed her, saying:

'It's all right, dearest. Guns, I think.'

Never could Ernest remember being so utterly worn out in mind and body. Long hours at the laundry, strain and anxiety at home, aid post duties three nights out of seven, had brought him to the point when all he desired was to sink into a purely animal slumber. Tonight, his first free evening since the weekend, he had put his head heavily and thankfully on to the pillow, and felt himself falling blissfully asleep, when the screaming death-knell of the siren wakened him.

He arose and dressed in stoic calm, anxiously observing Evie, for her time was near and she needed all the love and care he had to give her. Now they sat side by side in darkness and discomfort, a twentieth-century Englishman and his wife, sheltering, he thought bitterly, like primitive savages from the beasts of the air.

He stared into the blackness of the hall, wondering if the world he had known would ever return. The security of a land at peace seemed wonderfully blessed when he looked back on it. It was like a vision of childhood, a time of innocent games and trivial pursuits, of un-noted and unvalued happiness. It had vanished so completely that Ernest could scarcely remember what it was like to walk along a lighted street.

During the past few years he had heard endless arguments and read endless articles on the trend of world affairs; but now once again he asked himself how the world had come to a point when, to preserve human liberty, men had been driven to this last expedient of bombing and sheltering and outfacing death beneath the stairs. But he knew the answer. Great nations had been content to watch the extinguishing of small ones, to see power pass into the hands of evil men, and murder and persecution go unchecked. The Christian nations had said no word, so long as these crimes were committed outside their own political boundaries. They had denied the brotherhood of man.

None of it had really moved Ernest, either. He had disapproved of it, of course, but it had not moved him. Only now, amidst the wreck of a faulty world, did his imagination reach out to the world as it might be – spacious, and full of sunlit dancing places, of joyful labour and leisure and beauty; ideas that were just that necessary shade in advance of attainable reality, to give imagination spur. But he had not thought of them before the war. All he had thought about was 'success' and 'efficiency,' the realisation of his own private and circumscribed Utopia, and the vanity of 'personal development'.

Now he sat with his young wife beneath the stairs, life and death hanging upon chance.

'Listen!' Evie sat up, gripping his arm.

'I can't hear anything.'

A succession of dull thuds sounded in the distance, like the dropping of enormous weights. The sound pricked him fully awake, he raised his head. There was a pause, then further heavy thuds. Devilishly methodical was the timing of these repetitions.

Evie shuddered. 'They're bombing Kilworth. What are they aiming at? There's nothing here.'

Ernest took her hand in his; they leaned forward together. There was a whir of engines soaring across the town, a burst of firing, then again the whir of engines on a different course. It was impossible to tell what was happening. Thus they sat for a long time, huddled and silent.

'They've passed over, I think,' he said, relaxing the tension.

Immediately there was an instant's terrible stillness. The house seemed to hold its breath; then came a whistling and a crash and the walls shook. From the street came the sound of shouting and hurrying feet.

'Someone's hurt!' He half rose, listening.

Evie burst out sobbing. 'I can't stand it! I can't! Dear God, help me!'

He put his arm about her and drew her close. He felt utterly helpless.

'Have courage, darling!'

He heard her murmuring a prayer. It was like a child's prayer; she clung to him like a child, so that his heart melted. But he could not pray as Evie did. He could not believe that prayer could deflect a bomb from its destined course. From where it was released, there it must fall. Courage was the thing; to endure if it so chanced, to die manfully if need be. For himself that was all that mattered.

If this was to be the end of life, he wondered what in it had been most worthwhile. Surely, only those moments of vision when it seemed a veil was rent, and all mundane things were seen for an instant to be unreal and transitory. It was then man realised his inward self. A chord of Beethoven, a sunset, the sight of beauty in the fields, or the ecstasy of love at home, called such moments forth. They lasted only for an instant, and lived for years in memory, golden grains amidst the chaff. By these and not by length of days was a man's life measured. Evie's prayer went up beside him like the heart cry of a child; but the only reachings out he knew were the aspirations of his spirit.

Sitting there, his dark eyes focused on the chink in the letterbox, Ernest was touched with an instinct deeper than thought, a communication too subtle for the mind. Every intense aspiration was a prayer. One prayed according to one's need and conscience. He could not with any faith ask God merely to preserve his life, for how, amidst a hail of bombs, could such a prayer be answered? But for the higher human qualities he could rightly pray; and for him there was only one intense desire. Silently, from his heart, and with perfect faith, Ernest uttered the first spontaneous prayer of his manhood, that he might be given the spiritual quality of courage.

He pressed Evie close to him and looked into the shadows, his eyes full of thought. She had ceased weeping, and lay limply against his shoulder. For a long time all was quiet. Suddenly his hat fell off the stand and rolled on its brim into a corner.

Both started and drew together, staring.

'What was that?'

'My hat, I think,' and there was a pause and some laughter that relaxed the tension.

'Mind you don't tread on it and ruin it,' she said, becoming housewifely. 'It's your best.'

The diversion of the hat seemed to ease the strain. All sound of gunfire had ceased. Evie sat up and wiped her eyes; he could feel her smiling at him in the darkness. He withdrew the stiffened arm that had been supporting her and asked:

'Feeling better?'

'Yes – a bit. I think I'll be all right.'

'Let me light a cigarette.' A match flickered, showing her white face.

'Wait! I think they're coming back.'

'Oh, damn!' He put out the match and listened.

Bombs began to fall. They sounded like the first ones, but somehow not so startling. They grew louder; came rapidly towards them, like a striding giant.

'They're coming nearer. They'll hit us.'

'No,' said Ernest.

As though to belie his words, a whistling crescendo hurtled over the roof, the door shook as if a giant hand tugged at its fastenings. The crockery on the Welsh dresser tinkled and slid on to the floor, and there came several detonations like body-blows viciously repeated.

'Stick to me,' said Ernest, between his teeth; but she slipped from his arms slowly, and the stool upset. He bent over her, flashing his torch, aware that the house had not, at all events, collapsed upon them. He did not recognise the face that looked up at him.

'You'll have to get the doctor. It's – it's – '

'But, my dear! I can't leave you here alone.'

'The doctor – '

He paused irresolute; his wits scattered. There was no one in the flat above, no friendly person near at hand. Frantically she shrieked at him:

'The doctor, you fool! Get the doctor. Don't you understand?'

'All right, dear, I'll go,' he said patiently, and rose and spread a coat carefully over her. Then he put on his raincoat and went to the door.

'Ernest!'

'Yes?' He came back and knelt beside her. Out of the darkness he felt her arms encircling his neck, and heard her whisper against his cheek: 'I'm sorry, I didn't mean it.'

'That's all right, sweetheart. I'll hurry.'

He closed the door and stood on the step, looking across the town. The lower rim of the sky was lurid with the flames of incendiary bombs. Above the blazing buildings, searchlights crept in converging cones, their reflections flickering ghostlike on lightless windows. Splashes of anti-aircraft shells dotted the sky with miniature lightning, and the crashing roar of it all seemed to shake the rooted earth.

As a picture of horror it was complete, and Ernest stood before it as though he looked upon the ultimate worst that organised evil could bring against his strength of spirit, and measured himself against it. Here at last was the naked weapon; here was raging the fight for the eternal verities in which his life was, and could be, of no account. Rising within him he felt the courage to endure and triumph which is man's sure proof of immortality.

As he stood there he heard the downward hurtle of a diving plane, and the random spattering of machine gun bullets on the roofs. He crouched against the door jamb, following the course of the invisible raider as it swept upwards to the safety of the clouds. It was as though he had seen some particularly odious exploit of an odious young man. Having seen this performance Ernest believed it, but it remained incomprehensible. That, he supposed, was German frightfulness in action. His lips curled. Not often had he felt such complete contempt as he did for that particular hooligan of the air.

He ran to the gate and turned swiftly up the road. Almost the first person he met was a woman in a cloak and a brimmed hat. Halting, he called after her.

'Are you a nurse?'

'Yes. Is someone hurt?'

Ernest discovered he was out of breath. 'My wife – the air raid.'

She seemed to recognise all the signs of a young husband in distress. Her voice, interrupting his gasping explanations, made light of his excitement.

'All right, young fellow. Take me to her.'

They entered the flat. He switched on the light and saw his visitor as a middle-aged, rosy, and competent-looking woman. Together they helped Evie upstairs to the bedroom.

'You're not afraid of being up here with all this going on outside?'

'Not likely! Got something else to think of. You get some hot water ready, and stay downstairs, young fellow. If I want you I'll shout.'

Ernest stood on the rug before the fireplace in a mood of peculiar perturbation. Irresistibly he crossed to the cupboard where they kept the whisky for Mr Bunting. He had often heard of husbands drinking whilst their wives were having babies, and thought it extremely callous. Nevertheless, he poured himself a good dose, and immediately felt better for it, though temporarily breathless. It occurred to him that if he had to go upstairs the nurse would smell his breath, and draw unfortunate conclusions. Even though he had taken to the whisky, he was not quite as other husbands. Hunting round he found Evie's bag of sweets, and took a mint lozenge; then he lit a cigarette to disguise the suspicious odour of the mint and stood, legs apart, listening to the movements of the woman overhead.

In the mirror he saw his image also listening and looking very white about the gills, he thought. He studied this image, made company of it. It was a responsive image; when he smiled it smiled back at him. He was going to be a father; the fellow in the mirror was going to be a father. Amazing! What did he care about air raids? Not, to use Evie's expression, an old tacket, whatever that was. A plane whooshed over the roof; he heard shells screaming upward and exploding with a muffled sound. He took up the glass to toast the silent reflection who looked, Ernest thought, a decent type of chap and, above all, intelligent. But the glass was empty. He discovered this first by trying to drink out of it, and then by holding it unsteadily against the light. Also by a slight giddiness as he replaced it on the table.

It came to him that he was a callous brute like all other callous brutes. He was full of contrition which passed almost instantly into anger against the Germans. 'Swine!' he muttered. 'Swine!' He went out to listen on the stairs, came back and looked round the room, his spirits running swiftly down to zero.

Everything that was the work of Evie's hands met him with an appealing look, her embroidered cushions, her rug, her knitted jumper. From all these her gentleness and patience spoke to him. They had just now a forlorn appearance of having been finally abandoned. He pressed his hands together in an agony of fear, and listened between the bursts of gunfire. But no foot moved upstairs. He went into the hall and climbed halfway up the stairs. The balustrade vibrated beneath his hand and he heard the whizz of falling splinters, but did not heed it. The raid was dying down, he thought. It was strange to remember that it had been going on all these hours, ever since he and Evie got up to shelter in the hall. Ages ago, that seemed now. He felt that she had travelled far from him since then.

With a beating heart he climbed higher till he stood in front of the landing window, afraid to venture farther. Drawing the curtains aside, he saw the first grey streaks of morning and felt his heart leap at the sound of a baby's cry.

Thus, puny and before his time, Ernest's son was born into a world struggling between light and darkness.

Summoned by the departing nurse, Mrs Bunting arrived early in the morning, and with her came Julie and Mr Bunting, all looking weary and grimy and dishevelled.

'What an awful time for you both!'

'It's all over now, mother,' said Ernest. Though his head ached and his mouth felt dry, he was full of thankfulness.

The front of Mr Bunting's suit was caked with mud. He had been obliged to get down to it quickly, had fallen flat on his face in the street to avoid being blown to pieces.

(He knew the exact spot; had mentally affixed a commemorative tablet on it). Patiently, between gulps of tea, he repeated what he obviously thought should be conceded without endless reiteration, that it had been unavoidable. Laburnum Villa was undamaged; nothing more serious had happened close at hand than the shattering of Oskey's greenhouse roof. The house that morning had been the scene of a reunion that brought relief to all concerned when Mr Bunting, anxious and bedraggled, returned from the control room.

'Thank God we're safe!' murmured Mrs Bunting. 'Especially Evie!' It was terrible in the town, they said; fires blazing everywhere and no end of casualties.

'Yes, Kilworth's taken a packet,' said Mr Bunting, draining off his tea and rising to put an end to the discussion. 'Must get off to business. Come on, Julie.'

Left alone with his mother, Ernest sat down to rest. He had a heavy day in front of him. Wednesday was always a heavy day at the laundry. Mrs Bunting enjoyed the luxury of mothering him, setting a stool for his feet and bringing his breakfast on a tray to the table corner. She had gone through the air raid sitting with a set face in the dugout. Having endured the loss of Chris, she was prepared to endure anything the war could bring to her. But the birth had given her a new life to reach out to and to care for, and Ernest saw her old smile make its reappearance.

Before he left for work he tiptoed upstairs and looked at Evie and her baby lying fast asleep. The joy of fatherhood was not completely dimmed by the happenings around him. Among tremendous events it seemed not the least tremendous, another human birth with all its unpredictable possibilities. He came downstairs, a mist of emotion clouding his vision, bade his mother goodbye and set off for the laundry. When he came to it he found nothing but a heap of ashes.

The sight pulled him up with a catching of the breath; then he walked slowly round surveying the wreckage. The outer walls still stood precariously, but a glance told him there was nothing to be saved. Twisted wheels and bent shafting lay under scorched tiles and timber, a smoking, sodden mass. He picked his way through it, recognising a machine here and there and wondering how everything could have become so displaced and tangled. Poking about the debris of his own office, he saw one or two private treasures: a book, a picture, a broken flower vase; he let them lie.

All he had worked for lay at his feet – a black ruin. It was like the ruin of men's hopes in the world around him. One had to build on the ashes or succumb. But he felt no sharp sense of shock as he would have done earlier in the war. In a war waged as this was being waged, it seemed the most natural thing that a man should find his own wrecked business amongst the discoveries of the morning.

He saw Mr Eagle, muffled in his greatcoat, hobbling towards him on his stick, and felt for him a great pity that stifled utterance. They stood side by side for a moment without speaking. Then Eagle said: 'Well, that's the end of the laundry.'

The words were so at variance with Ernest's thoughts that he turned in surprise. 'The end? Oh, no! It'll rise again. We'll build a new one.'

'You might, my boy, but not me.' The old man threw out his hands with a feeble gesture. 'I'm too old for new enterprises. Besides, there's nothing left to build on.'

Ernest tried to hearten him. 'It won't be rebuilding. It'll be something new and better. Better planned, with more sunlight in it and no dark corners.'

Ernest saw it rising before him as he spoke, a building of steel and glass, compact but well proportioned, with no sooty chimney stacks and clinker heaps. He saw it under a sunny sky, glinting white, with a suggestion of green lawns and shrubs around it, better far than the reality could ever be. But the inspiration of it warmed his heart. After the war, rebuilding would be opportunity and adventure, and not laundries only. His vision shifted; he saw other and vaster things, bright new things born out of the old worn-out ones.

'Ah! These ideas, Ernest,' exclaimed Eagle, quizzing him. Then his voice changed; he turned with a confiding air, his stiff fingers grasped Ernest's arm like claws. 'Hey, but I'd like to see it. Yes, I'd like to see it, Ernest boy. I'm getting old, but I'll have to hang on, eh?' His eyes peered out of his wrinkles, eager and anxious.

'I hope you will, sir,' replied Ernest, and stood immersed in thoughts that had travelled far from the ruins at his feet which he felt were significant rather than important. Compared with other things, the burning of the laundry was, indeed, quite trivial, but it was part of the great world argument. Brutality made no converts. Not by these methods would men be made to accept a way of life they did not believe in. Some day he would bring his son to this spot and tell him how, on the day of his birth, he stood here and vowed that out of all the mess and muddle he would help to build something better.

Meanwhile that was not the issue. If anything was to survive, his duty lay elsewhere. There were things in life that had to be fought for; they could not be preserved by non-combatants. At last Ernest saw his duty straight as a furrow.

'There's one thing, sir. I'm liberated at last. I'm free to join the army.'

'What? You're going to join?'

'I'm going into the infantry. I'm going to fight.'

Eagle blinked at him. 'To fight – *you*?' and his old puzzled regard came back. 'You're a rum fellow, Ernest. I could never understand you.'

'I'm going to fight,' repeated Ernest, and shut his teeth on further words. Whether there were decent Germans or not didn't matter; it had seemed important before, but not now. If there were men in Germany who thought as he did, and had weakly let themselves be silenced, he would fight for their liberation too.

A few echoes of *Mein Kampf* came back to him. In all its turgid wandering sentences he recalled no word that satisfied a single aspiration of the human soul. Its doctrine was a blood-stained mysticism, based on sophistry and fraud, setting up the State as a god. Men like himself were to cast away all individuality and merge themselves into a grey amorphous mass of assenting nonentities, dressing alike, thinking alike, moving with antic saluting and goose-stepping gestures, past the tribal leader. One would have thought such a mad conception would have been jeered out of existence at its birth.

Yet an entire nation had accepted it. All the authority and resources of a modern state had been organised to insinuate this perverted doctrine into millions of minds, and to the stifling of millions of consciences.

To Ernest, as he stood there, it seemed amazing that the ideals of the English-speaking races had never been preached with a tithe of the fervour that had attended the gospelling of one small clique of Nazi zealots. Neither Britain nor America had ever striven with such passion to instil into the minds of youth their national ideals. Yet these ideals represented everything that was man's brightest heritage: tolerance, justice, freedom for the individual mind. Only through these could there be any hope of human progress.

He put these thoughts from him.

'Goodbye, sir.'

'Goodbye, Ernest.'

Mr Eagle regarded him with a look of affection and farewell. There was a deadly calculated resolution observable in Ernest at times; he had a spirit for forlorn hopes and desperate assaults. No matter how many fell beside him Ernest would go on unswerving; if beaten to his knees he would crawl on, sustained by an idea. But he was slim, and not robust, his hands delicate almost as a girl's; he lived only on the fire within him.

'God keep you safe and bring you home again,' said Mr Eagle, and his voice had a gruffness and a huskiness beyond the ordinary, the grip of his talon fingers tightened with emotion. Whatever happened to this boy he felt that, on his side, it was the last goodbye. He stood amongst the ruins of the laundry watching Ernest striding energetically away.

EIGHTEEN

DOUGHTILY MR BUNTING set off every morning for London, where the bombs were dropping. His preparations for departure were made with conspicuous briskness. He brushed his bowler, rolled his umbrella, and packed his eleven-o'clock sandwiches in his attaché case to the accompaniment of a whistle like a blackbird's. One might have thought he was packing for Margate. All of which was designed to make light of Mrs Bunting's fears, but only made her go into the kitchen and wipe her eyes with a corner of her apron behind the door. There was a touch of feeling beyond the customary between them at the moment of goodbye.

Though Mr Bunting made light of the frequent raids, he had private moments of uneasiness. He started at unexpected noises, felt his heart sink, and all the breath go out of him. These sensations were brief; he recovered instantly. They were caused by the unexpected acceleration of motor engines, or gusts of wind, or the careless dropping of articles of ironmongery outside the cubby-hole. He blamed his nerves for such lapses as testily as he blamed his stomach for his indigestion, as though he found fault with portions of his physical apparatus not amenable to act of will.

The slow battering of London had no longer much interest as a carriage-window spectacle. There were many mornings when he travelled after insufficient sleep, and found even the *Siren* too great an effort. If he could get a corner seat, he tried relaxing according to the system described by that paper's medical correspondent. Once he dozed throughout the entire thirty minutes' journey, and was awakened by a fellow traveller at the terminus.

'There's an alert, sir.'

Mr Bunting thanked the stranger for his warning, and shook himself awake, pleased by his success with the relaxing exercise. He saw the sky to the north dotted with shell bursts, a handful only; some single Jerry mooching round. Coming in sight of Brockleys, he examined the building floor by floor, and window by window, as though he were inspecting his own property. All his old nerve and spirit flowed back in these familiar surroundings.

'Been lucky lately,' he told the porter, as he passed indoors with his habitual bustle.

Business was now confined to one or two departments – a mere trickle running through the others. But Mr Bunting was fully occupied. He was the oldest and most knowledgeable of the Brockley staff, and almost the only man of managerial status now left to them. He had climbed to a high place in his chief's regard. Other men might be quicker in understanding and execution, but none could be more painstaking or reliable. If he were sent into an unfamiliar department to dispatch a number of yards of a certain pattern of linoleum, Mr Bickerton could be certain, not only that he found the right material, but that he checked the label once more before cutting off the precise length asked for. He was as dependable as his own callipers. Often nowadays he was required to go into unfamiliar departments, but he never crossed into the carpets and rugs unless he had to. There were too many echoes of Brutus and Horatio sleeping incongruously amongst the piles of carpets, and there was no Joe Corder.

One of Mr Bickerton's tasks just now was to reconstitute records destroyed in the bombing of his office. One or two evasive customers were inclined to dispute details of deliveries and, to cope with them, he relied largely on Mr Bunting's pertinacity in getting at the roots of things. By making calculations from the amount of stock in hand, by cross-examining the packers, and even doing a little detective work amongst the empties in the cellar, it was possible to piece together a large proportion of the invoice file. But on all matters concerning the ironmongery department they relied entirely on Mr Bunting's pocketbook.

Pursuing this task, Mr Bickerton, portly and pink-headed, sat at one side of the table in the upstairs office, with Mr Bunting, also portly but coarser in texture, at the other. These were the occasions when they met almost as equals, for the chief had long since ceased to be tersely authoritative when they went into discussion.

Keeping his place with his finger, and steering past such items as verses, mottoes, and recipes for tasty dishes which were intermingled with the ironmongery jottings, Mr Bunting read aloud:

'Forty at three-eighths mesh.' Sensing the familiar pause of incomprehension on the other side of the table, he added: 'Netting, sir, wire netting.' He hoped this made it clear.

'I see. Continue.'

'I thought I heard a – bomb – drop,' remarked Mr Bunting, pronouncing these words very distinctly because he occasionally stumbled over them, being infected with the silly distortions of his daughter.

'Over there, sir.' He made a vague indication with the pocketbook.

A faint but active humming like a mosquito hung between them.

'Amazing how the Huns persist in this sort of thing,' remarked Mr Bickerton, pushing back his chair and crossing to the window. There he stood peering out whilst Mr Bunting sharpened the end of his pencil, and reflected pleasantly that it was Saturday, and the sun nicely coming out.

'Amazing type, Hitler, don't you think?' said Mr Bickerton, crossing to the fireplace. 'I don't suppose he's ever known any decent people. Megalomaniac really.'

'You're right there, sir,' said Mr Bunting, mentally endorsing half of this description and making a note of the remainder so he could look it up in the *bijou*.

'Of course, we've had autocratic rule in England. In the past, of course. That divine right business. Mistaken idea; but the fellows were at least gentlemen. We never submitted to a pack of cads.'

'He was only a house-painter, sir. Not that that's anything against him. Still, it's a queer thought; if you'd been over there ten years ago you might have seen old Hitler doing up a bit of eaves-spout!'

Mr Bickerton's eye rested on his manager thoughtfully. 'I suppose so. I never thought of it. Shall we continue?'

'Might as well, till they get a bit nearer.'

Mr Bickerton sat down, and as though brushing aside some thought of his companion's limitations, said: 'Ah! You're a good fellow, Bunting.'

'Me, sir?' His look was one of sharp surprise; a moment later it turned to a flush of pleasure. 'Not at all,' he remarked. He was considerably embarrassed.

Coming downstairs he found the shop closed, for the chief had no regard for time. The only sound was a pail being moved from point to point, and the rubbing and humming of Mrs Musgrave beginning her happy labours of the Saturday afternoon. Feeling pleased with the compliment still maturing inside him, he greeted her cheerfully and refrained from pointing out that the brass yard measures fixed to the counters needed no attention and that the chief result of polishing them was a lot of messy stinking polish on everybody's fingers.

'Mr Bunting,' she said, in a tone of confidence. 'You must excuse me not mentioning it before, but I was right sorry to hear about your boy being killed.'

He was instantly on his guard. 'Thank you, Mrs Musgrave.'

'Yes, I was. Right sorry. Poor boy, and all on account of that Hitler. Him so young, too. He was a pilot, wasn't he?'

'Yes,' he said, his eyes adhering fixedly to the counter where Mrs Musgrave's duster went to and fro.

She appeared to compose herself for a friendly sympathetic chat. 'And how does his poor mother take it? It must be dreadful for her. How did it happen?'

He perceived that his feelings were to be wrung. He had an inspiration.

'How's Charlie?' he asked suddenly.

'Didn't I tell you?' She relinquished the duster and leaned her diminutive body across the counter. 'They dropped a bomb right where he's camping last week. Right in the same field, the devils.'

'Was he hurt?'

'No, but he heard it go off. I reckon the War Office ought to move troops out of a place like that. Don't you?'

'They certainly should,' said Mr Bunting gravely, passing on to the cubby-hole where he put on his hat and coat, and stood for a few minutes still and silent, disturbed by the stirrings of old griefs. Then, as though one of his simple mottoes came back to him, he took a deep breath, and walked through the salesroom to mingle with the crowds of London's streets and platforms.

Walking homewards during the afternoon, after visiting Oskey's seedsman for a new and phenomenal dwarf pea, Mr Bunting saw young Rollo loom up before him, like an intercepting battleship. His signals were all at friendly; the meeting struck him as the most amazing chance encounter in the world. By his lusty handshake and his vociferous greeting he demonstrated how pleased, even delighted, he knew Mr Bunting must be to see him. Yes, he was on leave. Mr Bunting had not known it, perhaps? He had travelled all night, and hit the hay at two ack-emma. Now he was bursting with good fellowship and, by a lucky chance, had the Corton-David with him. Wouldn't take him five minutes to run up to Laburnum Villa.

'Um!' said Mr Bunting, looking doubtfully at the car, which had to him the threatening purr of some particularly dangerous machine.

'No trouble at all,' Bert assured him, opening the door and compelling him to enter by a large encircling gesture. Almost immediately he leapt in at the other side, and the thing was in motion. 'Glides like velvet,' he commented. He seemed to miss the familiar clang and rattle of the transits of the Armoured Corps.

As they swept along he confided that he had spent the morning looking round the bombed parts of Kilworth. They were indelibly engraved upon his memory. The motions of his gear-changing took on a muted wrath. 'Got something else chalked up against 'em now,' he said. Then he thought. minute. 'Yeah! And don't forget it.'

'Mind the pillar box!' shouted Mr Bunting, as they swung into Cumberland Avenue. He was aware that young Rollo gave him the curious glance of one who detects that peculiar weakness – nerves. The pillar box flew past them safely, it receded into the distance erect and quite undamaged, as Mr Bunting's startled backward glance testified.

'Can't understand why they put 'em so near the kerb,' mused Bert thoughtfully. Course, it didn't matter when you were driving tanks.

At Laburnum Villa Mr Bunting dismounted with an odd impression that the universe had just hit something and jolted to a standstill. His feet sought the familiar, steady ground. Relieved, but still feeling as though accompanied by a whirlwind, he opened the door and admitted his visitor to the living room. Evie, bare-armed, was dressing the baby after his bath, and with her was a much smudged Julie with a dust cap and a duster.

Both turned and stared transfixed, the baby kicking nakedly between them. 'No good blaming me,' thought Mr Bunting. If there was a tactless way of doing anything you could bank on Bert Rollo finding it.

'Bert!' exclaimed Julie; and there was an exchange of glances and a pause broken by the answering: 'Julie!' so that Mr Bunting cocked his ears. He felt that for all practical purposes he was not present. When Bert was about he never felt the house or any of his possessions were his own. Even now the enormous khaki-clad figure filled the room, the huge limbs and broad shoulders gave one a desire to open windows and let in air.

'Gosh! Is that Ernest's nipper?'

'Yes,' smiled Evie. 'What do you think of him?'

'He's swell!' said Bert. He had apparently not till now seen a baby at such close quarters. He seemed astounded that anything human could be so small; he observed its completeness as to toe and finger nails with a sort of wonder. 'Cute!' he pronounced, but kept clear of the baby as though afraid he might catch it in some inadvertent movement and do irreparable damage.

'Sit down, Bert,' invited Mr Bunting hospitably, for Bert, after all, was a soldier of the king, and a DCM, and no doubt a useful man for dealing with Germans. His sole preoccupation and desire, in fact, seemed to be to deal with Germans; he had few other subjects of conversation.

All these months, it transpired, Bert had been waiting for the invasion. He had the tank ready. Night after night he had gone hopefully on duty; morning after morning had dawned coldly with no word of Germans being on the way. One got an impression of Bert growing more and more bored by this inaction and presently concluding the whole invasion racket was boloney. But a pal of his, who read articles in the papers, and was a wide-awake guy in every respect, pointed out that this might be Hitler's very game with chaps like Bert who liked quick action; catch them with the covers on their guns, playing pontoon in the YMCA. Whereupon, after smoking a pipe or two on this proposition, Bert had suddenly muttered: 'I get it, pal,' and started up and gone round his tank carefully, giving it an extra look over in vital places. But he was tired of waiting for the enemy to come to him. The Armoured Corps had handed Musso a few snifty ones in Africa, and there was much disappointment in Bert's part of the country at their not having been asked to the party.

'Africa's all right; real tank country,' he observed. 'But it's the Jerrys I want to get at more than the Ities. And – you wait, Mr Bunting.'

'You chaps going to start something?'

'Ah!' said Bert, and looked at his boots, and from his boots to the door through which Julie had vanished, and from thence through the window into the garden where there was no sign of her.

'Nice to see you, you know,' remarked Mr Bunting, breaking a stiff silence. He feared his reception of Bert had been somewhat frosty, though it was by no means certain that Bert noticed it. Mr Bunting's remark was received with an appreciative nod. Bert's eyes fixed themselves on a minute garment hanging near the fire, the smallest article of clothing he had ever set eyes on. He appeared to come slowly to the conclusion that, in spite of its Lilliputian dimensions, that's what it was – a vest.

'Ernest's in the foot-sloggers, isn't he?' he asked Evie.

'He's in the Derwent regiment.'

'That's what I thought. The infantry.' He ruminated on unaccountable preferences. 'Some chaps must fancy it. I guess that's the reason.'

Julie was heard coming down the stairs, and she reappeared without the dust cap and the smudges. She had instead a certain radiance of cheek and lustre of curl that were dazzling. As she made her entrance in her most sporty frock and jumper everyone was momentarily arrested by the transformation. Mr Bunting had the look of puzzled wonder with which he watched quick-change effects and conjuring on the stage. He turned his head to follow her movements. But Julie was aware of none of this, nor, apparently, of anything unusual. Her manner quite definitely assumed that whoever had gone upstairs it was the normal everyday Julie who had come down again. She halted in the doorway, holding something above her head.

'Look what I found in the cupboard in the spare bedroom.'

For an instant Mr Bunting almost doubted his eyes. But there the object was, held high in Julie's hands and unmistakably labelled, a bottle of 'Bonnie Prince Charlie,' the second bottle bought to forestall the Chancellor's wartime budget.

'Whoops!' she exclaimed, and threw it up and caught it.

'For God's sake, Julie!' Mr Bunting exclaimed in alarm.

'Whoops!' she cried, and once more caught the bottle with careless ease.

With three quick strides he was upon her, had taken firm but careful possession of the whisky, and was looking for some place to stand it. 'You little fool!' he remonstrated, for his heart was fluttering. 'Give me quite a turn.'

Julie turned her smile on Bert. 'Why, you've been made a sergeant. Daddy, did you notice Bert's got his third stripe up?'

Mr Bunting had not noticed, nor did he pay much attention now, even though Bert pointed out it was one more than pin-head Adolf got in four years of the last war. To speak truth, he felt the slight sickness of a man who has been for a moment completely unnerved.

'You ought to drink a toast, daddy, especially as Bert 's here,' said Julie, and, without waiting for assent, calmly put out two glasses and went to fetch the water jug; preparations which, Mr Bunting observed, were watched appreciatively by young Rollo.

'Very well, we will,' he said, and poured and raised his glass.

'Absent friends!' he said solemnly, and felt the delightful warmth and comfort seeping into his very centre. 'Absent friends!' and he thought of Chris and Ernest, and all the young men from Brockleys far away on land and sea.

'*Some* whisky!' commented Bert, after an exhalation. 'Got a kick.' He sat holding his empty glass and knitting his brows over the label on the bottle, every word of which he slowly read whilst Mr Bunting sipped his glass empty and replaced it on the table with an air of finality. The action, however, only moved Bert to suggest that 'whilst they were at it' they ought to drink the baby's health. He put this forward with an air of being willing to do the right thing. He also inquired, as a matter of interest, how much a whisky bottle held.

With admirable calm, but less generously, Mr Bunting poured again. He could not help noticing that they had already got a measurable distance below the neck.

'To young George Christopher!' he said. If he recollected aright, it must be near George Christopher's feeding time; but Evie was much too shy to feed him in the presence of a stranger. The glasses were emptied and replaced on the table, and Mr Bunting grew a shade uneasy. This juxtaposition of bottle, jug, and glasses had an inviting look, there was an air of the flowing bowl about them. Left there long enough they might inspire Bert to suggest further toasts; Mr Churchill for instance, or President Roosevelt, whom Bert particularly admired. Julie, in Mr Bunting's opinion, should have had sense enough to clear the things away; it would be too pointed if he did it himself. But Julie never had sense; she had disappeared again, and all he could do was to screw the cork down in an absent-minded way, but very tightly.

Presently she returned wearing her coat and drawing on her gloves with a certain air. Bert seemed to take in first her general effect of charm, and only secondarily the fact that she was going out.

'Say, going anywhere particular?'

'Only just down town, Bert.'

'I've got the car. Run you down, if you like.'

Her brows arched in surprise. 'Will you really? Oh, thanks awfully. So long, daddy darling.'

Rising thankfully as the door closed behind them, Mr Bunting stowed 'Bonnie Prince Charlie' in the long vacant corner of the sideboard devoted to his ancestors. Bought at twelve and six and completely forgotten, rediscovered when the tax had pushed it up to sixteen bob; it was like finding buried treasure.

'Bit of all right, Evie, eh?' he remarked, closing the cupboard door.

Evie sat with the baby at her breast, her eyes happy and thoughtful.

She was a gentle, tender, timid thing; one would never know she was in the house except for her dark smile, which, Mr Bunting imagined, always went out to him with particular warmth, and the low voice that had not a harsh note in all its compass. There was nothing more natural and lovely, he thought, than what he now saw before him, a mother with a baby at her breast. Evie had the look of a woman whose life is fulfilled. Watching her, his thoughts turned to Monica, whom the war had robbed of the best of heart's desire. He never saw Monica these days, but he heard stories about her that distressed him. Dancing, cocktail parties, and a whirl of headlong gaieties were Monica's life now. Disappointment took some people one way and some another. You couldn't reach across the years to these young people.

He put on his overcoat and went out to look at his rain-sodden garden, bare of everything except a few ravaged winter greens. He would have to do better next year, make a great effort. That was the way to win wars or anything else – put out that extra ounce of strength and see the job through to the end. That had always been the British way; and it was an odd thing, he thought, that other countries forgot what all our history taught them. They claimed the victory before the fight was half begun, but a man like himself believed in stamina and tenacity: get your teeth in like a bulldog and, however clawed and mangled, learn to breathe without letting go.

But the country was getting into its stride; Winston, whose words he weighed almost one by one, had said so. Soon we should meet the Huns on equal terms; he knew no fighting man who wished for more than that.

Whether it was Chris, who saw things with a clear eye, and, knowing what he was risking, had taken on eight Messerschmitts alone; or Ernest, who magnified dangers and yet remained unshaken, or even Rollo, who hadn't sense enough to recognise danger when he saw it, they were all better fellows than the Germans. And there were thousands, scores of thousands, like them, here and in the empire overseas.

He plugged a fill of 'Lighthouse' into his burnt-down pipe and became aware that Oskey was approaching the fence. He could always be relied on to appear when Mr Bunting was deep in thought.

'Few seeds for you, Bunting. "Ailsa Craig".' He handed an envelope thus inscribed in pencil.

'Give a good dressing of bone meal and sow thinly. Watch for the fly.'

'Thanks, Oskey. Don't think I got any of these. There's no reason we shouldn't have a few flowers just because of Hitler.'

'Flowers! Them ain't flowers. They're onions.'

'Onions? Oh, of course;' Mr Bunting was sensible of the faint familiar note of derision. 'They'll come in handy. Bone meal, you said?'

He wrote it on the envelope and passed on to avoid argument about a gardener's wartime duty, of which Oskey took the sternest view. Lilies that neither toiled nor spun, as it were, in the interests of the national larder, were frowned upon by Oskey. Even too many green peas was unpatriotic. Root crops for the winter were Oskey's theme; and he knew every detail of the proper way to store them.

Passing to the front of the house, Mr Bunting bent over the clumps of arabis and aubrietia in his rockery and looked at the spaces where he would see the crocus and the rockrose in their season. He looked at the laburnum he had forgotten to trim and came to his almond near the gate. Above all else the blossoming of the almond tree was Mr Bunting's most looked-for sign of spring. Here already were the first buds and, secretly glowing within them, lay folded all the delicate pink loveliness that moved his heart whenever he first saw it. Its image in his mind stirred him now with a wonderful sense of hope and faith as in a certain promise of the things man can neither repress, retard, nor hasten. They ripen and increase in obedience to eternal law, as the tide of liberty rises even under the oppressor. But the flowery image in his mind was faint, and the reality far away, an event of the future. It would come forth to a word spoken in its own ear only.

He went indoors, took his seed box from the kitchen shelf, and put the 'Ailsa Craig' inside it. It was not often he was permitted to claim the smallest bit of indoor space for his purely personal activities, but, after much demanding, Mrs Bunting had made a place for him to keep the seed box. Everything was in it, packets of vegetable seeds in comforting profusion, and when Mr Bunting examined them he thought pleasantly of the expected saving in terms of cash. But it was over the coloured packets of the annuals that his eye brightened: candytuft, larkspur, sweet rocket, and some real old-fashioned nasturtiums, all glowingly depicted. Hitler or no Hitler, the borders at Laburnum Villa were going to look gay this summer. He returned the seed box to its shelf. He knew by introducing it he had disorganised the whole arrangement of the kitchen, but he was very insistent that it should remain precisely where it was. He took it down from time to time to read and re-read the instructions on the packets by the fire on February evenings, and he forbade anyone else to touch it.

NINETEEN

WHEN MR BUNTING was not actually engaged on functions of control at the control-centre telephone he sometimes spent an hour in the back room with Mr Rollo acquiring the art of throwing darts. An organisation like ARP, Mr Rollo declared, needed a social side, and particularly a sporting side, and the more he thought and talked about it, the more did he see himself as the right man to organise these activities, for he had discovered since the war that he had remarkable organising powers. His immediate aim was to recruit a darts team at the control centre and, when this was trained to a high state of efficiency, to organise a competition and win the cup.

'Be a nice souvenir after the war.'

'Good idea,' agreed Mr Bunting, who gathered that the cup was to stand on the mantelshelf in Mr Rollo's office at the garage.

As an instructor he displayed the greatest patience. Even when Mr Bunting missed the board altogether he only corrected his stance thoughtfully, and advised a 'more deliberate aim'.

'Hang it! I'll never do it.'

'Yes, you will,' replied Mr Rollo quietly and confidently, and for encouragement handed Mr Bunting one of his famous black cheroots. 'Let's have a tonic.'

With an air of initiating a novice into official secrets he took a couple of letter files off the shelf, and revealed behind them a small stock of bottled beer. 'Any time you want to bring something in shove it up here. But don't shout about it – I dare say it's against regulations. Of course this arrangement is only for the select few.'

'Course!' said Mr Bunting, expanding a little, as he always did when he smoked a cigar. That he was included amongst the select few seemed right and fitting and most agreeable. He drank with the zest of a man who sees his favourite label on the bottle.

Dart throwing at the control centre naturally led to dart throwing at home. Having practised a few flighting motions of the wrist on his way there in the dark, Mr Bunting got out his homemade dart board, and invited Julie to a practice. The social side of civil defence made a strong appeal to him; its gossip and good fellowship, its privileges for the select few, all reminded him of the freedom and mild doggishness of his bachelor days, and he desired to enter into it more fully. So, in spite of Mrs Bunting's protests, the dart board had its place during the evenings behind the kitchen door. During the day she took it down and hid it in the pantry, declaring it reminded her of a taproom. Though she had never been in a public house she knew where the lowest characters congregated.

She also drew her husband's attention to various scars and scratches on the door itself which, in consequence of his wilder aiming, was 'ruined'. But Mr Bunting, hitherto so regardful and even fussy about his property, considered that a bit of putty and paint would make the door as good as new after the war – if the whole place wasn't blown to smithereens first. These misses had a hollow impact, which was always followed in the kitchen by a silent exchange of glances between father and daughter; and, in the living room, by a sigh which Mrs Bunting set up, not so much for the kitchen door, as for her husband, who used to give his evenings to a serious study of the problems of the war and now spent them larking about like a boy.

One evening he was focusing his eye and concentrating his mind on the only double that would save him from being routed, when Julie said: 'Listen! There's a plane over. I'll just look out.'

'What for?'

'I'm fire-watching. Put the light out, daddy.'

Mr Bunting turned the switch, and waited with his thumb on it whilst she opened the door. On his way home he believed he had got into the knack; now he had lost it, and the game had reached a stage when he ceased to have any interest in counting.

Julie called excitedly: 'Daddy, come here. I can see fire bombs.'

'But the siren hasn't gone.'

'All the same there 's Huns about. Look!'

Looking out, he saw the whole skyline lit with an unearthly glow. Roofs and spires and gables were outlined against a blinding whiteness. They looked like geometrical patterns, black and sharply edged and very tiny; above them the sky paled as over a furnace.

He caught his breath; his first thought was that the whole town was alight.

Mrs Bunting came pattering through the kitchen. 'Oh,' she gasped, 'those terrible people!'

He took her arm and listened, and looked uncertainly towards the sky, for after the incendiaries came the high explosive.

'Here he comes again,' called Julie.

A second batch of incendiaries came whistling through the air. The nearer darkness leapt into life as though a hundred flaming torches had been flung down at random. They burned with a peculiar fierce intensity, their glow enlarging itself, whitening and spreading, illuminating chimney stacks and trees with a thievish light. Faintly, from overhead, came the drone of the bomber wheeling in a slow circle. In its wake the searchlights crossed and interlaced, and became lost in cloud. One could imagine the crew up there, a few muffed-up young men, looking down from the security of height and darkness on a town which lay completely at their mercy, where they could maim and blind and kill without even knowing who their victims were, or what of man's priceless treasure they destroyed.

The Buntings drew back into the kitchen doorway, staring at the ring of flares. Away to the west one of these slowly turned a sullen red, and sparks streamed upwards.

'Oh dear!' shuddered Mrs Bunting. 'There'll be nothing left of Kilworth.'

'Yes, there will!' he said. 'We got to tackle some of this. Come on, Julie!'

They hurried down the path, leaving Mrs Bunting and Evie beneath the stairs. A peculiar excitement filled Mr Bunting, but the greater part of it, he knew, was fear: a deep-rooted primitive fear of fire as a destroyer, which dried his lips and shortened his breath. With his mouth open and his heart thumping he panted a yard behind his daughter.

She stopped suddenly: 'Did you bring the bomb scoop, daddy?'

'Course I brought it!' he retorted, nettled. What would be the sense of rushing about without taking the equipment? Julie's question gave him a feeling that he had, at any rate, kept his head.

'There's one here,' he said, pausing over a sizzling object which looked less like an incendiary than a damp squib trying to go off.

'It's not a very good one,' remarked Julie.

'Better dot it with a bit of sand.'

He found a sandbag near a lamppost, and flung it on the bomb, vaguely wondering if it represented a case of sabotage; one of these Poles or Czechs who occasionally filled a high-explosive bomb with concrete. The thought gave him a peculiar feeling of comradeship, as though the bomb were a message from some nameless enslaved citizen of Europe relying on him to see things through. The spluttering in the gutter ceased, and apparently the bomb went out. He stood back watching carefully to make quite sure this had happened; then it occurred to him it might explode. The Huns' natural talent for murder and mutilation had led them to the manufacture of fire bombs that exploded; he had been warned about them on the wireless.

'Come on,' he said, and picked up his scoop and hastened on.

Round the corner they came upon what Julie called 'a real one'. It lay on the pavement shooting out its tongue of flame and hissing fiercely. Mr Bunting looked round for a sandbag, but was too dazzled by the glare to see. The only thing was to fill his scoop with earth from somebody's front garden. He pushed a gate open.

'Here's a sandbag,' said Julie, hoisting one on to her shoulder.

'Let me – '

'You watch. Up the Buntings!' she cried, and ran forward, flung the bag accurately over the bomb, and dashed back dusting her hands and panting.

'Rake some sand over it, daddy.'

'You be more careful,' he admonished her, as the bomb was damped down, and a sudden blackness enveloped them. 'Be getting your dress on fire.'

'But, darling, you can't be careful in a war.'

They walked on. Much of the glare had already vanished from the sky; what had looked like a blazing city was now reduced to a few ominous points of flame. They reached the end of the avenue, and stood looking this way and that. Now and then there came a sudden blackening as a fire bomb was dealt with or burnt out behind the shadows of the street.

'Better get back home,' said Mr Bunting, reflecting that there would be scores of people out attending to the bombs.

Julie took his arm. 'Oh, there's bound to be some more somewhere. Come on, cowboy!'

Reluctantly he followed her. He was entirely out of sympathy with his daughter's zest for incendiary bombs, and he was irritated by her increasing habit of addressing him in terms borrowed from young Rollo. They passed the end of one peacefully sleeping street where there was neither light nor sound nor movement, and on to the next where he paused staring, unable to decide whether what he saw was a fire bomb or a fire, and whether it was near or far away.

Julie ran on ahead; her voice, girlish and shrill, reached him out of the darkness.

'There's one on a roof. Blazing like billy-ho.'

Mr Bunting swore softly. Incendiaries on streets and gardens were easy, but, on roofs – Why, he wondered, didn't they sound the siren and get people up? Everybody was too slack. There was no one about except himself and Julie, who sounded as excited as though a fire bomb were a four-leaved clover. He hurried on, grasping his scoop, and wondering how best to call assistance. He could see the bomb plainly now, caught between some broken roof tiles, and burning away in this quiet street unnoticed except by one old lady who leant over her gate as he passed to tell him it was 'There!' She seemed, by this action, to make him responsible for the bomb, as though he had appeared in some official capacity, for she immediately went indoors.

It was only when he got closer and saw the sundial on the lawn and the Virginia creeper on the gable that he recognised the house as 'Mandalay,' the home of Colonel Saunders. He immediately became excited, hammering on the door and shouting through the letter box: 'Hurry! 'Cendry bombs! 'Cendry bombs!'

'Excuse me,' said Julie, as the door opened, 'but your roof's on fire.'

The colonel, his grey hair looking even more silvery in the moonlight, stepped out on to the lawn and glanced upwards.

'Got a ladder?' asked Mr Bunting, with no certain idea who was to use it.

'No; we'll have to try from the roof space.'

He went indoors and began to climb the stairs, the Buntings unceremoniously following. Though made alert and active by danger, there was something odd about the colonel's gait that Mr Bunting had never noticed on the level. He was reminded of some gossip which circulated on the estate when Saunders had been given command of a company of the Home Guard. It was then said, not only that he was too old, but also that he was lame, Oskey even going so far as to assert that he had an artificial leg. Mr Bunting had never believed this, but now, as he saw, the colonel climbed the stairs by advancing one foot at a time, and bringing the other up to rest beside it with an effort.

Now he paused to lean over the balustrade and address his wife, who appeared out of the shadows staring at Mr Bunting and Julie with astonishment. She cupped her hand behind her ear and the colonel spoke into it.

'There's an incendiary on the roof, my dear.'

'Shall I send for William?'

'I'm afraid the matter's too urgent. We must do what we can ourselves,' and they moved on in the glow of his torch until they stood beneath the trap-door of the roof. As Mr Bunting forced it open with the handle of his scoop a hissing and a smell of smoke were wafted down to them.

Mrs Saunders appeared carrying a highchair. There was a momentary hesitation, a matter of seconds only, but long enough for Mr Bunting to feel a pang of shame at inviting a man older than himself to display his infirmities.

'I'll go up,' he said, and got upon the chair.

Pushed from below he clambered through the trap and emerged on to the ceiling joists upon his knees. Somebody handed him a stirrup pump.

'We'll pass up water from the bathroom,' said the colonel, who was being helped up after him.

'That's no good. Use the tank in the roof.'

Meeting the colonel's uncomprehending stare, he said impatiently, rather as though he were speaking to old Turner: 'The tank. Right in front of you.'

'Oh, of course.'

Coughing and spitting, Mr Bunting crawled towards a glowing object in the corner of the loft, and tried to get his scoop beneath it. Whether he succeeded in this he could not tell, for the smoke blinded him and forced him back. The rafters were now on fire, and the bomb had fallen through the roof on to the timbers below. Unless dealt with quickly it would burn its way through and start other fires. So Mr Bunting ignored the rafters; the bomb was the thing, and he glared at it fiercely and returned to the attack. A piece of hose, accurately thrown, fell across his arm and the next instant water spurted.

'That's better. Pump like blazes.'

He glanced round and saw that the colonel had somehow reached the tank. He had tied a wet handkerchief across his face; above it his eyes were anxious and determined as though he were going into action. Behind him, with her head and shoulders through the trapdoor, was Julie, red-eyed with the smoke, but immensely interested.

Lying flat upon his stomach, his lungs almost bursting, Mr Bunting turned his jet upon the flames. He had got the bomb at last, and was now dealing with the rafters. They cracked frighteningly as the fire consumed them, and sparks fell around him. Nevertheless, he sprayed with all the method of a practical man who does not allow the merely spectacular to divert him from his vital target. Sweat trickled down his forehead and into his eyes. When he brushed it away his fingers streaked his face with grime. What his clothes were like he could not imagine. But he was keyed up and full of fight. At last he was really in the war.

Suddenly the siren began to screech. Julie turned and addressed it ironically:

'Say! You're telling me, comrade!'

He turned on her fiercely; he had enough to contend with, he considered, without silly remarks.

'Take cover, you little fool. Doing no good there.'

'How's it going?' asked the colonel presently.

'Getting it under. Best give it a good soaking. Wind might start it again.'

For a time nothing was heard except the rattle of the stirrup pump and the colonel panting. His stroke became slower and slower; finally it ceased.

'I'm done, Bunting. Isn't it out yet?' he gasped. He had seen no flames for several minutes, and had continued pumping simply because Mr Bunting was so obviously a man who, when he put a fire out, intended it to stay out.

Even now he peered and poked amongst the sodden mass of ash and water in the corner before replying.

'Yes, it's out,' he reported finally, as though, after due thought, he could give a guarantee.

'Thank God for that!' exclaimed Colonel Saunders, untying the handkerchief, and mopping his brow with it.

Mr Bunting rose from his stomach. It was not possible to stand upright, and, after trying several positions, he crouched against the roof truss, rubbing his knees. Thus they sat, silent and perspiring, in the dim pillar of light that streamed faintly through the trap into the loft. A fantastic situation, Mr Bunting thought, for two elderly men. Yet you had either to put up with happenings like this or hand over everything you'd got, and resign yourself to living under a lot of swaggering Germans. He had never thought he would live to face such strange alternatives. The colonel certainly looked all in; every line of his seventy odd years was stamped on his face in the pallor of exhaustion. He wiped his brow slowly and wearily.

They became aware of the quietness of the house.

'Siren's driven them to cover, I suppose.'

Mr Bunting did not answer; he was too dry about the mouth, Neither did he wish to move. All he longed for was a drink, a draught of vintage cool and aged, as Corder would have said – bottled beer or anything. He wanted it now before he washed, or brushed his clothes, or went downstairs. It was hardly a desire he could, in the circumstances, express aloud.

A plane flew over; he recognised the thud-thud of a German bomber, and was reminded that the siren had sounded. The guns spoke and their reverberation shook the loft.

'Now for the heavy stuff,' remarked the colonel.

Neither of them moved. To Mr Bunting, the cramped and darkened space beneath the roof seemed as safe as any dugout. One got used to life being in the balance, got used to looking back with thankfulness on what one had enjoyed of life, knowing much more might not be granted. It was the actual concussions that scared you, the blasting explosions of the bombs, and the sickening thought of what was happening where they fell.

Now they screamed through the air, and the house quivered; some loose tiles slid off the roof with a smash like breaking crockery. From close at hand came the heaviest explosion of his experience; the timber against which he leaned struck him in the back, the tank vibrated like a bell, and he plainly heard the sound of a collapsing building. He glanced at the colonel, who gave no sign of being aware of these happenings. Such stoicism was beyond Mr Bunting, whose thoughts flew to his wife sheltering with Evie and the baby beneath the stairs. There welled up within him an anger and hatred of everything German that surpassed in intensity any emotion he remembered. Never, in the last war, had he felt such a deep and bitter hatred of the enemy. He was a slow and reluctant hater, but at that moment he hoped the war would never end until the Germans had suffered in their own country what they had so wantonly wreaked on others.

Downstairs a door slammed, and feet came hurrying and stumbling up the stairs. He heard Julie mount the chair, and the next instant she appeared at the trapdoor.

'More incendiaries. Bags of 'em.'

He stared. 'Good God! Have you been wandering about in this?'

'Don't be silly, daddy. I've got to fire-watch.'

He made a helpless gesture, and glanced at the colonel, wondering if he, too, had daughters. But the colonel's ear was inclined towards Julie. There was an exchange of explanatory gestures.

'One on the flat roof apparently.'

Mr Bunting was at first disinclined to believe this. He descended to the level of mere domestic irritation. When there were thousands of roofs in Kilworth he couldn't see why a second bomb should fall on 'Mandalay'. Anything outrageous and unfair always first appeared to him in the guise of the incredible.

'But they've dropped hundreds this time,' insisted Julie. 'Thousands!'

'We'd better look out,' said the colonel, and began fumbling with the skylight. He was unable to open it, and Mr Bunting picked his way across the joists and lifted the catch.

'I'm awfully sorry, Bunting, after all you've done – '

'That's all right. How do we get up?'

The colonel crooked his knee and pointed at it. 'Stand on that, you can't hurt it.'

Never in all his life had Mr Bunting even imagined himself doing such an absurd thing. But there was no alternative. He stepped on to the colonel's knee, squeezed his head and shoulders through the skylight, and appeared above the tiles. The cool night breeze blew about him, the freshest and sweetest air he had ever breathed. He filled his lungs and felt revived, though sharply awakened to a sense of danger. Just below him the tiles sloped down to a small area of flat roof, and there the bomb was burning. The roof would be leaded, he knew, and fairly safe unless there were overhanging timbers.

'Pass the scoop,' he said, and having grasped it, bent down. Then he edged himself farther out and bent down lower.

'No!' he said, and ducked as a volley of anti-aircraft shells screamed upwards at what sounded like a dangerous angle.

Cautiously he looked out again. 'Can you hold me if I go a bit higher?' he asked, and felt his shin and ankle grasped more firmly.

He leaned out over the tiles. If the colonel let go he would only slide down on to the flat roof where there was a parapet to prevent him falling off. His position was not so much heroic as awkward and uncomfortable. He pushed his scoop forward, lifted the bomb, and let it fall.

'Damn!' he muttered, and wondered if he could stretch lower still, but decided against it. A silly business, he thought, a man of his age being suspended out of a skylight. The whole thing was lunatic and maddening. He put this reflection from him, and calmed himself. Gathering up the bomb once more, he edged it towards the parapet. Again it fell, and, for a second or two, he stared at it, and turned the scoop over, wondering what was wrong.

'Here goes,' he thought, and very slowly and carefully and almost bristling with determination he took the bomb with a ladling motion and pitched it into the garden.

Downstairs in the relaxation that followed the 'Raiders passed,' Mr Bunting drank his glass of beer. He had washed, but was still being brushed intermittently by Mrs Saunders, who examined him, brush in hand, whilst he drank. The colonel opened beer bottles with an absent-minded unobtrusiveness, but always hospitably in advance of his guest's requirements. His wife, who was concerned even for Mr Bunting's sodden trouser ends, seemed to him to be excessively grateful. They were old people, ten years older than himself at least. They had a stately, old-fashioned drawing-room, and manners to match, and their kindness embarrassed him.

To Julie the colonel was particularly gallant.

'Does your daughter take sherry, Mr Bunting?'

'Oh, rather!' put in Julie. 'Thanks awfully,' for this wine was unknown at Laburnum Villa.

He filled her glass. 'I shall always think of you, my dear,' he said gravely, 'as the girl who "had to fire-watch" – even though the bombs were dropping'.

'But I like doing it.'

'Ah!' he smiled. 'We still produce the right kind of young people. Eh, Mr Bunting?'

Though not quite certain what the colonel was alluding to, Mr Bunting assented. He also said it was 'jolly good beer,' but hastily declined a third glass, fearing his remark had been misunderstood. He had a dread of what he called 'taking advantage' of people's kindness. Before starting for home he examined his clothes in the long Saunders mirror, pulling his coat this way and that, and twisting his neck to get a back view of his trousers.

'Do you think your mother will notice anything?'

Julie suddenly choked, and put down her glass, a paroxysm of coughing overpowered her. Then she gave him a glance of teasing affection.

'No, darling,' she said, her eyes wide and mock-serious. '*She* won't notice anything.'

'That stuff's too strong for you,' he remarked, when they got outside, and offered her his arm for safety. She grasped it warmly.

'Best say nothing at home about climbing on roofs, dearie. Your mother's easily upset.'

He spent some time after supper drawing with his stub of pencil on a Brockley memorandum. Now and then he went into the kitchen and ran his steel ruler over various details of the bomb scoop. The sides were not the right shape, in his opinion, and there should be a depression in the middle. He finished his drawing, dimensioned it, and examined it with pride.

Then he wrote across it – not because he was likely to forget, but because he loved to elaborate everything with jottings – 'Sketch for Mr Bickerton'. He folded it carefully, and put it into his attaché case ready for the morning.

TWENTY

IN THE FOLLOWING weeks it sometimes seemed to Mr Bunting that there was a lull in the war. He had no external evidence of such a lull, for the bombings still went on, but he definitely had the feeling. Daily and nightly hazards, however terrifying, take on in time the pattern of routine, and the mind accommodates itself to meet them. But Mr Bunting's mind had been accommodated to more than these; he had expected even worse horrors. He had looked for a rising tide of horrors, cities burnt and bombed and paralysed by an incessant pounding from the sky. There was to be murder and mutilation on a scale that outran the most bestial massacres in history. So far as any human mind can prepare itself to face such things, his mind had been prepared, and the preparation had been done for him by Dr Goebbels and his minions who had warned him that these things would inevitably happen.

War had been threatened and war had come; the blitzkrieg had been threatened and now was here. Mr Bunting, who had greatly feared these ordeals, waited and observed. If he had a British lack of imagination he had much British phlegm and practicality. He was descended from the man who, though singed and scarred by the pursuing dragon, was still able to tell St George that the tongue of flame, though pretty deadly, was not the full seven feet of rumour. Only by such men and methods can dragons be approached and conquered.

Observing in this spirit, amidst alarms and air raids, frequent scares and perpetual anxieties, Mr Bunting perceived that the blitzkrieg was already at full blast. All the steam was on, there was no more in the *Führer's* boiler. And yet the world was not shaken. His own life was reorganised to meet it, so was Brockleys, so was the city. Though no hero, he found himself meeting it with as much defiance as a breathless middle-aged man can muster, or with a calm tinged with contempt for an enemy who can so underrate him. Yes, there was a lull. It was in his mind, and in the minds and hearts of those around him.

Through this strange world of war he walked, taking note of burgeoning leaves. Not for him the consolations of far-away Utopias. Such things were all right for Ernest, but he lived from day to day, his satisfaction being to see the first green spears of his two dozen daffodils pierce the soil, and watch the gradual opening of the primroses transplanted years ago from Kilworth woods. And at weekends there was the planning of the garden, with a solitary robin, identifiable from all other robins, hopping at his heels for crumbs.

One day Mrs Bunting startled him by asking the question that occurred to her about four times a year.

'How's Mr Corder?' It was followed by a palpable silence, during which he felt his heart turn over.

'George, I believe you're getting a little deaf.'

The irritation he felt at this imputation helped him over the bad moment. Moistening the roof of his mouth, he answered:

'Corder's all right, Mary. Same as usual.'

It was the first time he had deliberately lied to her. These shocks! They came from all quarters – inside, outside, with warnings and without. He got up and walked into the garden, but seeing Oskey there, turned and sought the empty front room. There he stood before the cold grate biting his upper lip, his face grey.

He had found Corder lying at the top of Brockley's basement stairs. Everybody had been in the cellar throughout the raid, he thought. He himself had been there when the first bomb fell, and he'd seen Corder come down with the others. He had motioned to him, but it must have been without Corder noticing. The cellar was full of crates and sacks and boxes, and the staff sat about here and there in twos and threes. When things grew quiet Mr Bunting rose from his corner to follow the rest upstairs. It was then he heard shouting of an urgent quality and, hastening forward, found one of the men bending over something that looked like a crumpled heap of clothes. He did not at first recognise who it was.

Then, pushing the others aside, he knelt and bent over his friend. Corder's head turned painfully towards him, and his lips moved. 'What's he say?'

'Don't know, sir. Queer stuff; can't make sense of it.'

''Lirious, I expeck. Poor Joe!'

Mr Bunting's heart was torn. 'Joe!' he murmured, and bending closer, repeated the name softly. He ached for one last sign of recognition, for instinctively he knew that Corder was past human aid.

Corder raised himself up; his eyes, alight but vacant, stared into Mr Bunting's. There was something, something he was struggling to say. Then, like the turning of a switch, the light went out, and he collapsed on his side, and lay inert and still.

For a moment Mr Bunting did not comprehend. 'Joe,' he repeated; his hand pressed the warm hand; he refused to accept the fact of death. He looked up at the faces around him, appealing to them for he knew not what.

'Come away, Mr Bunting, you can do no good,' said Mr Bickerton, and dejectedly he rose, and walked through the awful silence of the shop to the cubby-hole and shut the door. There he sat haggardly staring, but not, for a while, seeing anything.

Presently he became aware of a shiny object on the floor. Stooping, he picked up Corder's green fountain pen. It took him a long time to realise how it got there.

Now he leaned against his front room mantelshelf, whilst every detail of this scene passed across the mirror of his mind as remorselessly as it did in the night when he could not sleep. All his working life he had known Joe Corder. He knew about his son in Australia, and his married daughter in the States. He had a mental picture of Corder's home like the image one forms of a house in a novel, and he knew all the ups and downs of the family history. But he had never seen any of the Corders.

He sighed. How needlessly lives were wasted in the war and on what slender threads they hung. Corder had gone from the cellar to the cubby-hole, as once before, in the mistaken idea that Mr Bunting had not heard the siren.

What could one do to pay a debt like that? Nothing – except strive impossibly to be worthy of it.

Julie put her head round the door. 'What are you doing in here, daddy? You do look off colour. Is it your tummy?'

'Just meditating, dearie.'

'Cos if it's your tummy you'll have to have some more of Mrs Bunting's arrowroot.'

'I'm all right,' replied Mr Bunting in a tone that protested against the threat of arrowroot. 'Meditating, that's all.'

'Come and meditate where it's comfortable, darling. Have you seen the evening paper? Our chaps are socking the wops all over Africa.'

'Ah!' he exclaimed, appreciatively. One had to come back from private griefs, had to hide them even from the uncanny intuition of one's wife. Nor must any private grief sap his resolution, nor his desire to see the enemy pounded and punished for his loathsome crimes. So far he had seen only the cheerful headlines of the news from Africa; there was still the inspiring full report. There was the war map to examine, for Mr Bunting had bought another war map, and this time he hoped to follow up the victories. Frequently he expounded the strategical situation to Mrs Bunting, particularly in Abyssinia. There, in his opinion, the whole of Europe's trouble started, and there the first retributive stroke was going to fall.

'Musso can't get his men in or out; see?' and his blunt finger pointed. They were hemmed in by Australians and South Africans, the British, and the Navy. He enlarged on these points with gusto.

'Then these Abyssinians will rise spontaneously. Shoot behind rocks and trees. Gorilla tactics. That's what Musso 's done for his men, put 'em in a trap with no back door.'

'Oh, dear! What's going to happen to them?' exclaimed Mrs Bunting, whose old-fashioned idea was that they were all somebody's boys.

'Same as is going to happen to the Huns in Poland and a few other places before this job's finished. Get their blocks knocked off.'

'George, what an expression!' She appealed to Evie, whose influence with Mr Bunting was unbounded.

'Get their blocks knocked off,' repeated Mr Bunting, aware of

Evie's sparkle of approval. 'Teach 'em to stay in their own back yard. And when these rotten Germans cry out to us to stop, what do you think we're going to say to them?'

Here he leaned across the table, his face reddening, his moustache bristling. 'We're going to say: "You wait, you rotten swine, we ain't half started yet. We're going to teach you something before we stop."'

'Hooray!' shouted Julie. 'The mucky old *drecksacks*.'

'Well!' exclaimed Mrs Bunting, shocked at the pair of them.

'The *schmutzig* old – '

'That's quite enough, Julie,' interrupted Mr Bunting sharply, for though he approved his daughter's patriotism he feared that some of the words she used might mean more than Julie thought they did.

'Bert says our new tanks have armour plate on them, like a battleship. They can butt old Jerry's biggest ones right into the Rhine. Bust 'em to bits like salmon tins.'

'Bert?' repeated Mr Bunting, puzzled. He could be amazingly obtuse at times.

'Yes – Bert Rollo, silly!'

'Oh, *Bert*. Couldn't think who you meant. Don't tell me he's on leave again.'

'How should I know, daddy?'

'When Bert comes on leave, of course, he'll come to see us,' said Mrs Bunting.

Why of course? Mr Bunting thought, but diverted his interest to the supper preparations. There was an appetising smell and a promising sizzling in the kitchen. Fish cakes, or fritters, or possibly some of Julie's special nut rissoles which were really tasty. At any rate, not arrowroot. Things had come to a pretty pass when a man couldn't take a few extra soda mints without being sent to bed on arrowroot. Personally, he never found arrowroot agreed with him. Nothing, in fact, toned up his stomach like a tot of hot whisky. It was not stuff to chuck away on healthy young soldiers at sixteen bob a bottle.

'I wonder if those blighters will be over again tonight?' he said, as they prepared for bed. He went to the door to report upon the weather. Not a star was visible; there was a still air and a thick low mist which blotted out even his shed and garage and settled damply and gently on every leaf.

'Ah!' he breathed thankfully. 'Going to get a good night's sleep.' This would keep the bombers away. Do his celery a bit of good, too.

As Mr Bunting unhooked the blackout curtains before sitting down to breakfast, he saw the almond tree dressed in the first bridal beauty of the year and glittering in the sunshine. Its sudden beauty moved his heart, like music. It looked as though a thousand pink butterflies rested on the leafless branches, their wings gently fluttering.

He stayed his wife as she crossed the room and drew her to his side.

'Look, Mary! The almond tree's in blossom.'

'Looks pretty, doesn't it?'

'Yes,' he said softly, and he was aware of a warmth of hope stealing into his breast. The blossoming of the almond always marked the turning of a corner in the year; it was the herald of the spring. These past months he had been haunted by a feeling, too foolish to impart to anyone, that its flowering would be especially significant this year. Often in the dark days of winter, when everything was bound with frost, leafless, bare, and grey, he had thought: 'By the time the almond flowers we'll have turned the corner in the war.'

Now here, like a new-lit lamp of hope, it shone in its full beauty. And who could say what events even now were shaping to bring men's best hopes to harvest?

He remembered standing here amidst the beauty of the past year's June, when a distracted France had surrendered and Britain stood alone, her armies imperilled on the Dunkirk beaches, her hands at home empty of weapons. Heavy, indeed, had been Mr Bunting's heart that day; it would have seemed impossible that he could be standing here nearly a year later with a renewed and rational hope, and fortified by the knowledge that across the Atlantic was streaming aid more generous than any country had ever offered to another. Thus, much had been won by human courage, the courage of the vast anonymous host of Britain. You could always turn the corner if you doggedly kept going.

Some words had come into his mind this morning, as he shaved: 'He that shall endure to the end.'

'What's that out of, Mary?'

Mrs Bunting puckered her brow.

'He that shall endure to the end shall be saved,' Evie told him. 'It's in the Bible.'

'Ah! he breathed. Life had brought him knowledge of many of his failings and the war had revealed more. He was not brilliant, nor heroic, but there was one thing he could do – endure. He could stick it out right to the end. It was the one thing he was good at, and it happened to be almost his sole duty.

He had been going to clear out the roof space lest an incendiary bomb came through the tiles, but Julie had done it for him. There was a heap of junk for him to take out to the garage for sorting, and to this task he gave the few minutes he had to spare before his train time. Amongst a mass of other things he found a Union Jack. Mr Bunting had no idea where the Union Jack could have come from; he was not the flag-waving sort; it embarrassed him rather. But, unfolding it, he found a piece of paper written in a boyish hand, the letters squeezed in as they reached the margin: *Chris Bunting's corronation flag.* Chris had put it out of his bedroom window for the coronation; he remembered seeing it flying there.

Tattered and frayed as it was, the flag had a noble and familiar look. A thousand memories of it, floating free or hanging listlessly, came back to him. A noble emblem. He had last seen it over the body of his son.

He held the fabric between his fingers. Bunting! He believed they called this stuff bunting; common, tawdry, ordinary stuff. Yet out of it were made the banners of victory.

He rolled it up and took it into the kitchen. 'I'm off to work,' he said to his wife. 'Take care of this, Mary. Be wanting to stick it out some day.'

At the gate he paused, and for a moment looked up at the window of what had been Chris's bedroom. The fresh morning air blended pleasantly with the fumes of Mr Bunting's 'Lighthouse', as he walked sturdily down the road.

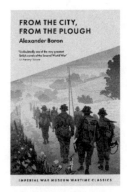

ISBN 9781912423071

£8.99

'Alexander Baron's *From the City, From the Plough* is undoubtedly one of the very greatest British novels of the Second World War and provides the most honest and authentic account of front line life for an infantryman in North West Europe.'

ANTONY BEEVOR

ISBN 9781912423163

£8.99

'Few other novels of the war describe the grinding claustrophobia, violence and lethal danger of being in a tank crew with the stark vividness of Peter Elstob... a forgotten classic that deserves to be read and read.'

JAMES HOLLAND

ISBN 9781912423422

£8.99

In January 1941 Griselda Green arrives at Blimpton, a place 'so far from anywhere as to be, for all practical purposes, nowhere'. Monica Felton's 1945 novel gives a lively account of the experiences of a group of men and women working in a munitions factory during the Second World War.

ISBN 9781912423491
£8.99

In 1943 John Foley is posted to command Five Troop and their trusty Churchill tanks *Avenger, Alert,* and *Angler* – thus begins his initiation into the Royal Armoured Corps. This intimate and detailed account follows the fate of this group of men in the latter stages of the Second World War.

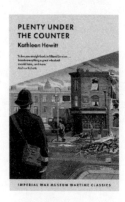

ISBN 9781912423095
£8.99

'Takes you straight back to Blitzed London... boasts everything a great whodunit should have, and more.'

ANDREW ROBERTS

ISBN 9781912423378
£8.99

'A highly unusual war novel with several confluent narratives; moving, interesting and of great literary value.'

LOUIS de BERNIÈRES

ISBN 9781912423156
£8.99

'When a man has been a soldier and seen action, he writes of war with true understanding, and with authority. When that man writes with with, elegance and imagination, as Fred Majdalany does in *Patrol*, he produces a military masterpiece.'

ALLAN MALLINSON

ISBN 9781912423088
£8.99

'A tremendous rediscovery of a brilliant novel. Extremely well-written, its effects are both sophisticated and visceral. Remarkable.'

WILLIAM BOYD

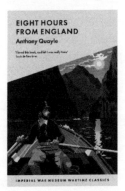

ISBN 9781912423101
£8.99

'Much more than a novel'

RODERICK BAILEY

'I loved this book, and felt I was really there'

LOUIS de BERNIÈRES

'One of the greatest adventure stories of the Second World War'

ANDREW ROBERTS

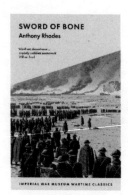

ISBN 9781912423385
£8.99

'Brilliant... a quietly confident masterwork'
WILLIAM BOYD

'One of the best books to come out of the Second World War'
JOSHUA LEVINE

ISBN 9781912423279
£8.99

'A hidden masterpiece, crackling with authenticity'
PATRICK BISHOP

'Supposedly fiction, but these pages live – and so, for a brief inspiring hour, do the young men who live in them.'
FREDERICK FORSYTH

ISBN 9781912423262
£8.99

'Whitty, warm and hugely endearing... a lovely novel'
AJ PEARCE

'Evokes the highs and lows, joys and agonies of being a Land Girl'
JULIE SUMMERS